JANIE CONWAY HERRON

With love from
Janie

another Song about love

another Song about love

JANIE CONWAY HERRON

Another Song About Love
Janie Conway Herron – June, 2020

Cover design and interior - ©Tall Story
www.tallstorydesigns.com

Cover art - Vashti Ilanya
www.vashtillanya.com

For Tamlin,
who tells me he can still hear
the music in my writing.

Song is the precious addition to a blank message, entirely contained within its address, for what I give by singing is at once my body (by my voice) and the silence into which you cast that body. (Love is mute, Novalis says; only poetry makes it speak). *Song means nothing*: it is in this that you will understand at last what it is I give you; as useless as the wisp of yarn, the pebble held out to his mother by the child.
(Roland Barthes, *A Lover's Discourse*, 1990: 77)

1

THE VISITORS

THE SUMMER OF 1982 FELT dangerous. Bushfires raged in the hills, blowing ominous red clouds across the sky, while the heat that shimmered on the streets of Melbourne made people brittle and as likely to snap as twigs on a dry forest bed. But I loved the feeling of hot sun sinking into my skin. It connected me to a sense of childish freedom and the smell of salt sea air. When I moved from the northern beaches of Sydney, the ocean disappeared and the world I had known up to then faded into memory.

JANIE CONWAY HERRON

The wide, tree-lined streets, large double-brick houses and the many parks and gardens a short walk from home made suburban Melbourne a marvellous place to grow up in. But all through those first few southern winters, I longed for the warmth of the little beachside shack where we'd lived. Mum and I often spent hours walking along the shore collecting shells.

When an eagle flew out from the bush to circle the ocean's edge, Mum pointed at it and exclaimed, 'Wouldn't you just love to fly like that?' Picking up curly shells, she held them close to my ear so I could hear the low hissing of waves rolling into shore. 'Now you can take the ocean with you, no matter where you go,' she whispered.

Twenty years later, when that summer of 1982 began, I was a young woman flying high on the wings of hope. I was a singer pinning my dreams on the songs I'd written making it in the world of popular music. I was the single mother of a beautiful boy, Jesse, whose presence brought me joy every day. Yet behind my smile was the uncertainty of a girl still searching for the ocean in her heart.

I first noticed Anna playing bass in a folk band. I'd never seen a woman play and sing so effortlessly. She performed with almost everyone I knew in the Melbourne folk scene of the 1970s. We were all young

another song about love

idealists then, taking our cue from the singers of the British Isles or America, singing songs about the hardships of life. Most of the songs had little to do with our inner-city, urban reality, yet we sang them passionately, our voices rising over a chorus of acoustic guitar picking, banjos, fiddles and flutes. Occasionally someone played an electric guitar but until Bob Dylan was booed off the stage at the Newport Folk Festival and British bands like Fairport Convention revolutionised the sound of traditional British ballads, this was frowned upon. Women singers sang high, their beautiful plaintive melodies filled with the pain of unrequited love. The songs were of heartbreak and unmarried pregnancy, of leaning our backs against oaks and thinking they were trusty trees. Women were rarely seen as instrumentalists, even if they did play guitar. Amongst those unwritten rules of the folk clubs Anna stood out as a multi-instrumentalist. People relaxed into the music that poured out of her like liquid toffee, strong and sweet.

When we first started playing together, my high nervous energy cut through Anna's easy pace. She mellowed me out, smoothing the rough edges of my playing and making the rhythm steady and strong. In Scarlet Sisters, Anna played electric bass and I played electric guitar. Folk-rock was breaking down the taboos around amplified instruments in folk clubs but we wanted to try out our music in Melbourne's burgeoning pub rock scene where you were expected to play rock and roll. There were no role models for women playing electric guitar in rock bands in the 1980s, but with Anna's encouragement, I began playing and writing songs with a tougher edge. They suited the musical style we were aiming for.

'Playing electric guitar is the same as playing acoustic,' Anna advised. 'Only instead of trying to coax the sound out of the guitar, the art of playing electric is holding the sound back.' She showed me how to dampen the strings and use percussive techniques to create a funky feel with a bluesy edge. Making the rhythm clean and crisp, all that energy at my fingertips. Watching it ripple out to catch at the audience's dancing feet was exciting and new.

When he heard we were getting a band together, Ali suggested that he become our drummer. We enthusiastically agreed. Having recently toured South East Asia in a soul covers band, Ali fitted naturally into the musical style we were aiming for. He was keen to play original music too, rather than what he described as the hackneyed old songs he'd been playing in covers bands. Ali also knew a guitarist called Stevie who'd played in bands in the Sydney club circuit. He'd recently moved to Melbourne and was also looking to join a band that played original material. If Stevie worked out our band would be complete.

another song about love

With our ardent politics and experiments in free love, my friends and I held, steadfast, to our ideals of sexual freedom. That summer, desire simmered in the intensity of the long hot nights. We were close but not too close. We were lovers and friends without the trappings of commitment – at least that's what we told one another. If love was free why not have plenty of it?

My marriage had ended. Joe's absence left a space that I tried to satisfy with Paul, but it was just an affair and didn't fill my need for intimacy.

'Another time in our lives we might even have got married,' I laughed, 'but now's not the right time, is it?'

'Guess not,' Paul shrugged, his face screwing up in an expression half way between humour and dread. 'It's so easy to slide out of one relationship into another; we'd just repeat old habits.'

The languor of the way Paul said this strengthened my resolve. Paul was right; it was all too easy to drift from one relationship to another. Joe and I truly loved each other but once Jesse was born things changed. As Joe and I juggled our musical career with being parents the beautiful cocoon of our life together disintegrated. Now nothing held the promise of love and commitment I'd hoped for. No longer willing to risk the vulnerability of monogamy, I experimented with the open relationships Joe and I had toyed with in the last stages of our marriage. I liked the idea that you could have more than one lover without feeling jealousy or a sense of entitlement over others and in many ways I still do. It scared me though, especially when I felt that deep yearning for a special person. Romantic love was what I'd been brought up on. All the songs of my childhood had been about it.

Inspired by my next-door neighbour Jonathon, I'd also started growing marijuana in my backyard. He had a small crop of his own and was meticulous in his approach to growing ganja, as he called it, refusing the negative connotations of dope. When it came to growing ganja, his methods verged on the mystical.

'It helps if you talk to them,' he told me, as he pruned a couple of sweet-smelling heads from his own plants. 'They respond to your voice. They like to be loved and nurtured just like any other living thing.'

I saved the seeds from smoke my friends shared with me and planted them in pots the way Jonathon showed me. I was proud of my homegrown crop in the same way someone might be pleased with a good batch of home brewed beer. I nurtured and pruned them through the balmy spring and into the heat of summer until I had four beautiful bushy females ready for harvest.

When my friends came round, I mulled up a bowl of my best heads, the smell of marijuana permeating my fingers as I mixed the pungent herb into

another song about love

a fine, smooth smoke. I didn't deal though. Like Jonathon, I didn't want my precious plants to be tainted by the street dollar. My budget had never stretched to affording ganja but friends had always made sure there was enough to share. My reasons for growing it had more to do with payback to friends than profit from dealing. After inviting them in for a smoke, we fetched our guitars and sang, our voices flying high over the steady rhythm of the guitars. Outside the hot night sky moaned, whistling through telegraph wires and down the cobbled back lanes of the city.

On days when Jesse went to school, I rose early and padded quietly into his room. I loved to watch the rise and fall of his sleeping breath in the mornings, feeling the strength of my love rising as I lifted wispy curls from his forehead and gently woke him. Sometimes I sneaked into his bed and traced the fine contours of his childish cheeks with my finger, remembering the quiet stillness of those early mornings when Jesse was a baby. How he had nuzzled into me as I offered my breast, spurting with sweet mother's milk that stained my clothing and made me smell both sweet and sour.

One school day morning I lay in bed savouring the light breeze from the window blowing across my body and listening to the murmur of city traffic. It was time to wake Jesse but Eddie was sleeping beside me, his broad back curved against my side.

I'd met Eddie at a Rock Against Racism gig where we'd both been performing. Jesse was having a sleep over so I'd invited him home. I smiled, thinking of his hands caressing my breasts as he whispered, 'I want to make that cream come thick and strong, let me taste it.' Chin resting on my belly, he watched me, a cheeky grin breaking across his face as he urged me on to orgasm with his fingers. Eddie was good at negotiating the delicate balance between intimacy and independence that open relationships required. He wasn't afraid of my generosity, like others were. He always gave plenty in return.

In the week that he stayed with me we spent a lot of time singing songs together, my voice in tandem with his, our rhythms in sync. I loved Eddie's stories and his Islander songs lilting like ocean waves coming into shore. I wanted him to take me home and introduce me to his people but he was due to leave in a couple of days. I knew I'd miss his company but I'd be glad of the distance as well.

When I opened Jesse's bedroom door he was already awake.

'I think you slept in, Mum,' he said curtly.

I checked my watch. 'You're right Jesse, it's after eight. We'd better get a move on if we're going to get you to school on time.'

another song about love

'Everyone'll look at me and ask stupid questions if I'm late getting to school,' Jesse complained. 'Can't I stay home just for today?' His eyes grew wistful.

It was a look he knew I found hard to refuse. It wasn't as if I let him miss school often, I reasoned. Besides, we hadn't hung out together for a while.

'Okay, on one condition,' I relented.

'What's that, Mum?'

'You let me get in bed with you. Come on, hop over.'

Grinning, Jesse moved over to the edge of his bed and pulled back the covers. Comfortable lying together we fell into one of our regular question and answer sessions where Jesse asked the questions and I answered as best I could.

'Hey Mama, what was it like when I was born?'

'Beautiful, Jesse, I'd love to do it all over again.'

'Would you, Mama?' Jesse thought for a minute and then prodded my arm. 'But you couldn't.'

'Why not?'

'Cause I'm already born, you couldn't have me again.'

'You're certainly one in a million Jesse, but I could have another baby.'   'You'd have to get back with Dad though.'

'No I wouldn't. I could have a baby with another father.'

'But they wouldn't be my brother or sister.'

'Of course they would, Jesse.'

'But you'd have to get married again.'

'You don't have to get married to have babies, Jesse.'

'Oh?' Jesse went quiet then he turned towards me. 'Mama, if you had a baby now, how would you know who the father was?'

'I couldn't be sure, Jesse.'

'Then it wouldn't have a father.'

'It'd have lots of fathers.'

Jesse squirmed and his knees dug into my hip. 'But fathers mightn't want to be fathers if they didn't know who the real dad was.'

'Come on Jesse, don't be so old fashioned.'

'Did my dad know he was my father?'

'Of course he did.'

'But how?'

'He was the only one I was with then.'

'Did he want me?' Jesse's big brown eyes became pools of vulnerability. 'Of course he wanted you,' I reassured. I never liked it when we talked about Joe like this but I'd become practiced at diverting Jesse before his questions became too complicated. 'Let's wake Eddie up and go out for breakfast,' I prompted.

'Can I get an ice cream sundae?'

'Only if you eat something that's good for you first.'

Jesse jumped out of bed and made a dash for my bedroom. 'Eddie!' he yelled. 'It's time to wake up. We're going out for breakfast.'

another song about love

At the Black Cat Café, Jesse grinned as he attacked a huge dish of ice cream. It looked like a sci-fi landscape with different flavours poured over it, topped off with chocolate jelly babies and multicoloured snakes curled round a big dollop of cream.

'Shame on you,' Eddie jibed. 'How can you let your boy eat such junk?'

'Mum doesn't usually let me. This is my special treat 'cause she made me miss school.'

'Oh shut up, both of you,' I snapped.

'Ho, touchy are we?' Eddie's arm crept round my waist.

'As a matter of fact I am, so watch it,' I answered, smiling.

'You gonna miss me or something?' Eddie quipped.

'What, me miss you? You must be kidding.'

In the silence that followed Jesse let a long snake slide slowly into his mouth. With his face covered in ice cream and his uncombed hair sticking out, he flashed me one of his best grins and I couldn't stay grumpy anymore.

We walked down Brunswick Street, past the funky shops, restaurants and galleries that had brought this once deserted industrial area back to life. Jesse swung between Eddie and me, his sticky fingers gripping our hands. When we reached the Edinburgh Gardens he ran up the tree-lined path toward the old steam train. It was a remnant of the innercity rail line that had run through the park nearly a century earlier. The new black and red paint job they'd given the train made it look like it had jumped straight out of a storybook. Whooping with joy, Jesse climbed into the driver's seat, while Eddie and I sat together on a park bench watching him play.

'Jesse's dad and I used to come here when Jesse was a baby,' I offered quietly. 'He still loves coming here. I think it reminds him of his dad. He doesn't get to see him much these days, only when he comes down from Tamworth or we can afford to fly him up there. Joe's new family keeps him almost permanently in country music land.'

Eddie took my hand. 'A train, a bit like this one, runs from Cairns to Kurandah. I used to ride on it when I went to visit my auntie. I was my auntie's favourite. She brought me up after Mum died.'

'How old were you?' I asked.

'About six.'

'God, you were so young. That must have been hard.'

'It was harder for Dad. He had four kids to look after on his own. They were battling even before Mum died.'

'Did your auntie take all the kids?'

'Nope. Only me. She had four kids of her own.'

'Shit, I'm finding it hard with just one!' Eddie's warrior aunt made my own struggles with Jesse pale into insignificance.

another song about love

'My auntie had nothing else she was trying to do. She wasn't a career woman. Besides, up in north Queensland there are always plenty of relations to help out. People aren't isolated like they are here in the city.'

'I'm not isolated,' I replied. 'Anna and I share babysitters and the kids love being together when we're at gigs. My parents always love having Jesse to stay too. Since they've moved away from Melbourne it isn't as easy as it used to be when they were living close by though.'

'Yeh, having a strong community helps when there are kids to be taken care of,' Eddie continued, unaware of my discomfort. 'My auntie didn't have a chance to be a pop star. She's a great singer though, country and western too. She knows all the classics. She was my first singing teacher.'

'Maybe I could take lessons from her some time,' I ventured.

'Maybe.' Eddie grinned then quickly changed the subject. 'What're you doing this afternoon, Sis?'

'I've got a rehearsal at Anna's place. We're auditioning that guitarist I told you about.'

'Do you want me to look after Jesse?'

'Would you? I was going to take him with me.'

'Nah, he'll be bored at a rehearsal. I'm much more interesting. If Jesse doesn't mind, I'll take him round with me for a while.'

As my skinny, tousle-headed son walked away with this tall, broad islander, I wondered how Joe would feel. A quick flash of pain stabbed at my heart. I was thankful for the geographical distance from Joe. It helped me forget the awfulness that had crept between us before he headed for Tamworth.

I walked up the streets of North Fitzroy towards home. A hot wind whipped around my legs, picking up leaves and making little whirlwind patterns with them. The house I rented was in a row of single-storey, semi-detached cottages. Mine was the last one. The rent was cheap but the house was dilapidated. The bathroom and toilet were outside in a glorified tin shed. I was glad the long hot summer had dispelled the prospect of a frosty early-morning dash to the bathroom across the cement backyard. Parched brown leaves of the morning glory in my tiny front yard wound up around the posts of the front porch and hung from the guttering. The delicate purple flowers had withered and dropped, their skeletons crunching under my feet as I opened the gate. The old tin letterbox burned my fingers as I pulled out a bright yellow envelope with red, black and green borders. It was a letter from my friend Claude. Inside, a black and white photo of an impossibly good-looking man with dreadlocks framing his face gave significance to the reggae colours on the envelope. The photo was slightly out of focus, accentuating the softness around his eyes, but his smile was broad. On the back of the photo Claude had scrawled a short note. 'This is René; I'm sending him to you. He is the real Rasta. Take good care of him.' I turned the photo over

14

another song about love

again, trying to make out something of René's character. The soft focus blurred the definition and René was lost in the grey of its edges. I dropped the photo on my bed as my eyes adjusted to the half-light of the bedroom then grabbed my guitar and headed for the tram stop.

Soon my tram was rounding a distant curve in the road, clattering slowly forward on the shimmering tracks. Overhead the sky had taken on a strange orange hue as clouds of smoke formed on the horizon. I juggled the guitar under the tram seat and sat down. Behind me, two women talked about the fires in the same tone of voice people used for car accidents or murders.

'Ooh it's terrible, you know, five people killed in one house, everyone gone just like that. Still, I suppose that's a blessing in disguise, if you know what I mean.'

'Oh I know. I'd never get over it if I were the only one who survived something like that. I mean, you're better off dead, aren't you?'

'I guess so. There's no telling how the hand of fate will strike when it comes.'

Opposite me a man read the sports page of the newspaper. The headlines shouted across the space between us: HILLS ABLAZE! FIRE CLAIMS MORE LIVES! A photo showed the charred skeleton of a house with a lonely stone chimney, still standing. Next door to it, another house stood untouched. I struggled to understand how the hand of fate could make such decisions.

The tram lumbered up High street towards the top of the hill near the Northcote Town Hall. At my stop, a red, black and yellow Aboriginal flag welcomed people to the suburb while "Pay the Rent: This is Aboriginal Land" was written underneath. As I stepped off the tram I wondered whether the hand of fate had more to do with rent being way overdue.

The night before, as we'd watched the devastating aftermath of the fires on the news, Eddie told me about Framlingham, an old mission in country Victoria that was now run by Aboriginal people. Fires had destroyed everything around it but hadn't touched anything on the mission. It was plain, he said, that the spirits had protected them. I didn't know whether to believe him or not but I was impressed with the idea that such spiritual protection could exist.

I paused before walking down the steep hill that sloped towards Anna's house. The stunning view reached out to the mountains. A brown cloud fanned across the skyline, obscuring the tops of the hills where the distinctive TV towers disappeared into the smoke. The long rows of houses nestled in the foothills of suburbia spread their tiled roofs towards the city, while the heat and the view made the fires seem frighteningly close.

In the cool of her house, Anna and I smoked a joint and drank the first cup of tea for the afternoon. Anna's two

another song about love

children, Sam and Antonia, were at school and we had a bit of time before rehearsal was due to start.

'Do you think Stevie might be a toker?' Anna let out a long exhale.

'More of a Scotch drinker,' I grinned. 'He looks like Clark Kent with those glasses, don't you think?'

'Yeah, but I'm hoping he's Superman on guitar.' A wave of crinkling lines spread across Anna's cheeks as we both laughed.

Anna picked up her bass. 'Got any new songs? Play me something new, Lil.'

I felt the rush of nervousness I always had when playing something new. 'This one's about friendship,' I explained. 'You know, the kind of friendship that lovers can sometimes have but mostly don't.'

'Play it, Lil,' Anna insisted as she plugged her bass in.

I played the first chord loud and strong, still rapidly firing explanations about the song's origins. 'I stole this chord from Joan Armatrading but Eddie reckons it's a Hendrix chord.'

'Sing it, Lil. The PA's on,' Anna persisted.

I played the intro, sinking into the safety of Anna's bass line as it pushed the rhythm along. When I let the words out, I sang them hard and guttural so that the questions sounded like demands. *'Will you be constant? Will you be my friend? Will you still be there after the passion ends?'*

Anna followed as if she had a sixth sense and the song took shape. Playing it over and over again we found a steady groove, losing ourselves in the sound and feel until, startled by the silhouetted figure standing in the back door, we tumbled to an ending.

'I couldn't get you to hear me out the front so I came down the back lane. The gate was open. I hope that's all right.' Stevie smiled as we stood, mouths agape, guitars hanging around our necks. 'What was that song you were playing?'

Anna thrummed the rhythm on her bass with her thumb. 'It's a new song Lillie wrote. Do you like it?'

'It's great,' Stevie answered. 'I like the Hendrix chord.'

Anna put her bass down. 'Want a cuppa, Stevie? What's your poison?'

'Coffee, thanks.' Stevie stared at the array of musical instruments, leads and microphones before heading towards a couch full of just-washed children's clothes looking for a space to sit down.

'Make yourself comfortable, don't mind the washing.' Anna flicked a match under the gas. 'Ali will be here any minute, then we can get started.'

I sat down at the table and pulled a small bowl closer. 'Eddie's been teaching me how to make a proper mull,' I explained as I rubbed the mixture between my fingers. 'He mixes it real fine so you get all the sticks and stems out of it. Want a smoke, Stevie? It's home grown!'

When the tiny flame flickered at the end of the joint and lit first time, Stevie inhaled deeply. As he was

another song about love

about to have another toke, Ali came in, looking for a space to set up his drums.

'Now that's a nice smelling spliff.' Hand outstretched, Ali took the joint from Stevie. 'How're you going, man?'

'I'm going great,' Stevie answered. 'Looking forward to playing with you all this afternoon. I've got some more gear to bring in. I'll go get it.' He returned with his amp and pedals, plus a six-pack of beer.

'Doesn't look like he's a whisky man,' Anna whispered.

'Still could be Superman in disguise,' I laughed.

Once everyone was set up, Anna played a slow, steady riff. Ali was right there with his bass drum in sync as Stevie played some light licks in the spaces, hesitating as he tried to suss out the levels.

I leaned over to him. 'It's okay, you can play loud,' I said. Picking up my guitar I strummed that Hendrix chord as hard as I could, listening intently as the music swirled around me.

Stevie pushed a few pedals until he got a singing edge on his guitar, turned up the volume and went for it. As the band swung out on the edges of the notes Stevie played, the song picked up and moved into a heavier beat. We played round and round the arrangement until Stevie cut his volume back, sliding a few chords in behind my rhythm as Anna and Ali eased it down.

JANIE CONWAY HERRON

I leant into the microphone. The words were loud and clear and it felt good to hear my voice soar over the music. *'Can you hear my heartbeat? Can you feel my heartache? I can give so easily. Still I wonder what you'll take. Will you keep coming round, after you've come for the first time?'* I repeated the last line and the band brought the volume down. When a drum roll from Ali brought us to a stop, we were all smiling.

'I like it, I like it.' Anna rubbed her hands together and laughed.

'Thanks, that was great, Stevie,' I said.

'It's a pleasure, especially when it's such a good song.'

'You think so?' I asked. 'Do you really like it?'

'I wouldn't say it unless I meant it,' Stevie replied, ensuring his inclusion in the band.

Later that afternoon I opened my front door to the sound of the television blaring. I shouted at Jesse to turn it down, then regretted the cross edge in my voice. The north wind was making me cranky. When the familiar odour of yandi, as Eddie called it, beckoned me, I hurried to get a share of the joint. Jesse was sitting in the corner, glued to the television, ignoring the adults in the room.

Eddie handed me the last of the joint they'd been smoking. The mull bowl had been full that

another song about love

morning, but from the amount that was left, it was obvious they'd been smoking all afternoon. I took the joint and looked around at the others in the room. I hadn't the faintest idea who any of them were but they were all smiling. Stoned I thought as I said. 'Hey Eddie, you haven't introduced me to your friends.'

'Sorry Sis, I ran into this mob this afternoon.' He waved his hand in the direction of two men and a woman sitting together on the sofa.

The woman got up and offered her hand. 'Hi. I'm Cath,' she smiled warmly. 'We've been enjoying your yandi this afternoon. Eddie tells me you grew it yourself.'

'Yes I did,' I said.

'Deadly.' Cath pointed to the man sitting beside her. 'This here's my cousin Drew, from Townsville. He's going to take Eddie back home tomorrow.'

Out of the corner of my eye I noticed Jesse edging closer to the television, his head almost resting on the screen.

'Get away from the television Jesse, you'll ruin your eyes,' I snapped.

'But I can't hear it when you grownups start talking,' Jesse protested. 'Can't I take the T.V. into another room?' He looked up at me pleadingly.

Then the third visitor stood up, his hand outstretched towards me. 'Hi. I'm René, Claude's friend. I hope he wrote to you about me.'

I took his hand. 'I thought you looked familiar. Claude sent me a photo and a letter telling me to expect you.'

'Can I help Jesse put the television in the other room?' René asked, his accent making the simple request sound more exotic than it was.

'We found René on the door step when we got home, didn't we Jesse?' Eddie asked.

'Yes we did,' Jesse replied, watching closely as René unplugged the T.V. 'I'll show you where Mum's room is. She's got a connection.' As he followed René I heard him ask: 'Are you a real Rasta man?'

René's laugh rippled up the hall. 'Yes Jesse, I am.'

Eddie prepared a meal for us all that evening – vegetables and fish cooked in coconut cream, Islander style. He handed me a plate full of food. 'This is for Jesse,' he said. 'Why don't you take it in to him?'

Jesse had fallen asleep. Perhaps I should have woken him, but I didn't have the heart. I wondered what life was really like for him. He fitted in easily with the peripatetic way we lived but his was no ordinary childhood. What kind of mother was I, bringing so many people into his life? I looked at my son's peaceful sleeping face, kissed him gently, turned off the television and tiptoed out of the room.

It was after midnight when I saw Cath and her cousin to the front door. A gust of hot wind blew dried leaves

another song about love

down the hall and Drew backed away. 'Whoa, them spirits are restless tonight, we'd better be careful getting home.'

'Don't worry brother, they're looking after us. It's them white fellas that need to watch out,' Cath laughed and I wondered if I was included in her prediction.

'Thanks for the yandi, Sis,' Drew said, shaking my hand.

After they'd left, Eddie rolled another joint. 'Last one before bedtime,' he said as he used the rest of the mull in the bowl.

'Are you staying the night?' I asked René.

'If you don't mind, I have nowhere else to stay for the moment,' he replied. I sensed he planned to stay a while.

'Jesse's asleep in my room, so you can sleep in Jesse's bed for tonight. Eddie and I can sleep out here on the sofa bed.'

After making sure René was comfortable, I lay back listening to Eddie as he crooned one last lilting islander song then put the guitar in its case. With the click of each latch my desire increased and when he sat down I pulled him closer.

'I've been waiting all night for this. I want to make the most of our last night.'

'What makes you think this *is* our last night?'

'Tomorrow you go back home. I'll probably never see you again.'

JANIE CONWAY HERRON

'Never say never,' Eddie replied and lay down beside me. Tracing the line of my body from shoulder to hip he whispered. 'It's a two-way thing this one,' then folded me in his arms.

Next morning Eddie waved to us as Drew's car disappeared up the street. As I waved back I felt both glad and sorry. Distance was already replacing the intimacy we'd been sharing all week.

I smiled down at Jesse. 'Better get on with the day,' I said as I took his hand and led him back inside the house.

René was waiting for us in the kitchen. Rather than the instant coffee I often made for myself he'd brewed real coffee beans and the room smelled like one of the best cafés in Carlton. As we spent the morning together I noticed the way René took care to entertain Jesse and make him feel at ease. When we walked to the shops Jesse took René's hand eagerly and when René waved at some of Jesse's friends, his small chest swelled with pride. At the supermarket we bought lots of food and René insisted on paying for it all.

After René moved into a flat nearby, he remained a regular visitor. One night he stayed very late and I asked him if he wanted to share my bed for the night. When he accepted I undressed and got into bed feeling pleased that at last our friendship might become more intimate. René took off his jeans but left his T-shirt and underpants on. As he sat on the edge of the bed there was an awkward silence while we both worked out what to say.

'I want you to be my friend,' René offered first.

'We are friends, aren't we?'

René looked away. 'I just don't want to spoil things between us.'

'By what?' I turned towards him.

'By making love.' René tried to sound nonchalant.

I moved closer. 'Couldn't that make things better?'

'It could, but it might make things complicated too.' The muscles in René's cheek stiffened as his jaw clenched. 'I just don't want sex to spoil things anymore.' René pulled his knees up to his chest. 'I am waiting for someone, Lillie. I am waiting for her to decide to come back to me. She is trying to decide between me and someone else. Someone you know quite well.'

'Claude?'

'Correct.'

'Neither Claude nor myself find it easy to give our hearts away, even if we are generous with our bodies. It's too dangerous for us.'

A long low sigh escaped René's lips. 'Claude has Jemma convinced that she has his heart. We were just three friends and we travelled together for a long time without any sex happening at all. When Jemma and I became lovers, things went really awry. Claude started asking me very personal things about what

JANIE CONWAY HERRON

Jemma and I did together while making love. At first I joked with him, but after a while I avoided him. When he told me he'd made love with her too I couldn't believe it. I went running to her and asked if it was true. She said yes. Then she said she had always loved us both and that she wanted us both. I tried to handle it but I couldn't. That's when Claude suggested I come to Melbourne for a while and gave me your address.'

I laced my arms round René's shoulders. 'Love is never easy.'

'But I can't do without it,' René sighed.

'I'm trying to,' I replied.

René laughed. 'You do without love? You're surrounded by it. You have so many friends. And what about that little boy of yours?'

'That's different. He can't hurt me like lovers do. I'm learning to have no expectations in love. It's hard but I'm learning.'

'But if you're really in love with someone, that's impossible.'

I let go of René. 'Perhaps I don't fall in love anymore.'

'Oh Lillie, I have made you sad now, haven't I?'

'Sometimes I just feel lonely for it, that's all.'

'For what?'

'For being in love, in that way you describe.'

René kissed me on the cheek. 'I'm sorry to make you unhappy, I will have to make you feel better.' He moved behind me and massaged my

another song about love

shoulders slowly and firmly. 'I used to do this for a living in Paris. I got quite a reputation. Lots of ladies used to visit me. Sometimes they'd invite me home.'

'So you were a gigolo in Paris, were you? Now that is romantic.'

René kept massaging. 'No, I was not very good at that but I'm a good masseur.' He gestured to me to lie on my stomach and I sank into his deep caresses. I could feel the boniness of his buttocks and the soft fall of his testicles through his underpants as I relaxed and drifted off into a deep sleep.

I woke next morning to the smell of fresh coffee brewing and the sound of Jesse and René laughing together. When the door opened, Jesse stood there with a big grin on his face. Carefully balancing a tray of croissants and a mug of fresh coffee, he brought it over to me. 'René and I made breakfast for you this morning, Mum. René taught me how to make real coffee, so now I can do it for you too.'

Standing beside Jesse, René bowed saying, 'with love from both of us,' and our smiles filled the room.

2

THE OCEAN IN ME

ONE PERFECT BEACH DAY, WITH the sun shining in a clear blue sky and the surf rolling in, I squatted close to the waves that edged into shore. Letting my feet sink into the gritty wetness of the sand I felt the undertow build up around my heels, picked up a piece of driftwood lying on a stretch of sand and drew. It was a simple picture – a house with windows, a door, a chimney and a path running to the gate. Inside a fence, a woman and a man stood either side of a little stick-figure girl, her pigtails sticking out on either side of her head. When a wave rushed up around my feet taking most of the drawing with it, I stared at the smooth stretch of sand where my drawing had been, then ran up the beach towards my parents. Dad turned around opening his arms wide. I felt their strength and safety wrapping around me as he lifted me up, tossed me into the air and caught me again.

I wriggled out of his embrace and ran to the water's edge. 'Bet you can't catch me now,' I yelled before running away.

But Dad caught me easily, his unshaven face scratching my skin as he covered me with tickling kisses.

Later we sat on the beach eating ice creams and Dad talked about moving to Melbourne. He made moving sound like a big adventure but when I glanced across at Mum staring out across the ocean she looked as if she had lost something.

'Daddy, do they have beaches in Melbourne?' I asked.

Before he could answer, Mum turned towards me. In the silence of her unexpressed thoughts, the ocean's hissing and the call of the gulls helped me understand what was needed. Running back to the pile of shells I'd been collecting, I picked the biggest, curliest one I could find, making sure the ocean was still inside, before running back and offering it to my sad-eyed mother.

another song about love

Every Saturday morning Dad drove us down the coast road from our beachside paradise to my grandparents' place in Sydney. On Saturday afternoons Mum and I often took a bus into town and went to the movies. *Peter Pan, The King and I* and *Anastasia* were some of my favourites but one afternoon I saw a film that was life changing for me. It was one of the newsreels before the main movie. As I sat next to Mum and watched Russian ballerina Anna Pavlova, I was entranced. I wanted to be just like her, emulating the spirit of a dying swan in her graceful dance. When we got home I put on one of my parents' classical records. With my black hair pulled back from my forehead, I offered my face to the mirror and spinning like a multicoloured top, I danced. Head tilted, I stretched longer and longer, every movement conscious. Back straight and feet turned out, I tried to capture the essence of Pavlova's style.

Sometimes I went to the Saturday afternoon matinees with my grandfather the master of the Wurlitzer organ. As a younger man he'd been the accompanist for silent films but with the advent of talking movies he was relegated to playing the organ during interval. Then my grandfather appeared like magic from the bowels of the theatre stage, sitting in front of a giant Wurlitzer organ. Perched like a king, the master of the instrument before him, he expertly pulled and pushed the panel of knobs in front of him. The sound of oboes, violins, horns and even a chorus of angels came out of the

JANIE CONWAY HERRON

keyboard. My grandfather was the conductor of a huge orchestra whose sole inspiration came from his fingertips.

The theatre was often full of kids who'd come with their parents to see Cisco and Pancho, the two renegade Mexicans riding around the American countryside putting everything right. When Pancho's horse reared and he exclaimed, 'Oh Cisco' and Cisco's laughing face faded as he answered 'Oh Pancho,' I leant towards the stage in great anticipation. With the pomp and splendour of Pop's first chords, the curtain opened and the organ slowly rose into place from below the stage. Like some wicked goblin he looked around and grinned his gold-toothed smile while the jewelled rings on his fingers flashed. I felt superior to the other children who had to sit with their parents, while I had come with my grandfather, the magic man on stage. His first melody rose to an almost unbearable crescendo then with a rush and tumble of notes, he finished. Flashing me a grin he announced, 'I'd like to dedicate my next number to the finest little dancer in the world, my granddaughter Lil.' Standing up, he pointed me out to the audience. With all the kids staring at me, I leant forward. Listening for the opening notes of the next piece, I was aware of their eyes focused on me. When I left the theatre hand in hand with my grandfather, some of the kids pointed and stared but it didn't worry me. I basked in the notoriety my grandfather brought me.

another song about love

Occasionally he took me to a restaurant in town where all his friends met regularly. I felt grown up being invited to this smoky den, a meeting place for actors, artists and musicians. As Pop lit up a cigar he beamed down at me over his waist-coated belly. Describing my dancing prowess to them all, he announced that I would be a prima ballerina one day, just like Anna Pavlova. I drank in the aromatic perfume of my grandfather's women friends. They were all chiffon and powder puff pink and I was lost in their furs, as they whisked me up and carried me away in their feathery embraces. Their words sounded a hypnotic chant. 'Isn't she small, isn't she graceful and talented? Aren't you our little star?'

At family gatherings Pop played the piano while I performed. Faster and faster my grandfather played, his bejewelled hands skipping over the keys. A broad grin spread across his face, the cigar in his mouth exposing a glint in his gold tooth. I leant towards his shining, speckled head then pirouetted away. Around me spun the faces of my family. Born into music and cabaret, my grandfather and his brothers and sisters had performed in musical theatre since they were children. When Pop brought the music to a crashing finale, I curtsied deeply and waited for the applause. Silent tears flowed down my great aunts' powdery faces as they looked on adoringly, clapping and exclaiming. But something about their wide-eyed, tearful admiration made me shy. I may have wanted to be Pavlova but I was really Alice in Wonderland shrinking behind my mother's skirts, frozen like a rabbit caught in a headlight snare.

If I was the ballerina then my father was the clown. I loved it when Dad lifted me up. Poised gracefully on his hand, I sailed through the air, a dove in mid-flight, I cried out, 'Mummy, Mummy, look what we can do!'

Arms outstretched, my mother smiled as I floated into her waiting arms.

My bedroom was an old tram carriage next to our house. Coloured curtains hung in the windows and my dolls occupied the old passenger seat. At night, I turned the lights out and listened to the ocean crashing on the nearby shore. Staring into the dark, I imagined my dolls coming alive and talked to them about everything that bothered me. They listened intently, their wide eyes brimming with compassion. I confided in them, describing my friend Julie's dog biting me, or the boys down the road threatening to shoot me with their bows and arrows. When I cuddled them to me the world felt safe once more.

One night I was expecting my father to tuck me in. Impatient for the prickle of his moustache on my cheek I left the light on. When I heard footsteps outside the door I turned to greet him. But my father had turned into some grotesque ape. I screamed when he came loping through the door, words sliding out of his twisted mouth. He growled, 'Give us a kiss, Lillie. Give us a kiss.'

another song about love

Though I knew it was only Dad playing one of his tricks, my screams took on a life of their own, growing louder.

Dad knelt beside me trying to get me to look at him, but I was too scared. What if I was only able to see that horrible monster he was a minute before?

Then I felt the gentle stroke of Mum's hand, while Dad whispered. 'I'm sorry, Lillie. I didn't mean to frighten you. It was just a joke.'

'But the joke was too real, Daddy.' I reached up to hug my beloved father. After saying goodnight he tiptoed out of the room. Mum blew me a kiss from the door before turning out the light.

In the dark I tried to conjure up my sweet and loving dolls but all I could see were the faces of monsters. I pushed my back against the wall as they came closer.

'Turn on the light!' I cried out and Mum came rushing back to reassure me. It took many years before I could sleep with the light turned off again.

After we moved to Melbourne, I started ballet lessons at The Melbourne Academy of Russian Dance. It had a reputation for producing fine dancers and I wanted to be one of them. The trips to see my grandparents and the Saturday afternoon movie matinees with Pop were replaced by Saturday morning ballet classes in the city.

JANIE CONWAY HERRON

Through a tiny door that opened onto Elizabeth Street I'd take a steep flight of stairs up to a set of rooms where young girls like myself were transformed into ballerinas.

I flourished in this environment and within a couple of years I was preparing for my first Royal Academy of Dance exams. The morning of the exams Mum carefully laid out my uniform, a white tunic with a pink waistband, flesh-coloured tights and pink ballet shoes. She hung the tunic on a hanger before carrying it into the lounge room where Dad waited for us. When he reached out to hug me, I buried my nose in the comforting clean-cotton smell of his shirt.

As we drove into town, I sat in the back of the car listening as Dad advised me to stay calm and alert and give it my best. Mum was very quiet, which was usual when Dad was around. I watched the back of my mother's head, the proud, tight tilt of it. There was something slightly hurt in the stiff angle of her neck and the small sigh that slipped between her lips as Dad raved on. I put my arms around Mum's neck and felt her loosen a little as she patted my arm and smiled.

In the dressing rooms of Her Majesty's Theatre I met my friend Sarah. On our first day at the academy, all the students waited anxiously for our teacher to arrive. The classroom was large, one end walled floor-to-ceiling with mirrors. At the other end was a high stage where parents were allowed to sit and watch their

another song about love

children. Mum and Dad sat with the other parents as I took my place at the barre. All the girls wore the recommended pink leotards and flesh-coloured tights except for Sarah. Her mother stood beside her on the classroom floor, adjusting the net on Sarah's tutu to make it stand out. Sarah's spindly legs stuck out from under it like some ungainly doll. The door at the side of the room flew open and a small, dark-haired man stood in the doorway. Michel Rosenthal's entrance was exquisitely timed. Body straight, head held high, he stood still for a moment, his alert, dark eyes darting around the room as he sized up each student. Walking with the aid of a stick that echoed loudly on the bare polished-wood floors, he made his way directly to Sarah. Sarah's mother fiddled with her daughter's hair as Michel walked around the two of them. His stick beat a constant rhythm while he eyed them up and down. Sarah's face turned crimson but she kept direct eye contact with him.

'So,' he said dramatically, a deliberate pause making full use of the moment, 'we have a prima ballerina here already, eh? I suppose you'll be having her unformed feet in toe shoes next. Go and take that ridiculous thing off. This is a beginners' class, not the final act of Swan Lake!'

Her Majesty's Theatre, the name had gravity. Coupled with The Royal Academy of Dance and the grandeur of the foyer with its regal red carpet and marble staircase, it made my back rigid with anxiety. Inside the dressing room mothers helped their daughters into the same white uniforms with pink waistbands. Every girl was aware that she was being watched for the rare qualities that might make a prima ballerina. Being small, slim, straight-backed, flexible and strong was very important.

Mum brushed my hair and pulled it tightly into a bun as I stood in front of a long mirror, angling my head precisely in the way I'd been taught. Even without the mirror I was practiced at ballet positions and watching myself being watched.

Once I was ready, Mum and I made our way back to the foyer where Dad was chatting with Michel, who looked me over then nodded approvingly.

'You are lucky. My friend Peggy will be examining you.'

'Break a leg, Princess,' Dad said, grinning fiercely. 'That's stage talk. Your grandfather says it all the time. It means good luck.'

Mum put her hands on my shoulders. 'Just do your best Lil, that's the main thing, you can't do better than that.'

The exam room was bare, apart from the regulation barre, mirror and piano. Peggy, the examiner, smiled then introduced Miss Peters, who waited for us to start, her elegant hands poised over the piano keys.

'Now Lillie, we'll do barre work first. First position, please. Are we ready? Now one, two....'

another song about love

Peggy nodded to Miss Peters and the first piano chords rang out.

Once I began dancing, the thundering nervousness I felt dropped away. Michel often said that nervousness before a performance was a good thing, so long as you could utilise it. In the final mime piece I became the little match girl I was emulating. The pink and white tunic, the sunlit room, the pianist and the examiner all faded away and I became a little girl dressed in rags, shivering in a snowy St Petersburg street selling matches. At the end of the exam I curtsied, stepping wide and bending low, imagining an audience in front of me while Anna Pavlova watched my every move from above.

When the exam results were posted, Dad drove me into the academy. There were four levels you could attain, Honours was the highest. I was desperate to get Honours, anything less felt like failure. As we walked towards the front foyer, Sarah rushed down the stairs at the entrance with outstretched arms.

'We did it, Lillie. We did it!" she exclaimed. 'We're the only ones in the school to get Honours.'

Arms around each other, we waltzed inside in search of our mentor Michel, while my father and Sarah's mother looked on proudly.

JANIE CONWAY HERRON

In the heat of the summer, I made up for the lack of ocean by spending all day at the local pool and all evening roaming the streets with my gang. When heat waves simmered in suburban streets day after day, the red brick houses became ovens inside until the hot northerly winds turned south, bringing storms and cool relief. At night, when the air was fresher outside than in, families took their bedding into their gardens and slept in the open. In the crisp night air the children shook off the torpor of the day's heat and took over the streets, inventing games to while away the humid nights.

Mum had a policy of open house that made our home popular with the other kids, who loved to come and play in the relative freedom there. This openness caused some consternation amongst the other mothers, especially when I started playing with Wendy Harfourd, who lived down the road. Wendy wasn't considered a 'nice girl' or a good influence on the other children. Both of her parents were drinkers.

One day Wendy showed me how to piss in the gutter. She pulled her pants down around her ankles, squatted and leant forward, aiming the piss in a neat stream over her pants and into the gutter. Fascinated by Wendy's aim and intent on studying the yellow stream as it flowed down the hill, I was shocked to hear our neighbour Mrs. Tallow yelling at us. Her high-pitched voice called us dirty, dirty girls. Pointing at Wendy,

another song about love

she yelled at her to get home at once or she'd get the authorities on to her.

Wendy pulled her pants up slowly. She looked Mrs. Tallow straight in the face as she did, then turned on her heel and walked away.

Open-mouthed with respect for Wendy's blatant disdain for authority, I was hauled home by an indignant Mrs. Tallow. She admonished me for playing with Wendy, saying 'drinking is in the blood' and 'I'd better have a talk with your mother about this.'

I wanted to say something in Wendy's defence. I admired her and wanted to be able to piss in the gutter like she did.

Mum listened intently as Mrs. Tallow, shaking with righteous anger, told her the story of our escapade. As she embellished along the way and added details about Wendy's family my heart sank. The end of my newfound friendship with Wendy was certain.

'That may be so, Mrs. Tallow,' my mother replied, 'but I don't see anything very dishonest in Wendy's actions. She's only ten years old. As far as I'm concerned all the kids, including Wendy, are welcome here. Until such time as Wendy herself gives me reason to ban her, she's a welcome guest in my house.'

It took Mrs Tallow quite a while to recover enough to excuse herself and leave. When she'd gone Mum turned to me, her smile filled with delightful conspiracy. 'Go along now. You can tell Wendy it's all right to come over to our place any time.'

JANIE CONWAY HERRON

My feet grew wings as I sprinted to Wendy's place, an old weatherboard house with a rickety veranda at the corner of the lane.

Wendy's mother was a woman of enormous proportions. Large varicose veins ran up her bare calves and disappeared under a floral dress that hung loosely from her vast bosom. She stood in the doorway and looked me over before nodding silently and beckoning me inside. Wendy's mother was a woman of few words that came short and sharp like the flapping of her thongs on the linoleum. 'You can't stay long, you hear? Wendy's got chores to finish!'

Wendy was sprawled out on her bed reading the latest *True Confessions* comic. 'You'd better not get caught over here. Your mother will kill you,' she exclaimed, looking up briefly before returning to her comic.

'Mum doesn't care what Mrs. Tallow says,' I replied. 'She says you're welcome at our house any time!' My words sparkled into the room as we laughed at Mrs. Tallow's consternation. Emboldened by our triumph over the authorities, we plotted new escapades.

'We could get up at dawn when no-one's around and meet the milkman, see if he'll take us for a ride,' I suggested. 'It'll be great riding round early in the morning. It can be our secret, we won't tell anyone else, not a soul, God's honour.'

another song about love

Wendy ushered me down the hall and into the lounge room, observing me closely as I looked around. The floral carpet was vacuumed and the mantelpiece filled with framed photographs of Wendy's parents and other family members. Wendy's mother, surprisingly slim-waisted in a white silk wedding gown, smiled up at Wendy's father. He was handsome and self-assured, the slouch hat and khaki uniform giving him an air of confidence. This photo had been taken before her father went to the war. The lounge room was a shrine of remembrance where her parents kept their faded dreams clean.

When Wendy took me down the hallway into a grotty kitchen piled high with dishes and smelling of old fat, I glimpsed her father asleep on a single bed in a room out the back. There were no sheets or blankets, only an old, stained mattress. Flies buzzed round a bare light bulb and there was a strange acrid smell emanating from the room. I sensed Wendy watching for signs of my disapproval and looked away.

The next morning I woke before dawn. Putting on shorts and a T-shirt, I stuffed some biscuits into a small bag before sneaking down the hall past the sound of Dad's snores. Out on the back porch the air was warm even though the sun wasn't up yet.

'Sshh, Kerry, heel!' I bent in closer, looking my dog straight in the eye as he jumped up, his tail wagging furiously. Sticking close to my ankle, he followed me as I snuck down the street. Wendy was waiting in the lane at the side of her house. As dawn filtered over the horizon, throwing pink shadows in the sky, we heard the clip-clop of the milkman's horse.

'What'll we do now?' Wendy whispered.

'We'll just go up and ask him for a ride,' I answered. 'Come on!'

When the milkman saw two skinny brown girls and a dog standing on the road, all looking up at him with big pleading eyes, he couldn't say no. 'Come on then, hop up, the dog can sit in the front too.'

The dry crisp smell of Christmas hung in the air. The peaceful rhythm of horses' hooves on the asphalt made other children turn in their sleep, dreaming of gifts of bicycles and roller skates, snorkels and teddy bears.

At the end of his round the milkman dropped us off. 'You'd better be careful, young ladies! Do your mum and dad know you two get about the streets like this?'

'We're always careful,' we replied, before pleading with him to let us come again. Perhaps he was thinking of his grandchildren, or perhaps he remembered his own childhood, but the milkman soon became a regular party to our secret rides.

We spent most of the summer holidays at the local pool, where Wendy was admired instead of ostracized for her renegade spirit. Happy with her newfound popularity, Wendy became my mother's secret admirer, hanging out at our place whenever Mum had

another song about love

friends over for afternoon drinks. Wendy said Mum was very beautiful. She asked me why my father didn't spend more time with Mum and her glamorous women friends, who didn't seem to have husbands around either. I didn't know why.

When we asked Mum she laughed. 'We're all grass widows, temporarily without husbands because they're too busy becoming successful,' she explained.

We couldn't make sense of her words. It was only as an adult that I understood my mother's discontentment with her lonely housewife role.

Sometimes Mum seemed cranky after her glamorous friends had been around. It wasn't like her to snap at me to tidy my room. She sighed, preparing dinner as if it was the most boring thing in the world to do. I thought Mum didn't like her friends coming over, but Wendy said she couldn't imagine why she wouldn't enjoy those wonderful afternoons. We sat in the corner listening to them talking and laughing with their deep throaty voices. As they drank afternoon sherries and smoked tailor-made cigarettes, we imagined that when we grew up we'd be just like them.

We were over at Wendy's house one day when the phone rang.

'It's your Mum,' Wendy frowned as she handed me the phone. 'Her voice doesn't sound right.'

'I want you to come home right away.' Mum sounded angry and her words were slurred. 'I need you here at home, now!'

JANIE CONWAY HERRON

Panicking, I put the phone down. 'I don't know what's wrong,' I told Wendy. 'Mum never tells me to come home in the middle of the day. I'd better go straight away.'

I ran home as fast as I could. Bursting in the back door, I sprinted up the hall and into the kitchen where Mum was still sitting by the phone. She had her best suit on, the one that made her look like a film star – but she looked terrible. There was a peculiar expression on her face and her lipstick was all smudged. Red patches of it spread across her cheeks and chin.

Like an animal sensing danger I backed into a corner, overtaken by terror. Dad pulled Mum up by the shoulders and helped her out of the room. My knees shook as Dad pushed past me snarling, 'Your mother is too drunk to look after you!'

Mum stared at me wordlessly, her face awry and her mouth all crooked.

After they'd left the kitchen expanded, overwhelming me with its echoing enormity. I ran into the pantry but the pantry was too small. All the green and yellow canisters, lined up and labelled in neat and descending order, became sharply outlined and fell on top of me. Tea, coffee, sugar, biscuits, green on yellow words leapt out, hurling themselves from protective shelves onto my head. I ran out of the pantry, out of the kitchen, down the hall and out the back door as Wendy came down the path towards me. Shame rose up from

another song about love

the pit of my stomach. My mother couldn't be like Wendy's father. She didn't drink like he did. No! I didn't want people talking about my mother like that and I didn't want anyone, least of all Wendy, knowing what had happened.

Wendy stood still. She must have known something was terribly wrong and had prepared herself for some dreadful news, but neither of us was ready for what happened next. From deep inside me came a high-pitched scream that frightened us both. Wendy stumbled back up the driveway as I ran after her, waving wildly and yelling.

'Go away! Go away! Nothing's wrong. Just go away and don't come back. Don't you understand? I never want to see you again!'

3

ONE NIGHT STAND

I WAS TALKING FAST. MY voice rose on a wave of nervous enthusiasm as Stevie drove through the wide, winding streets of outer Melbourne suburbs to Scarlet Sisters' first gig. We were the support act for Frankie Brave, an up-and-coming singer songwriter who'd just signed a deal with AM Records. Anna had known Frankie since the 1970s when she'd played bass in his band. When Frankie asked her if she knew anyone who'd be a good support for his band she'd recommended Scarlet Sisters. Knowing Anna was our bass player, Frankie said yes straight away. Frankie was pulling large audiences all over Melbourne. It was a good opportunity to debut our band. We were all excited about it.

JANIE CONWAY HERRON

'There it is!' I yelled, pointing to a large, neon-lit hotel.

Stevie cruised slowly towards the pub.

'Have you been to The Doncaster Inn before?' I asked.

'Only as part of the audience,' Stevie answered. 'I saw you play here once.'

'Did you really? When was that?'

'About ten years ago. I was just getting interested in playing then. That guitarist you had was great.'

I smiled. 'That was Joe, Jesse's dad. He's living up in Tamworth, making it big in the country music scene these days. Joe's one of those musicians who can play almost anything well. If the marriage had lasted I'd still be in that band and we'd both be famous by now.' When I saw the sign out the front of the hotel my excitement rose again. 'Look, Scarlet Sisters! They've put our name on the billboard.' I wound down the window and leaned right out. There was a parking space over near the back entrance. 'Quick, let's get it!' I yelled.

'Calm down, Lillie,' Stevie replied. 'We're early.'

A musky dankness engulfed us as we moved through the dark cement corridor in the hotel basement. We climbed the stairs to the lounge and made our way across a luminous orange and blue carpet, sticky with many years of spilt drinks.

another song about love

Ali was meticulously setting the angles and distances between each drum as he tuned the toms, one by one. The warm, round sound rang out through the room.

Two of the roadies from the main band were huddled round the mixing desk. With Stevie close on my heels, I strode over to greet them. Shaking hands with these notoriously tough guys as firmly as I could, I introduced them to Stevie.

Adrian leant towards us in an almost conspiratorial way. 'You can use any other lights but the blue ones, alright?'

I jumped away from him. 'Fuck, man! What kind of deal is that?'

Adrian grinned. 'You can use any lights but the blue ones, okay?'

'But you told me on the phone the other day that on account of this promotion of Frankie's album all you have are blue lights.'

Adrian's grin widened. 'Yeah, that's right.'

'So what you're telling me is we have *no* lights.'

'Yep.'

'Frankie is a friend of mine, you know,' I said, desperate to reclaim some dignity.

'Well you can speak to him about it if you want – but he won't be here until after you're due to start.'

Only the clinking of Adrian's keys gave any sign of his hesitancy as I stomped off towards the stage. 'Well, that's rock and roll, man!' I heard him chuckle.

I kicked at the stage with short jabs that echoed through its wooden hollowness. 'Fucking arseholes! Who the hell do they think they are! 'I shouted. 'I'm going to tell everyone about this. No one will want to work with them.'

Ali did a neat roll across his toms then leant over to adjust them. 'Don't underestimate the power of a gig, Lillie. Even if all your friends refused to be the support band, there'd still be some young garage band willing to do it.'

'But they wouldn't be as good as we are,' I protested. 'I just wish someone would give us a break.'

'Don't worry, Lillie,' Stevie chipped in. 'They can still hear us in the dark and we'll sound great!'

It was Wendy who found a solution. We'd asked her to do lights for us, never dreaming she'd have to supply them as well. A practical woman, she organised to borrow lights from the theatre group she worked with. While we did our sound check, she methodically set up around Frankie's 'blue funk' as she called it, without acknowledging his road crew with so much as a look.

But, when Vincent arrived ready to mix the sound for Scarlet Sisters, Frankie's road crew had more rules in store. 'No changing the equalisation on the mix, it's already set up for Frankie.'

This was usual procedure for the support band, but Vincent had no time for such a practice. 'How can

another song about love

I make you sound good, when the EQ is set up for male voices? Female voices need entirely different equalisation. It's outrageous that they expect you to work under these conditions.'

'You're right, Vincent,' Anna agreed. 'But it's usual for the support band to have these limitations. Everyone accepts it and if you don't, you don't get asked to do supports. It's as simple as that.'

Vincent's thin face screwed up. 'Well then, don't work under these conditions. You're better off not doing this sort of gig.'

'We need the exposure, that's why we're doing it,' Anna and I chorused.

'What kind of exposure is this? You're better off doing things in a small independent way. Put gigs on locally and invite your friends. That's the way to do it.'

Out in the back room I leant against a wall and rolled a joint. Anna took it and lit it, then handed it back. It was a simple gesture that mirrored the balance of give and take in our relationship. We were both involved in juggling children with careers. Together, we helped each other keep the balls in the air. It wasn't easy but we were doing it. I handed the joint to Wendy and she took a long, deep toke. Her smile acknowledged the long history of our lives together.

After my childhood proclamation of never wanting to see Wendy again, she turned up at my house after school every day. Mum often let Wendy in before

JANIE CONWAY HERRON

I had a chance to freeze her out. Stomping down the hall I slammed my bedroom door, leaving Wendy and Mum to keep each other company.

One day, Mum sat me down and told me that she had a problem with drinking too much and that was why my father had been so angry the day she'd called me home from Wendy's place. Mum had been attending Alcoholics Anonymous meetings and trying to stop drinking, but Dad hadn't been much help. When she'd told him about it that terrible day, he'd declared: 'No wife of mine is an alcoholic'. Mum counselled me to have more empathy for Wendy's situation and be more supportive. If Mum was also making a plea for greater understanding of her own circumstances, I didn't understand it at the time. Over time, my shame about people knowing my mother was an alcoholic lessened while Dad continued to find Mum's alcoholism hard to comprehend. It was the beginning of a big rift between us.

Wendy and I understood each other at an intimate level that we shared with only a few others. Anna was one of those people. In places like this we didn't need words, just a shrug or a rolling of eyes. The yellowing walls of the room were covered in graffiti. Neither Anna nor I bothered to read beyond the first few deeply philosophical phrases like 'Johnny's got a 12 inch dick,' and 'Bob likes it both ways.' But Wendy read meticulously. With a quick rolling of her eyes, she pointed out a scrawled message above the doorway.

another song about love

NO GIRLS OR GROUPIES ALLOWED BEYOND THIS POINT.

Wendy took another long drag on the joint, her words rolling out slowly with the smoke. 'I wonder if that means us?'

'Na, we're women, not girls, and we certainly aren't groupies,' Anna replied.

'Speak for yourselves,' I added. 'I feel like a girl most of the time and I'm still a groupie, even if I am more choosy now.'

'Well girly, I'm afraid you'll have to leave then, even if you are the mother of a ten-year-old boy and the lead singer of the band!' Anna laughed.

Our set started. Looking across the empty dance floor I saw Wendy throw a spotlight on Anna playing the bass riff of the first song. Stevie's sweet guitar licks cruised over the top and Ali kept time with the high hat. Then the spotlight was on me and I introduced the song. 'I'd like to dedicate this first song to Wendy, who's out there doing lights for us tonight, and Anna, who's playing bass up here, plus all the other women out there in rock and roll land.' A woman's voice whooped across the darkness as I bent into the guitar and played.

Halfway into the first set, the pace picked up and we gathered momentum. At the beginning we played to a straggle of people, the majority of them Frankie's fans. But the band was tight and people felt it in their feet. Two by two, they trickled onto the dance floor. By the time we were halfway through our bracket, the dancers were struggling for space.

I could hardly believe the clarity of the fold-back speakers. I'd never been able to hear myself so well. Turning to adjust my amp I yelled across to Anna, 'Vincent is a genius!' before beginning the last song.

In the dim light behind the mixing desk, a man watched me. His white suit coat stood out in the darkness in striking contrast to his dark skin, while his black hair was brushed back flat. To my surprise, when I caught his eye, he grinned back at me. I couldn't help returning his smile before shyness made me look away. When I looked back, he'd disappeared. I spied him at the back of the room leaning against the wall and nodding approvingly. The startling blueness of his eyes was disarming. Even at that distance I could see their colour clearly. I kept on singing, but my attention was divided between the man with the blue eyes and the song. I launched into the last verse, hoping that I hadn't missed anything out and the band sailed along with me. After the third repeat of the chorus, some of the audience sang along with us. This was a good sign. It had been worth bowing and scraping to Frankie's roadies just to play to an appreciative audience. When we finished, the crowd yelled for more, the sound rising and falling as the house lights were turned on and taped music played through the speakers. The support band never did encores.

another song about love

Out in the back room, everyone congratulated each other.

Stevie grinned as I reached up and hugged him. 'You were great.'

'Yes,' Anna agreed, 'you were fantastic.'

When Vincent came into the room, his fair-skinned face flushed with excitement, we all cheered him. Tugging at his straw blond hair, he told us how he got such a great sound. 'It's all in the EQ settings, just like I told you.'

'You didn't!' Anna gasped.

Vincent nodded, the smile on his face a mixture of defiance and concern. 'But I reset to the original settings after we finished.'

'Thanks, Vincent,' I said quietly. This was the first time in my life anyone had taken so much care of the way I sounded.

'Well, I wasn't going to have my reputation as a mixer shot to pieces on my first gig in Australia, was I?' He laughed and I laughed with him.

Frankie stood inside the doorway for a moment, taking in the rise and fall of the laughter. He moved across the room, his black high-heeled boots ringing on the concrete floor.

'That was great.' His words slipped languidly from a lop-sided smile as his hand came to rest on Anna's back. 'Good to see you, Anna, how're you going?'

JANIE CONWAY HERRON

Anna smiled as Frankie's hand rested softly on her shoulder, but she didn't rush to tell him about the trials the band had had with his roadies. Neither did I.

The trauma of the early evening set up was almost forgotten until Wendy came into the room. Standing in the doorway, she brought us all back to the more practical aspects of band life. 'Hey you guys,' she yelled. 'I got you out of a jam. Now it's your turn to help me get these lights down! I don't want to be hanging around here all night. Can someone give me a hand, now!' She gave Frankie a special glare that sent furrows of surprise rippling along his forehead.

Anna snapped her bass case shut and followed Wendy out the door.

'What's up with her?' Frankie asked me, his face crinkling with puzzlement.

When I answered, my skin crawled with my own dishonesty. 'Oh nothing much, you know how road crew are.' I shrugged. 'I'd better go and see if I can give her a hand.'

Wendy was perched precariously on a ladder getting lights down and passing them to Anna. 'Just in time,' she yelled and leant towards me with another light.

I reached up but as the light dropped into my hand, the sudden weight made me stumble towards the ladder. Someone grabbed me tightly around the waist and pulled me upright, catching the light before it crashed to the floor. When he was sure I was steady, my blue-eyed admirer set me on my feet again.

another song about love

'Thanks. I owe you one,' I spluttered.

'I'll remember that.' The stranger grinned. Then Anna and Wendy were by my side, hugging me as if I might fly away at any moment.

'Jeezus, that was close,' Wendy exclaimed. 'I thought I was going to come off that ladder for sure. What's your name? Sir Galahad?'

The stranger's grin broadened. 'Matt.'

Anna and Wendy offered their hands.

'I'm Anna. Glad to meet you.'

'And I'm Wendy. Thanks for rescuing us.'

Matt bowed, clicking his heels together. 'Shucks, it was nothing,' he drawled, then took me by the arm. 'And what's your name, little girl?'

'Lillie.'

'Lillie, I like the sound of that. Do you float on water too?'

'Only on a good day.'

The four of us stood at the bar as Frankie's band began. When the crowd pressed to the outer edges of the room, Matt lifted me onto the edge of the bar so I could see. I was so taken by the feel of his hands on my waist I hardly noticed what the band sounded like. When I leant into him, he gently kissed the back of my neck. One hand moved under my top, cupping my breast and caressing my nipple as Damian sang and the crowd went wild.

After the gig, I stood on the steps of the hotel with Stevie and Matt. The night air was fresh, though still very warm and the sweet scent of suburban night flowers drifted across the car park.

'Want to come to St Kilda for a coffee?' Matt's invitation was for us both but Stevie declined.

'I've got Sunday lunch at the folks' place tomorrow. I'd better not look too bleary-eyed or they'll worry that I'm on drugs.'

I looked from Stevie to Matt, not sure of how to negotiate the next step. Jesse was over at Anna's and we'd paid for a babysitter. I was free for the evening but I didn't want to seem too eager.

Matt made it easy. 'Want to come, Lillie? I'll drive you home later.' He was grinning that cheeky grin again.

'Alright,' I replied, trying to sound indifferent. When disappointment fluttered momentarily across Stevie's face, I reached up and kissed him on the cheek. 'It was a great gig. I'm glad you're our guitar player.'

Stevie blushed. 'Nice meeting you,' he said to Matt. 'I hope we see you at our next gig.'

St Kilda's main drag had long been a popular spot for people whose way of life favoured late nights and early mornings. The café Matt took me to had windows offering a fine view of the street. When Matt guided me to a table, people nodded and smiled at him as they walked past.

'I used to work this street a while ago,' Matt said casually.

another song about love

'Work the street?'

'Sell my body.' Matt looked up at me, a bemused expression on his face.

'Oh?' I replied, trying to disguise my shock, 'I thought only women did that.'

Matt shook his head. 'I was a junkie but I've been out of that scene for over a year now.'

I pictured him soliciting rough trade then blowing all his hard-earned money on drugs, but his story was way beyond anything I could have imagined. I'd heard tales like his before, but never from someone who'd experienced the life. From gangland set-ups to police raids and girlfriends overdosing in his arms, Matt's story slowly unfolded.

When he asked me back to his place I accepted his offer enthusiastically. As we paid the bill together, I smiled at the bright-eyed waitress. She knew Matt well and I tried to imagine myself at the heart of this scene. It was a stupid thought. I might have been open to all sorts of ideas about sexuality and freedom but there was no way I'd sell myself like Matt had. Then again, I'd never been that desperate.

We stepped out onto the pavement. A light pink sky spread out across the bay and filtered through the branches of palm trees growing along the foreshore. I have always been glad to see the sun rise, relaxing into that heavy-bodied feeling of no sleep without giving in to it. I sank into the passenger seat of Matt's car and imagined the tiny flat that he was about to take me to. The overfull ashtrays, a week's worth of dishes in the sink crawling with unspeakable things, an interesting record collection with a complete set of Doors albums, an unmade bed with dirty brown sheets. I had taken it for granted that St Kilda was his stamping ground so when we headed away from there I had to ask where we were going.

'I live in Kew,' Matt answered. We drove on in silence until he turned down a wide suburban street lined with poplar trees and into the curved driveway of a fake Tudor mansion.

'My parents' place.' The car pulled up in front of a large double garage and he operated the remote control. 'Once I started going to rehab they said I could come back home. My parents are away this weekend so they won't bother us.'

My apocalyptic vision of Matt's living space faded as the garage door automatically closed behind us and he led the way up a narrow staircase to an immaculate kitchen.

Perched high on a stool I watched Matt make tea.

'My parents adopted me when I was a baby,' he explained.

'Really? Couldn't your mother have children?' I asked, my reply sounding so feeble and uncaring I felt ashamed.

'I was their charity case. I've got an older sister. My parents conceived her naturally, so-to-speak.' Matt's voice sounded like a kid braving schoolyard bullies. 'They adopted me to appease their

another song about love

conscience, I suppose. I made them pay through the nose for it too,' When Matt laughed, I laughed with him and his face softened. 'You're nice,' he said, reaching out to take my hand. 'I like you.'

'I like you too,' I replied, desire rising with the touch of his hand.

'You must be tired. Do you want to go to bed?' he asked.

I nodded.

Matt directed me upstairs with an arm round my waist but when I nestled my head into his shoulder, he didn't respond. He ushered me into a room that was so feminine I knew it couldn't be his. 'This is my sister's room,' he announced, pointing towards a single bed covered in dolls all neatly lined up in rows. He carefully put them on the floor. 'You can sleep here. Would you like a teddy to cuddle?'

I took my boots off and slipped under the sheet, wondering why he had become so distant. Perhaps it had something to do with being at his parents' place.

Matt was tender as he tucked me in. 'This one's my favourite.' He gave me a teddy and kissed me on the cheek. 'I'll see you later on.'

I drifted off to sleep, listening to the early morning bird sounds. When I woke my clothes were sticky with sweat. Certain that it must be late afternoon, I leapt out of bed, straightened my crumpled skirt and looked out into the hall before creeping downstairs. Matt was sitting outside.

JANIE CONWAY HERRON

'What time is it?' I asked.

'Just after midday.' Matt's face was smooth and newly shaved. Drops of water clung to hair hanging in curls round his shoulders. 'Do you want to have a shower?'

I declined, despite feeling very seedy. 'I have to be back before two. That's when Anna's going to drop my son Jesse off at home.'

Matt looked surprised. 'You look too young to have a child.'

'He's ten years old.'

'You must have been very young when you had him.'

'I was old enough.'

'Well, little mother, would you like a lift home?'

The sun sat high and hot in the sky as we drove across town. Inside Matt's car the intense heat made my head pound. When we pulled up outside my house, I leant over and kissed Matt on the cheek.

He gave me a dry kiss back. 'If you want to give me your phone number, I'll ring you sometime,' he said, with a lopsided grin.

'Sure.' I scrambled through my bag, looking for paper and pen. Pulling out a handbill advertising last night's gig I wrote my phone number on the back of it and gave it to him. 'Here's something to remember me by.'

'Thanks. I'll ring you soon.'

another song about love

'That'd be nice.' I opened the car door and got out. When Matt handed me my guitar, I sprinted across the road then turned to see him still watching me. 'Go on, off you go,' I laughed, flapping my hand at him.

Matt revved the car up, flashed his white teeth and took off.

'Cheeky man,' I mumbled. When I opened my front door the darkness of the house rushed to greet me with its coolness.

Once I'd showered and changed, the cool water and clean clothes made me feel fresher, but tiredness still pressed at the edges of my psyche. When Anna brought Jesse home, the kids asked if they could go to the local pool.

'Can I go please?' Jesse pleaded. 'It's *so* hot!'

'I don't know, I've hardly seen you all weekend,' I teased.

Jesse pushed his bottom lip into a pout.

'Okay, you can go,' I relented, 'but only if you help Sam look after Antonia, and make sure you keep plenty of sunscreen on.'

'I promise,' Jesse beamed.

The two boys walked up the street, looking like painted warriors with pink zinc stripes on their noses and cheeks. Antonia dawdled behind, her towel trailing on the footpath. At the corner, Jesse picked up Antonia's towel and Sam hoisted her onto his shoulders before they disappeared.

JANIE CONWAY HERRON

Anna and I stood watching the space where our children had just been. The afternoon sun burnt into my skin and the north wind blew gritty dust into my face.

'I'll be happy when this bushfire weather stops,' I said as I turned back towards the house.

'What did you do last night?' Anna asked.

'Not what you think, but I didn't get much sleep.'

'You should take better care of yourself, Lillie. All this hard living's getting to you,' Anna reprimanded.

'Yeah but it's fun,' I answered. 'That guy Matt's had a harder life than me but he still looks like a boy.'

'Probably acts like one too.'

'He used to be a junkie.'

'Used to be!' Anna snorted. 'There's no such thing as an ex-junkie.'

Irritated, I buried my head in my arms, sniffing the musty wood of the kitchen table.

'You don't want to run the risk of Jesse rubbing shoulders with junkies, do you?' Anna lectured. 'You owe it to your boy not to get involved with some half-grown man that needs taking care of. You spread yourself too thin, Lillie.'

'Yes Anna, you're right,' I answered wearily. 'Just give me a good night's sleep and I'll be right as rain.'

'Some rain might make us all feel better.'

another song about love

When the kids came back, we ordered pizza and sat the kids in front of the television while we drove round the corner to collect it. As I waited for the pizza, I remembered the morning sunrise and Matt's tender face bending over to kiss me.

The pizza man broke my reverie when he yelled out, 'One large vegetarian!'

'That's me,' I giggled then juggled the too-hot carton out to the car and threw it onto the back seat. 'Whoa, it's hot in that shop,' I exclaimed. 'I don't know how that poor man can stand it. It's a sweat shop in there.'

As we drove home, a gust of hot wind blew down the signs outside shops and blinds crashed against the awnings.

'God this is scary,' Anna said as she parked the car outside my house. 'It feels like the end of the world.'

We rushed inside, slamming the door behind us. Thinking of my precious ganja, I ran out into the backyard. Anna put the pizza down in front of the kids and followed me.

'I'm going to have to harvest them,' I said as I stared at my plants, grateful they hadn't been damaged by the wind.' Carefully, I took the pots across the cement backyard into the bathroom then turned the shower on. 'There you are, my babies,' I whispered as the water dropped like gentle rain on their pungent leaves. 'This is your last night together, tomorrow is harvest day.' I stepped back and surveyed the forest in the middle of the bath.

Anna put her arms round my shoulders. 'They're only plants, you know.'

'I know, I'm way too attached,' I sighed as I ushered Anna out of the bathroom and back inside.

The kids had finished off almost all of the pizza.

'We saved you some,' Jesse said, but the sodden pizza didn't appeal.

'I think it's time for us to go home,' Anna called to Sam and Antonia as Jesse greedily shoved the last of the pizza into his mouth.

'Hey Jesse, aren't you going to say goodbye to your friends?' I prompted.

'Bye,' Jesse answered absentmindedly.

When I stretched out on the couch and ruffled Jesse's hair, he moved in closer. Dropping his head into my lap he fell asleep. With some effort, I picked him up and carried him to his room. Whimpering, he slowly slithered down my body and flopped into bed.

I got into my own bed and looked around my room. Clothes were scattered all over the place. My life was perpetually on the edge of chaos and there was only one thing I could do to wrestle some control back from the gods of mayhem. I set the radio alarm clock early and turned out the light. The wind had died down and the air was dense and still. In the quiet stillness I drifted off to sleep.

another song about love

When the early morning news broadcast woke me, I tried to make sense of what the newsreader was saying.

'Fire swept through the small coastal town of Lakes Entrance early this morning. Residents had to be evacuated with only a minute's notice, taking whatever possessions they could with them.'

I listened as the disembodied voices of the evacuated travelled the airwaves to my bedroom. Many had escaped within seconds of the fire descending on their homes. One woman described driving down the road and looking in the rear vision mirror as her house exploded into flames. An excited reporter asked her inane questions. Caught up in the minute detail of her loss, she answered in a voice trembling with fatigue.

I remembered Lakes Entrance and the way the panorama of ocean and hills had panned out in front of me when I went hitchhiking as a teenager. It was easy to visualise the flames fanning out across the landscape. I imagined having to evacuate at the last minute and made a mental list of what I'd save first, starting with Jesse, then my guitars. In a bid to stop my wild thoughts, I turned the radio off. The early morning quiet was broken by the sounds of cars in the distance. I pulled back the curtains and looked out just in time to see Jonathon start out on his early morning run. When I waved, a quick smile and a nod acknowledged my presence, the muscles of his legs tensing and flexing with the regular rhythm of his running. Looking down at my legs I remembered the wiry child

I had once been. A layer of flesh fell smoothly over the strong calf muscles I had inherited from my dancing days. 'Muscle gone to fat,' I muttered. 'There's more than my house I need to get in order.'

By seven o'clock I had washed up and cleaned the kitchen. When I woke Jesse, breakfast was waiting for him.

Jesse attacked the pile of toast hungrily, his eyes darting round the room. 'You must have got up early this morning, Mum. The kitchen's all tidy and everything.'

'Yep.' I was pleased that Jesse had noticed. 'I even washed the floor.'

'Oh no!' Jesse's eyes rolled upwards in mock horror. 'Not the kitchen floor! My mum's turned normal.'

'Soon I'll start wearing tracksuits and watch you play football on Saturdays.'

'You don't expect me to be normal too, do you?'

'Why of course I do,' I said and my laughter blended with Jesse's.

As we walked to school, Jesse put his hand in mine. When I squeezed it a huge grin spread across his face. He crossed the schoolyard then turned to check if I was still there. I waited until he was playing with the other kids, then waved goodbye.

another song about love

On the way home I bought myself a roll of brown paper from the newsagent, in preparation for the harvest. By midday I was ready for the big task. The unrelenting heat made me sweat and the scissors slipped round in my hand as I cut huge swathes of brown paper. In the bathroom, the heady scent of the plants greeted me and I talked to them in a low voice before taking hold of the first plant and laying it on its side. I tugged at it gently and its pungent scent filled my nostrils. Once I'd finished pulling them out of their pots, I wrapped each plant in brown paper and hung them up to dry amongst my clothes, carefully arranging them so they couldn't be seen. Afterwards I threw the dirt from the pots onto the patch of garden in front of the house. The piles of moist, dark brown earth stood out in contrast to the brittle piles of brown leaves that had fallen from the morning glory.

As I made iced lemon tea for myself, and blackcurrant ice blocks for Jesse, it was easy to believe the smiling advertisements for domesticity offered in women's magazines. Today was a Hills Hoist day, as Anna liked to say. I looked out at my backyard, now bereft of carefully raised plants, and imagined lush flowering gardens filled with happy children, even a dog and cat.

The cool water of the shower washed over my body as I started singing. When I took a freshly washed dress off the washing line and put it on, the clean smell of sunshine-dried cotton made me happy. The cool crisp feel of the dress made my skin tingle. Fantasies of Matt floated around in my mind as I lay back on the couch. I imagined kissing him and the feel of his body through my thin cotton dress as we embraced. Then tiredness closed my eyes and I fell asleep.

I woke to black clouds rolling across the sky and the sound of thunder in the distance. Opening all the windows and doors, I ran out into the backyard as the first heavy drops of rain fell. Soaked to the skin, I danced, my bare feet splashing in the steamy puddles as I welcomed the cool change. The drought had broken.

4

SAIL AWAY

L IKE MANY AUSTRALIAN MEN OF the 1950s, my father forged a career on the back of the burgeoning national wool industry. He left school at fourteen and travelled into rural New South Wales where he worked as a wool classer until the outbreak of World War II. After the war, keen to resurrect his life and recently married, he began working as a wool buyer. We moved from the northern beaches of Sydney to suburban Melbourne because Dad had accepted a position managing the Australian arm of a French wool-buying firm. This position took him travelling a lot further than rural New South Wales. I loved the fact that my father travelled so much and learnt about different countries and cultures through his stories of the places he'd been to.

Every time Dad came home from his travels he'd bring back presents for me. Once he brought me a transistor all the way from Japan. I gingerly switched it on, hoping it didn't only play Japanese music. Johnny O'Keefe sang *Rock Around the Clock*, his voice made small by the tinny speakers. Thrilled with my present, I took it with me wherever I went. Knowing I loved dolls, Dad brought them back from all the different countries he had been to: a sailor from Amsterdam, a dancer from Spain, a peasant girl in an apron from Belgium and a bride from England. When I carefully lined them up on my bed, it felt like I'd travelled with Dad to far off places I'd only seen in pictures.

After one trip, Dad gave me something much better than all the previous presents. It was a photo of one of the dancers from the American Ballet, autographed to me personally. I found it hard to believe that my father knew this woman perched high in arabesque on the tips of her toes. I dreamed of meeting her, of going to New York and becoming one of the dancers in the corps-de-ballet through the connections my father had with this beautiful woman. I framed the picture and hung it above my bed, where she smiled at me.

another song about love

Late at night, my parents' heated whispers coming through the wall interrupted my dancing dreams and compelled me to listen. Ever since the day I ran home to find my mother drunk and my dad snarling and angry like never before, I watched closely for any signs of the terrible anger that surfaced between them that day. Apart from those heated whispers and Mum's quiet unhappiness, everything appeared to have returned to the way things were before.

One night, I heard my mother's angry voice and tried to catch snippets of their conversation. What was an affair? That's what Mum was angry about but I didn't have a clue what it meant.

I waited until Mum and I were alone to ask.

Mum's face reddened as she explained that an affair happened when one person who was already married wanted to be with someone else.

'So why were you and Dad talking about it?' I probed.

'When was that, darling?' The blush spreading across Mum's face made me wish I'd kept the question to myself.

'I don't know,' I answered. 'I overheard you and Dad talking the other night and you said something about having affairs.'

Mum looked away.

'I wasn't trying to listen,' I persisted as familiar, tight-wired anxiety rose up from the pit of my stomach. 'It's just that you sounded cross and I was scared you and Dad might start fighting again.'

Mum took my hands in hers. 'We were probably talking about an affair your father had when he was overseas. It's all sorted now though.'

'Where was he?' I felt an urgent need to know all the details.

'He was in New York, darling, and he had an affair with a dancer there.'

'What?'

'He thought he loved the dancer in the photo you have on the wall. It's all over now, so it's okay. We worked it out.'

My heart sank with the sudden knowledge that things could turn out to be so false. My father had had an affair with the same woman whose autographed photo hung on my bedroom wall. He'd loved the woman who smiled down on me every night. Whenever Mum went into my room, she'd been forced to look at the picture of that svelte woman frozen in arabesque. In an instant I hated every dance I had ever danced, every straight-backed graceful movement I had made and any aspiration I'd had to be like that smiling woman. I rushed from the kitchen, took the framed picture from my bedroom wall and smashed it on the floor. The glass fractured, splintering across the dancer's smiling face.

Mum sat down on the bed beside me. 'Lillie, please don't be so upset. These things happen in marriages. Besides, your father and I talked about it

another song about love

and now things are much better than they were before this happened. I asked your father to choose either the dancer or his family. That's us Lillie, you and me. We are his family. He chose us, not the American dancer. Your father loves you very much, Lillie, and he's not going to leave you, not ever.'

Looking into my mother's eyes I wanted to believe her assurances. But as I buried my head into the musky familiarity of Mum's embrace, I felt as fractured as the glass on my bedroom floor.

The regular ballet classes I went to after school meant a long walk from the tram stop to home and I was growing tired of making the journey. The classes were strenuous and left me exhausted, but the half hour walk home in the fading evening light was worse. Late one winter's evening, when the streetlights glowed in the dull evening light, I pulled my coat in tighter and stepped into the brightly lit milk bar to buy a bar of chocolate. I was always starving after ballet and the chocolate staved my hunger on the long walk home. As darkness closed in, I crept along the grassy verges of the backstreets close to home. A dog barked. When that set off another dog barking I broke into a run. My breath was a thick fog streaming past my cheeks. A dog leapt out of the gateway next door to our house, barking and snarling, its hackles standing straight up. I stopped still and held my breath. Dad had advised me to do this when I told him how the dogs barked and snarled at me on my way home from ballet. The dog sniffed around my ankles. His cold wet nose nudged my legs as he bared grimy old fangs in freckled gums, before walking away. I made the last dash home, my feet crunching on the pebbles in the driveway. Puffing and exhausted, I rushed to my room and threw myself onto my bed. When my own dog, Kerry, came in and nudged me under the arm I held him close, whispering. 'I can't go dancing any more. I don't want to. I can't, I just can't!'

Mum appeared in the doorway.

'I can't keep going to ballet classes after school, Mum. It's too hard,' I cried, hugging Kerry closely. 'It takes so long to get home and I have to walk all that way in the dark when it's winter. All the dogs in the neighbourhood bark at me and tonight that awful old bulldog next door nearly attacked me. Besides, I'm no good at dancing anymore. I'm not one of Michel's favourites. There are so many girls in the class better than I am, including Sarah. I'm just second rate, I'll never be a prima ballerina.'

'Don't be such a perfectionist, Lillie.' Mum sat down next to me. 'You don't have to be a prima ballerina; you could always be in the chorus. You're too hard on yourself. You need to enjoy dancing more. You can't always be the best at everything.'

While Mum's words were comforting, they echoed a looming sense of failure. Being anything less

another song about love

than a prima ballerina didn't feel right. As my enthusiasm for ballet waned I lost interest in everything else. I distracted myself with television dramas in the evenings, and during the day. When the screen flickered, I became lost in the drama of other people's lives instead of facing my own. Some days I didn't even go to school. When Dad was away I could do as I pleased and when he was home, he was too busy arguing with Mum to notice me. When he did show interest he'd go on about my potential, as if it was something I could retrieve. I became adept at not listening to him, finding a world inside my head where he couldn't reach me. While I watched television, Mum slept. Days often went by this way. We were both trying to forget: one through sleep, the other through fantasy – two misfits bound together.

When Dad was away, Mum and I often hopped into bed together. Nestling into each other we talked long into the night. Curled up against my mother, the softness of her belly in the small of my back made me feel safe. Mum stroked my hair and I pretended I was asleep; nestling in closer, tender, fragile feelings enveloped us both. Under the covers, in this bed, inside this room, our bonding was safe and warm. Outside, another world waited, one that threatened to shatter our intimacy, turning our bonding into a sentence, one reserved almost exclusively for women.

Dad was also critical of the way that I picked at my food and didn't eat at mealtimes. He hated it when I didn't eat. Mum asked Dad to be less critical.

JANIE CONWAY HERRON

Though he didn't say anything I was conscious of him watching me. The atmosphere at the dinner table became heavy with the tension of unsaid things. Every time I put my knife down on my plate, Dad's sighs made the food stick in my throat. I tried hard to push the food down, but it made me so sick I had to rush from the table.

Later on, I couldn't get enough to eat. No longer light, I protected myself with heaviness. I filled myself with warm pieces of toast, swimming in butter and honey, the sweet nectar comforting me and helping me forget my real emptiness. Layers of flesh bounced around me as I walked, hiding the gracefulness I once had. I tried to part the flesh and look inside for the tiny ballerina I once was, hiding in there.

Miss Daniels, the headmistress of the school Wendy and I went to, was a thin, severe woman whose ambitions for the girls in her care were predicated on women having a good education. Wendy and I often scoffed at this emphasis, saying our education was only so we could become the accomplished wives of upper-class lawyers and politicians. This may have been true, but Miss Daniels was determined that her girls' education was paramount. To this end she proposed that we all learn Latin before taking up other languages. Science was also highly valued, as were

another song about love

music and art. I loved singing and soon began performing in the madrigal group at morning assemblies. Excited, I took a deep breath as our music teacher raised her baton and we started singing. The sound of our young girl voices blending together, the way the harmonies merged and resolved, amazed me. When we finished, the applause from the rest of the school was exhilarating.

One day I was told to go to Miss Daniels' office to explain my absences from school. If she was concerned for my emotional welfare, it was lost on me.

'You see, my mother hasn't been all that well and I've been trying to look after her while my father's been away on business,' I tried to explain.

Miss Daniels leant back in her chair, pressing the tips of her fingers in and out in a way that implied she was weighing up the veracity of my words. 'Oh, I see. And what is it exactly that is wrong with your mother?'

'Um,' I struggled to find the right words, 'she's tired a lot and has to go to bed. I stay home to make sure she wakes up.' I didn't let on that my mother drank too much and I was trying to stop her by hiding the alcohol. This always became more urgent when my father was due home from interstate wool sales and was certain to cause a fight. I'd climb up on kitchen chairs and hide the whisky bottles she bought right at the back of the kitchen cupboard. Other times I'd put them behind the toilet cistern. I don't know why I didn't throw the alcohol out. Mum never questioned or commented but I know she often found my hiding places because the bottles disappeared. Sometimes Mum counselled me about the folly of hiding bottles from alcoholics but she never accused me of doing the hiding. That wasn't her style.

A frown travelled across Miss Daniels' forehead and she sat forward, spreading her fingers on the shiny polished wood of the desktop. 'Does your mother know that your absences are liable to make you fail at school?'

'No, she doesn't,' I stammered. 'I mean she wouldn't want that to happen.'

'Well that's what will happen if you don't start coming to school more often, young lady. I have a mind to get in touch with your father. I'm sure he has no idea that you are taking advantage of your mother's lack of discipline to hang out with your friends while he's away.'

'Oh no, that won't be necessary,' I tried to sound calm. 'I'll try to come to school more often, really I will, Miss Daniels!'

Miss Daniels' face softened. 'You're a very smart girl, Lillie. You could go a long way but you won't unless you apply yourself. We take pride in the standard of education at this school. We want you to do as well as you can and reach your full potential. I'll give you one more chance but any more absences will need a better explanation than you've given me today.'

another song about love

Heart pounding, I walked away from Miss Daniels' office. The headmistress sounded so much like my father, raving about me reaching my potential while he waved a hand above my head. Adults always had an invisible standard in mind that I could never reach. I couldn't stop Mum from drinking while I was at school.

That night Mum listened intently while I described my conversation with Miss Daniels. If she felt upset about what I told her she didn't show it. 'Don't worry, darling,' she said. 'I know you've been trying to help me, but it's not your responsibility. I should have realised that you were taking too much time off school. Leave it to me, I'll explain things to Miss Daniels.'

The following Monday I waited anxiously for Mum at the school gate. When she rounded the corner and waved I was relieved to see that she was sober. I could tell by the way she walked. She was dressed impeccably too, in a long, straight, close fitting linen dress with matching blue coat, white gloves and blue hat. I rushed to greet her. When Wendy ran across the yard, Mum took both our hands, beaming down at us as we walked proudly on either side of her.

Whatever Mum said to Miss Daniels during their meeting must have had a positive effect, because that afternoon in Latin Miss Daniels made a special point of praising me for the work I'd done. She even managed a smile for Wendy, whose forthright manner often put her offside with the headmistress.

Both Wendy and I knew what it was like to live in two worlds and keep up appearances. One day, Wendy came over to my place after school and we found Mum lying on the floor in the hall, unconscious. I was so embarrassed I stepped over her and closed the door into my bedroom as if nothing had happened. Wendy stood in my room open-mouthed with surprise.

'It's been happening a lot lately,' I said, trying to sound blasé. 'She'll come round soon and I'll put her to bed. Don't tell anyone about this, will you?'

'I promise.' Wendy said as she licked her finger, crossed her heart and entered the world of my darkest secrets.

Then Wendy told me how her father used to come into her room when he was drunk and do things to her that she knew were wrong. This had continued right up until the day he died. Wendy had never told anyone else. She didn't know whether her mother had any inkling of what had gone on. We both agreed that it explained why there had been so much tension between the two of them. Wendy's brother Geoffrey had always been the favourite. In the years since her father's death the friction between Wendy and her mum had mellowed out. Because of her own family life, Wendy understood my mother and would never judge her. We shared the precarious nature of our day-to-day lives and protected the secrets of each other's private worlds fiercely. Wendy was part of my inner circle whereas people like Miss Daniels were not.

My father, on the other hand, was a man I both loved and feared, someone on the periphery of both worlds who held enormous sway over how I saw myself.

At school one day a guitar, left in the middle of the music room, beckoned to me from its open case. I bent over and plucked a string. The guitar sang to me as the strings echoed in the belly of the instrument. I bent down and plucked the string again. I was fifteen years old when I fell in love with the guitar. I begged Dad to buy one for me. When Dad agreed to pay for lessons as well, I was ecstatic. He gave me another long talk about how I needed to practise regularly and not miss classes if I wanted to be any good at playing a musical instrument.

A parcel came from my grandfather with the score of Tchaikovsky's *Swan Lake* in it. It was a daunting expectation on behalf of my grandfather, but as Mum explained, he was old now and becoming forgetful. He was thinking of how I loved ballet and hadn't realised it was too soon for me to tackle a complicated piece of music that wasn't composed for guitar. But as I dreamt of impressing Pop with my guitar playing, a spark of interest in a future I could imagine for myself, returned.

One freezing winter morning, I walked to my first guitar lesson. I rang the doorbell of my teacher's house, thrust my hands under my armpits to warm them and waited. When the door opened I was surprised to be greeted by a young woman who smiled warmly and took me to a small, cheery room with a large window looking out onto the backyard. Outside, the bare trees stood stiffly in the wind; inside, the house was warm and comfortable.

When my teacher, Susan, picked up a guitar her fingers were pliable and fluid and the sound of her playing amazed me. Then it was my turn to try playing. I stretched out my fingers, one by one. They were as stiff as the trees outside and when I tried to play, they felt clumsy. At home after my first lesson, I played a D major chord over and over again until I got it right. With steady practice, I began to like the sound of my own playing.

Wendy and I often spent time together working out songs we knew from songbooks we'd collected. As I practised the chords, we worked on the harmonies to songs by The Everly Brothers and Buddy Holly until we thought we sounded pretty good.

Now, when my parents argued I shut out the sound of their fighting by turning on the radio in my room and listening to Stan Rofe play the latest hit songs on 3UZ. Fine-tuned to the times when the air

another song about love

between my mother and father was charged with electricity I turned up the radio as The Beatles sang *Can't Buy Me Love* or Cilla Black's golden voice sang about the man who was her world. One part of me was intent on drowning out my parents' voices with music while the other part couldn't resist listening to what they were saying. All the while The Beatles smiled benevolently from my bedroom wall. When I looked up at them it felt as if they understood my pain. If I moved around the room their eyes followed me and, as I dreamt of meeting them, they became the agents of my imaginary escape. Sometimes I'd marry one of them, mostly John, but then I switched my allegiance to George because he was a guitarist. The most exciting daydreams I had were the ones where I was playing in a group just as famous. The two groups would meet and George would fall in love with me and everything would be solved. My mother would stop drinking and come to live with us in England while my father would have to admit I'd made a success of my life and George would simply adore me like no one else ever had.

One night I turned the radio up loud, but still my parents' argument rose up and over the music. As Dad's voice came crashing through my reverie I found myself at the centre of their argument. 'She's only going to grow up and get married. Why is her education so important? It's costing us a fortune to send her to that school. Why does it matter what school she goes to?'

JANIE CONWAY HERRON

'You wouldn't say that if she were a boy, would you?' I could tell Mum had been drinking by the way she was yelling. Soon I'd be in there fighting with them. Later Dad would be sorry and want to make it up to me; he'd tell me it was just the strain of working so hard and having to look after Mum as well. But it was really me who looked after her. In return Mum protected me from my father's high expectations. What Dad didn't understand was that I was looking after him as well, trying to smooth the troubled waters for us all.

I turned the radio off and padded down the hall to the kitchen. Fetching a bowl of ice cream and a packet of chocolate biscuits, I took them back to the bedroom. Slamming the door wasn't satisfying enough, so I ate the ice cream so fast that it made my head ache. I picked up the guitar and tried to drown out the sound of my parents' voices with my own, but the soft phrases my guitar teacher had taught me didn't express enough anger. I played some open major chords and strummed them loudly, found a tune inside my head and screamed it. The sound pleased me so much I played and sang as loudly as I could. When I stopped playing the house was silent.

I recognised the sound of Mum's car as it coughed and spluttered before starting up. I wondered if she was too drunk to drive but I couldn't be bothered trying to stop her. Perhaps Dad was driving. I listened again. The house was still silent. After taking the biscuits back to the kitchen, I checked. I was alone. I caught sight of myself in my parents' full-length mirror. Turning this way and that I pinched the rolls of fat around my waist and held my stomach in. The roundness of my belly was still obvious and my breasts stood out way too much. I sighed, hating myself.

The next weekend Wendy was having a party. After her father's death, Wendy's mother went back to work as a nurse at the local hospital, doing shifts at night and on weekends. Wendy's house was often free from a watchful parental eye so there were constant visitors on weekends. If her mother suspected anything, she didn't let on. She had little choice but to leave her children alone.

At Wendy's last party, I had split my jeans. Ashamed, I sat on the grass in the front yard poking at my stubborn flesh, trying to get it inside the tight denim. I stayed outside until Wendy came looking for me and gave me a big old jumper to wear that hid the offending flesh. But the rubbing of thigh on jean all evening served as a continual reminder of my fatness. Standing in front of the mirror I made a vow. 'I won't eat anything but salads all week. I'll be sure to be thin enough for the party if I do that.' Then I went back to the kitchen for another biscuit.

I kept to my diet all week and the scales showed that I had lost half a stone. My new jeans fitted me like a glove, the tightness flattening my stomach right out. When I lifted my jumper I almost felt skinny.

JANIE CONWAY HERRON

When I arrived at the party, a small group of people had collected in Wendy's bedroom. Wendy sat on the top bunk, her thin neck stretching out as she reached for a high note and caught it. The guitars beat a steady rhythm. Everyone played the same chords. Each right hand synchronised with the left; the players synchronised with each other. We were all beginners and we watched each other fiercely as we ploughed through songs from the latest American songbook.

Sean sat next to Wendy, his green eyes and fair skin contrasting sharply with the straight black hair that hung in his eyes as he bent over his guitar. He was the only one with any musical experience and his Irish background gave him a certain status in this world of budding folk singers. Everyone looked to him when they were unsure of a chord or the way a song should go. He carried his authority with a nonchalance that made him extremely attractive to me. I found some space on the bottom bunk behind Wendy's desert-booted feet swinging in time to the music. When I reached up to grab one foot she leant over and handed me a flagon of red.

'Here, get some of this into you.' She had the wicked grin on her face that I loved. It always gave me a feeling of complicity.

After taking a swig from the flagon I took my guitar out of its case and strummed a chord, thankful it was in tune. The sound of it steadied me, blending easily with Wendy's singing and Sean's playing, while Wendy's brother Geoffrey tapped lightly on the

another song about love

bongos. The music spun a web around us all. Mesmerised, I kept playing until a shadow over my head made me look up. Paul was towering above me, his long legs miraculously holding him upright as he swayed over me. In a single, almost graceful motion, he sat at my feet. I lowered my head closer to the guitar and concentrated on Sean's playing.

Paul stopped the strings with his hand. 'When you play the guitar you look like a princess, did you know that?'

'If I look so great playing the guitar, then why the hell are you stopping me from playing?' I pushed Paul's arm away. If Paul wanted to impress me, this was no way to do it.

In the silence that followed, Paul lurched out of the room. Seconds later we could hear him throwing up in the bathroom.

Wendy jumped down from the top bunk. 'Jesus, Lillie, did you have to be so hard on him? You know how much he likes you.'

'Should I stop playing guitar every time some dickhead comes along and tells me I look like a princess?' I snapped.

Wendy glared at me. 'You're such a bitch sometimes,' she snarled and stomped out of the room.

Sean continued playing soft runs on his guitar. 'Hey,' he beckoned to me, 'you want to come up here and play that guitar?'

When Wendy returned, Sean and I were playing duets, while Geoffrey continued to tap on the bongos. If Wendy felt betrayed she was a proficient sword-swallower. Seconds later her singing flew out over the sound of our guitars. When she smiled at me, our eyes met in the same embrace as the two young girls who had sworn allegiance to each other all those years ago.

When Dad dropped me off at the Campus Folk Club, I scurried inside hoping no one had noticed him cruising slowly back up the street, checking people out. It was dark but I spied Wendy's long profile and swaggering stance. She whooped a loud greeting when I sidled up to her.

Throughout the evening my eyes kept wandering towards Sean. Gradually, subtle body talk was translated into verbal language.

'Do you want to go for a walk outside?' Sean asked.

I feigned indifference, answering flatly, 'Okay, if you like.'

Outside in the cold night air, Sean drew me close, pulled a small hipflask out of his pocket and offered me some whisky. I took a big swallow and we walked a little further, our boots clicking on the pavement. Going for a walk outside meant a long session of kissing on a park bench, or for the more daring, lying on the grass. Trees hanging over the

another song about love

pavement waved in the wind as Sean stopped and kissed me. His lips were moist and whisky tasting, his tongue pushed between my teeth, moving around in my mouth like an eel. When he kissed my neck, I offered it eagerly.

'Wanna go sit in the park?' Sean asked and when I nodded we turned off the pavement on to the soft grass. Then we realised there had been more than two sets of boots sounding on the pavement. The hair on the nape of my neck stood up in fright. When I turned around I was even more startled to find Dad behind us. Struck dumb with humiliation I looked desperately from Sean to my father and back again. Dad was so furious he couldn't speak. A silent charade took place as he grabbed me by the shoulder and pointed to the car.

Sean broke the silence. Shrugging nonchalantly, he turned back towards the club saying: 'See ya next time.' His eyes were still sparkling.

I watched Sean disappear while Dad clung onto my shoulder as if I might run off after him. I glared at Dad, pulled his hand away and stomped back to the car. Slamming the car door, I sat inside, fists clenched and lips tight, too enraged to speak. We drove home in silence.

5

GETTING HIGH
ON LOVE

EXCITED THAT RENÉ AND I were going to look at Vincent's studio, I climbed the stairs to his flat. Small and light, the apartment looked over a smoky neon-lit cafe where men sat drinking cups of thick, sweet, coffee. Tough sadness lined their faces as they talked about the old country and revisited the places of their youth in endless reminiscence. As I climbed the stairs at the side of the café I could feel the heat of their gaze on the back of my legs. I could be their daughter, wife, or sister, with my dark hair and olive skin, but I had been brought up in a completely different culture.

Up in René's flat, another coffee ritual happened. Sitting in an old office chair René had found abandoned in a lane, I leaned on the table he'd made out of a discarded wooden door and stacked milk crates. René heated the milk as the coffee percolated. When I told him about meeting Matt at Scarlet Sisters' first gig, René frowned and shook his head, dreadlocks dancing around his face.

'Not another one, Lillie, you have too many lovers.' He was thumbing through the small record collection he had accumulated since living in Melbourne. He put one on the turntable and stepped back. 'You will like this music, I know.'

There was the slight click and hiss of the needle making contact with the record and the first track started with a snappy drum roll. When the bass and guitars wound up into a reggae rhythm I recognised Peter Tosh singing. The infectious beat caught my fingers and I sang along with the chorus, keeping time by drumming on the edge of the wooden table.

'Always playing, aren't you?' René remarked as he placed a mug of delicious smelling coffee in front of me.

'What do you mean?'

'You're always playing along with the music.'

'I thought you were talking about my love life,' I teased.

another song about love

René took the bait. 'All these men in your life, it's not healthy for a woman.'

'And I suppose it is for a man?'

'It's different for a man. They don't fall in love so easily.' René believed in distinct biological differences between men and women and couldn't understand why I resisted the idea so much.

'Look who's calling the kettle black.'

'I'm not talking about being black,' René sounded offended.

'I'm not talking about that either, René. In this room there's one woman and one man. That's you and me, no matter what colour we are. You're the one who's all fucked up by love, not me.'

'I'm not fucked up by love. I know what I'm doing. Soon Jemma will leave Claude. Then we will see who has a broken heart.'

'Where does that get you?' I insisted. 'The three of you were better off as friends who cared about each other. As soon as romance came into it, you all freaked out. You should forget about romantic love and just have a good time. You can all love each other but not with that romantic, you-are-mine type of love.' I crossed my hands over my heart and accentuated the word love with a mocking tone. 'Believe me, that kind of love gets you nowhere.'

René tilted his head to one side. 'Jemma is the only one for me.'

I sighed. 'You're an attractive man, you could have anyone you wanted.'

'I want to be with Jemma but I don't have her, as you say.'

'Why did you leave, then?'

'She asked me to go, so I went. I thought she'd miss me but it's been over two months now.' René's voice trailed off into the music as Peter Tosh sang about the pitfalls of falling in love.

'You should take notice of what Peter Tosh is singing, René,' I warned.

René danced across the room towards me. Laughing, he pulled me to my feet. 'I promise I will,' he said making light intricate steps in front of me. Watching closely, I fell into step with him. As the music rose up under my feet I closed my eyes, found the centre of the rhythm between the bass and drums and moved with it. As the music took me somewhere else, a great burst of energy released inside me. A cushion of air under my feet made sure they hardly touched the floor. As the last track faded out on the drum and bass riff, I spun around and dropped to the floor.

'Where did you learn to dance like that?' René asked.

'I've always been able to dance,' I replied, feeling pleased René had noticed.

The men in the café nodded their heads and grinned as we passed the front of the cafe and waited at the lights on the corner.

another song about love

'Those men assume I'm your lover,' I told René.

René shrugged. 'Let them. It's better that way.'

'But I hate assumptions like that.'

'It's just their curiosity, that's all,' René answered.

'But they think I'm a slut, don't they, René?'

'A slut?' René looked surprised. 'That's way too strong.'

'But I can feel them staring at me.'

'Lillie, those men have seen a lot in their lives. They're not interested in what you do.'

'They see me going up to your place and they assume things.'

When the lights changed, we stepped out onto the road together and René fell back into step with me. 'They probably don't put any moral judgment on it. And if they do, so what? It doesn't matter.'

'It matters to me.'

'Don't blame them for your own opinion of yourself, Lillie.'

'But it's men who started it all.'

'Started what?'

'The idea of whore versus angel; if it weren't for men I wouldn't have to worry about it at all.'

'Which would you rather be, Lillie, whore or angel?'

'Both, not one or the other.'

René put his arm around my shoulder. 'You can be anything you want.'

'But it's all too narrow, you're either this or you're that.' I swung free of René's arm and skipped backwards up the street, yelling. 'I want to be everything at once. I want to be a star, that's what I really want. I want to be number one on the charts. I want, I want, I want!'

When we reached the next corner, I pointed to a long, low, cream brick building with a loading bay out the front and Vincent's car parked in it. 'That must be the studio. I can't wait to see what it's like inside.'

'The first step to becoming number one, eh?' René quipped.

'First step? This must be the nine hundred and ninety-ninth step and I'm still stepping. Come on, I'll race you.' I ran as fast as I could but René passed me easily, his long legs making short work of the distance.

When René pushed the heavy studio door, it opened with a thud into a small airless room. Through a double glass window we could see Vincent leaning over the mixing desk, concentrating. His limp grey overalls hanging loosely on his thin body made him look more like a car mechanic than a recording engineer.

I pressed a buzzer by the door. Vincent looked up, a big smile spreading across his face as he greeted us. Inside the studio, the soundproofing absorbed our voices. René said he thought a recording studio would be like being in his local church. As a young boy, he imagined the swelling voices of the congregation being picked up by the coloured beams of light that

another song about love

streamed in through the windows, floating right up to the angels.

'It can sound like that once something's been mixed,' Vincent explained, 'but when music is recorded it needs to be clean and dry, that's why we have the studio soundproofed. Here, I'll show you,' he added, as he took us back to the mixing console. There was no furniture yet so we sat on the cement floor. I scrounged around in the bottom of my bag and handed a small tin to René.

René rolled a neat spliff as Vincent described his plans to get the studio up and running.

'If I could get some help with the finishing touches, from you and anyone else you can rustle up, we could start recording in a couple of weeks' time. There's not a lot to be done. We could finish it in a couple of days.'

'We'll help, won't we, René? The band might chip in too.'

René nodded silent assent as he handed a large, cone-shaped joint to Vincent. 'This is some spliff, man,' Vincent exclaimed. 'Right off the cover of that Wailers album … what's it called again?'

'*Catch a Fire*,' René answered.

'Yeah, that's the one.' Vincent took a deep draw on the joint and exhaled. The smoke floated in rings across the air between us. 'What's your instrument, René?'

René shook his head. 'No, man, I'm not a musician.'

JANIE CONWAY HERRON

'I thought being a friend of Lillie's ...'

'No, I'm happy to be a listener.'

'René's a great dancer.'

'Everyone expects a black man to play music,' René explained. 'I dance and I listen. I respond to any good music, but especially reggae music.'

'You should use him in the film clip,' Vincent suggested.

'Great idea,' I replied, hardly able to believe I was talking about such things.

'Keep positive and it will happen. Do you want to hear something I recorded in England?' He pulled out a tape from behind the mixing desk. 'This is the last thing I did in London. I'm using it as a test for this studio.'

Vincent pressed play. 'I like sound scapes,' he said as the first crash of symbols heralded a cacophony of percussion then eased out into the sound of waves. A flute wove a melody round the room, crossing from one speaker to another. It created an aural panorama that belonged to wide-open spaces rather than the tiny studio we were in. A woman sang, her rich voice flowing over and around the melody of the flute. I closed my eyes and pictured her, arms stretched towards the sea, a salty wind blowing her long dress around her body and whipping the waves into a crescendo. When she stopped singing, the waves continued to lap gently underneath the fading flute and into silence. We waited for the next track. A husky saxophone cut through the air. Like the flute, its

another song about love

melody wove around the room and it became a smoky bar. From one corner, the same woman's voice whispered slow, sad phrases, while the saxophone haunted the background. Sometimes it coaxed the words from her mouth, at others it entered into a dialogue with her. Her phrases were answered with long weeping notes as she breathed the words into her listeners' ears. When her voice faded away the saxophone took over. Its wild, screaming notes ripped at the air, tearing it to shreds, rising higher and higher, until it disappeared on one last echoing scream. Silence returned to the room.

'Julia wrote the words to that last piece.' Vincent beamed with pleasure.

'Is that her singing?' I asked.

'Yes, she did most of the singing on our recordings. The concepts are mostly based on her ideas too.'

'It's great,' René offered. 'Reminds me of Linton Kwesi Johnson's poetry and the way he used music.'

'A great poet.' Vincent said, then described working with Linton, telling us casually, as if it had been part of his everyday life to work with famous artists.

As we left, I pushed a wad of ganja into Vincent's hand.

Vincent looked pleased. 'Thanks.' He sniffed at it. 'Smells good.'

'It is good.' I beamed.

JANIE CONWAY HERRON

I walked home from René's place, humming softly. Words formed inside my head and I skipped along, searching for an appropriate melody. When I turned into my street I sprinted inside. Picking up my acoustic guitar I worked out a few chords, then played round with a riff. I wrote down the words and sang the melody. Soon I had the core of a new song.

In the evening, I sat with Jesse watching television and playing the riff on my electric guitar without it being plugged in. The soft click of the plectrum on the strings was all that could be heard. I enjoyed the pattern of my fingers as they moved across the fret board and liked the discipline of making them dance. I put my head close to the guitar and became so absorbed I didn't hear the knock on the door.

Jesse ran up the corridor. 'Who are you?' he asked, when he opened the door.

'I'm a friend of your mother's.'

I breathed in sharply at the sound of Matt's voice.

'Not another one.' Jesse sounded exasperated.

I put the guitar down and rushed to the front door. 'Jesse, don't be so rude to our visitor.'

'He's just protecting you from strangers. Aren't you, Jesse?'

'Yep.' Jesse stepped back as Matt ruffled his hair. 'Mum has too many visitors.'

I hugged Jesse against me as we followed Matt into the lounge room.

another song about love

'I like to surprise people rather than make plans.' Matt looked towards the television as the ads blared into the room.

I turned the volume down. 'You can sit on the couch if you want, Matt.' I pointed to my guitar.

Matt bent down and picked it up. 'I've never met a woman who owns a Stratocaster before.'

I faked nonchalance. 'There are a few of us around.'

He dragged his thumb across the strings. 'I'm not much of a player, but I can strum a few chords.'

'I wrote a song today.'

'Play it for me.'

Jesse turned the television up. 'Mum, I'm watching this.'

'Okay, I'll play it later.' I put the guitar in its case and clicked the latches shut.

'You've got it good,' Matt told Jesse. 'When I was a boy, I had to go to bed by eight o'clock. We weren't even allowed to watch television on weeknights.'

Jesse shrugged and went on staring at the screen.

'Want a cuppa?' I asked and Matt followed me into the kitchen. When I told him about going to visit Vincent, he asked if we needed any extra hands putting the finishing touches on the studio.

'I'm pretty good with a paint brush,' he added. 'I used to work for a woman who bought old houses and did them up. Then I got busted and had to go dry out. She didn't trust me after that, but I'm still pretty good with a paint brush'

I poured strong, hot coffee into two mugs. 'Milk?' I asked, careful not to show too much reaction to Matt's blithe description of his chequered history.

Matt nodded and when I handed him his cup, he took hold of my wrist. 'You're a very beautiful woman,' he said, staring at me intently.

I laughed, dropping my gaze.

Matt let go of my hand. 'Shall we go keep Jesse company?' he asked. There was that enigmatic smile again.

When I put Jesse to bed, he put his arms around my neck and kissed me goodnight.

'You're not going to sleep with Matt are you?' he whispered in my ear.

'I might.'

'You will.' Jesse sounded disappointed.

'How do you know?'

'You're acting nervous.'

'Nervous? Me?' I tried to laugh it off. 'Don't you like Matt?'

'I don't know. It's just that when you get nervous, I get nervous too.'

'Well, I'll stop being nervous, then everything'll be all right.'

'All right, Momma.' Jesse kissed my cheek then turned away.

another song about love

I stood in the doorway looking at Jesse's tousled head on the pillow. He was my beautiful boy, my one-and-only child. There was no reason to be nervous.

In my bedroom I reached into my wardrobe and broke off a piece of ganja, brushed my hair and put some sweet-smelling oil behind my ears, wrists and my inner thighs. Then I padded down the hall towards the flickering light of the television and leant as casually as I could against the doorframe.

'Care for a smoke?' I asked.

'Sure,' Matt turned the television off.

Matt watched me as I stood at the mantelpiece rolling a number. I handed him a neatly rolled joint. He inhaled deeply, greedy for the effect. When he passed the joint back to me, our hands touched, lingering for a delicious second. I beckoned Matt up the passageway to my room. Once we were inside, he stood looking at me, undressing me with his startling blue eyes. Unsure of what to do, I undressed quickly. My desire went into overdrive as I eagerly unbuttoned his shirt and undid his trousers, slowly pulling his underpants down to his ankles. He stepped out of them and stood naked in the dimly lit room, his erection bobbing as I knelt in front of him. I kissed his cock and went to take it in my mouth but Matt grasped my shoulders and drew me up to standing. I threw my arms around his neck as we kissed our first passionate kiss, pushing my breasts against his chest and twining my legs around his waist. Matt fell backwards onto the bed. Covering him in soft feathery kisses, I moved over him until he entered me. Taking pleasure from each other we moved in a slow regular rhythm.

Later, I curled into Matt as he pulled me close. 'There's something elusive about you,' I murmured into his ear.

'That's my charm,' he chuckled and I fell silent as he stroked my hair.

I wanted to say something witty and sharp that expressed my feelings. But the words didn't come.

In Vincent's studio, I painted the windowsill of the mixing booth bright purple, with precise, even strokes and imagined the speakers, the furniture, everything turning from brown to purple.

Jesse and Sam carefully filled up the holes in the unpainted walls. Their young boy faces frowned with their sudden transcendence into manhood, as they pushed filler into cracks and smoothed it over.

Anna stood in a corner shouting directions while Matt, Stevie and Ali slowly rolled carpet out.

Wendy helped Vincent rewire the speakers, making over-confident suggestions in an effort to show her knowledge of sound systems.

'Perhaps you should move the speaker out of the corner, in order to make better use of the audio dynamics,' she advised.

another song about love

Vincent resisted. Seeing the frustration on Wendy's face, he turned on the microphone in the studio and announced time for a break.

I pointed a purple finger at the back pocket of my jeans and Wendy pulled out my stash.

'Mind if I roll one?' Vincent asked and Wendy begrudgingly handed it to him.

'Typical,' she muttered under her breath so that only I could hear. When I raised my eyebrows she shrugged and walked away.

'Anyone want to go get coffee?' Anna said, opening a tin of home-baked biscuits. 'I brought something for those who get the munchies.'

'I'll get the coffees,' Matt offered.

'I'll come with you,' I added, wiping purple paint on the back of my jeans.

'Can we come too?' Jesse pleaded.

I knew he was angling for sweets. 'No, you stay here and I'll bring you back a surprise.'

'Bring me back a Mars Bar.' Jesse grinned hopefully.

'No Jesse, not a Mars Bar.'

'What's wrong with Mars Bars?' Matt asked.

'Too much sugar,' I snapped.

'But these boys have been working hard. They need a bit of sugar to keep their energy up.'

'Yeah.' The boys chimed together.

I looked over at Anna and we both frowned.

'Just this once, but you can't eat biscuits as well,' Anna capitulated.

'I hate biscuits anyway,' Jesse answered.

'Liar,' whispered Sam and Jesse dug him in the ribs.

Matt and I walked to the shop in silence.

'What's wrong, little mother?

'You know,' I said curtly.

'No, I don't. I can guess but I'd rather you told me.'

A small bubble of anger burst inside me. 'Look, I have enough trouble battling against all those ads on television telling Jesse it's okay to eat that shit without having *you* encourage him.'

'But you don't want him to look on it as forbidden fruit, do you? First chance he gets, he'll buy a whole packet and eat them all at once.'

'I know. That's what I used to do,' I answered quietly.

'A whole carton of Mars Bars! No wonder you don't want Jesse eating them.'

'Not Mars Bars, packets of biscuits. I used to ask my mother to stop me from eating them and then sneak packets into my room in the middle of the night. I'd scoff the whole lot then put my fingers down my throat to make myself sick. My mother must have known I was eating them, but she never said anything.'

'You must have been very unhappy.'

'Not always, only sometimes.' I kicked at a stone on the footpath and it flew across the gutter into the middle of the road.

another song about love

'That makes two of us.' Matt took my hand.

I held it to my cheek. 'I'm happy now,'

'Ditto,' Matt replied.

As we rounded the corner near the shops, René appeared with a thin, blond-haired woman by his side.

'Look who's got a new girlfriend,' I whispered.

When we met up outside the milk bar, René held the woman by the shoulders and pushed her toward me. Hardly able to conceal his joy he introduced her. 'Lillie this is Jemma. She's finally come to visit me.'

Jemma took my hand in hers. 'René has told me all about you. I'm so thankful he has a friend like you.'

I jerked my head towards the studio. 'We were just getting some coffees for everyone.'

'And we were just coming down to help.' Jemma linked her arm in mine as we stepped inside the shop.

'Looks like we've both found love this weekend,' René whispered to me.

'Maybe?' I smiled.

'Of course we have.' René laughed.

As we walked back to the studio, Jemma linked arms with me again and we fell behind the two men. The intimacy Jemma assumed made me uneasy. The slight ache in my heart, the quick, close comparison between Jemma and myself didn't sit comfortably.

111

JANIE CONWAY HERRON

'René didn't tell me you were coming to Melbourne,' I said.

Jemma smiled. 'I didn't tell him I was coming. I just arrived on his doorstep this morning. It was a big surprise for him.'

'I bet it was.' I imagined the men in the cafe staring as Jemma climbed the stairs. I looked at her small wiry figure and couldn't help comparing it with my own. Physically, Jemma was everything that I wanted to be and I was conscious of my soft flesh moving as I walked. 'You're not fat,' people said to me, 'just pleasantly plump.'

Joe had never understood my self-consciousness. 'You're strong' he'd say. 'You're beautiful. I love your body. You remind me of a Robert Crumb woman and I love the way they look.' I cringed inside not knowing what to say, hating his comparison with those big-breasted muscular caricatures of women in Crumb cartoons. I tuned into Jemma's voice once more. She told me about being with Claude and I pictured my charming old friend beguiling and seducing her with romantic talk.

'But one morning I woke up and decided I had been completely wrong,' Jemma exclaimed. 'I looked at Claude and I felt nothing, absolutely nothing. All I could think about was being with René. After Claude went to work, I booked myself on the next bus to Melbourne, packed some things and left Claude a letter on the kitchen table. The bus left yesterday evening and I arrived on René's doorstep early this morning.'

another song about love

Jemma flicked her hands up in the air to indicate the end of her story.

'What would you have done if you'd found René in bed with someone else when you arrived?' I asked.

Jemma frowned. 'René's not like that. If he'd fallen in love with someone he'd have written and told me.'

'But he could have had a one-night stand or something,' I persisted.

'René's just not like that.' Jemma's mouth tightened. Now she'd come back to the man who really loved her, there was no possibility of an unhappy ending. Jemma's certainty astounded me. I'd never been that sure of anyone's feelings.

Whatever Matt and René were talking about was extremely funny. I watched them walking in front of us as René laughed and slapped Matt on the back. Matt diligently tried to keep the coffees balanced.

'Hey you guys, wait for us!' I yelled and broke into a sprint, relieved to be leaving Jemma to catch up.

During the afternoon René and Jemma were often in my line of vision. Kissing and cuddling, they took obvious delight in each other's company. Matt was helping Ali and Stevie lay the carpet. I tried to will him to come over and keep me company. He didn't even turn around so I concentrated on painting purple windowsills. When my eyes strayed towards René and Jemma again, I gave up in exasperation and sprawled out on the floor. Everyone else went on working. Only Wendy was tuned in to my feelings. She sat down beside me and nodded towards the loving couple.

'Pathetic, isn't it? All that heterosexist bullshit.'

'Yeah,' I laughed.

'Why don't you give up on men, Lillie?'

'Give me time and I might,' I answered.

'Women are better for you.'

'I don't know, Wendy. Look what a mess women lovers made of you.'

'They didn't make a mess of me. I made a mess of myself.'

'Same thing applies to men.'

'No, it's different,' Wendy insisted. 'Men have different values to women, it's an unequal relationship from the start.'

'That's what makes it interesting to me. I like to even the odds out,' I answered.

'Don't let Matt make a mess of you.'

'There's no way I'd do that.'

'I saw the way you were looking at René and what's-her-name.'

'Jemma.'

'Yeah Jemma. You had that wistful look like you wished you were her.'

'Sometimes I get lonely for commitment and long-term relationships but then I remember how trapped I felt being married to Joe,' I said. 'I've never been with a woman sexually. I'm not sure I'd like it.'

another song about love

Wendy put her face up close to my ear and whispered. 'Come on, Lillie, I thought you were an adventurer. You could always try it and see.'

'Is that an offer?' I grinned.

'Might be. There's only one way to find out. Take me up on it.' Wendy kissed me on the lips. 'Remember the first time we kissed?'

'At school?'

'Yep.' Wendy kissed me again. 'I've never forgotten that. Do you remember the next time? We were still at school and after the swimming carnival you showed me how to kiss boys, in the changing rooms. You kept pushing your tongue into my mouth. When you pushed my head back I could see Janet Hathaway staring at us over the wall.'

Laughing, I pushed Wendy away. 'She was horrified.'

'No she wasn't. She was curious,' Wendy hissed.

'How do you know?'

'Because afterwards she asked me to do it to her.' Wendy laughed. 'She was my first girlfriend really. We used to practise together all the time. I thought we were practising so we could to it with boys. When I tried it with boys it wasn't the same and it was nothing like that with my father. He didn't like kissing.'

'But you've had heaps of boyfriends,' I countered.

'I know. I had to try it to prove to myself I was normal.' Wendy hugged her knees to her chest. 'When I started having relationships with women I found out what I was missing.'

I reached over and hugged Wendy.

'I'll show you how to kiss properly,' Wendy teased as I turned my head from side to side, laughingly avoiding her kisses.

Out of the corner of my eye I became aware of the others watching, then Jesse latched onto Wendy's back yelling: 'Hey, get off my mum!' He was laughing, but his laughter soon turned to tears when Wendy wrestled with him.

'I want to go home,' Jesse wailed as I hugged him to me.

Anna touched my shoulder. 'I'll take the kids back to my place if you want to keep on working.'

'No, I want to go home and I want Mum to come with me!' Jesse yelled.

'Okay I'll give you both a lift.' Anna spoke in the quiet voice she used when things needed to calm down.

'What happened? Did the kid hurt himself?' Matt asked.

'No, he's just tired. It's been a long day.'

'He probably ate too many Mars Bars, eh?' Matt joked as Jesse buried his face further into my shoulder.

'All that sugar has hyped him up.' I glared at Matt. 'I'd better take him home.'

another song about love

'Shall I come too?' Matt patted Jesse tentatively.

'I think Jesse needs some time alone with me,' I replied.

'I'll see you later then.'

I wanted to ask when but I stopped myself.

When René took Jesse's hand, Jesse smiled through his tears. 'Hey, Jesse, things aren't that bad. Now you take good care of your mum.' René gave us both a kiss. 'Hey Bro', gimme five.' René offered his palm and Jesse slapped it resoundingly.

Slumped in the back seat, Jesse and Sam leaned on each other's shoulders, their faces all sweaty in the late afternoon sun.

'They're both really tired.' I sighed.

'And bored,' Anna added. 'It's not much fun for kids to be cooped up in a room with no windows all afternoon.'

'But Jesse wanted to come,' I pleaded. 'They both really enjoyed themselves.'

'Jesse is always trying to be one of the adults, when he needs to be a kid. How could he possibly know what it was going to be like today? He said he wanted to come because he wanted to be with you, or keep up with Matt or whoever else you're going out with.'

'You let Sam come.'

'Sam wanted to come because Jesse was going. Only Antonia had the good sense to go play with another friend today.' Anna put her hand out to touch mine. 'I know how hard it is bringing up kids on your own, Lillie. At least Sam and Ant have each other. Jesse only has you. He needs more time with you, doing things that he wants to do.'

I slumped down in the seat. 'I know he does. There just never seems to be enough time.'

'Then make time.'

When Anna pulled up outside my house I shook Jesse gently. 'Come on, we're home.'

Jesse didn't respond but when I opened the back door to pull him out he opened his eyes and grinned.

'Have a good evening,' Anna yelled as her car disappeared round the corner.

I hugged Jesse to me. 'Well, it looks like there's just you and me this evening. What do you want to do?'

Jesse looked puzzled. 'We could watch television.'

'No, that's what we always do.' I checked my purse. I had twenty dollars and some change. 'How about we go out for dinner?'

'Yeah!'

'Your choice.'

Jesse grinned. 'We could have pizza.'

We sat at a table in the back of the café watching the pizza-man throw a circle of dough in the air and catch it. Jesse laughed gleefully each time he did.

another song about love

The pizza-man grinned. 'So, you are taking your girlfriend out for dinner.'   'No! This is my mum,' Jesse exclaimed.

'You look like brother and sister.' The pizza-man winked at me.

I smoothed out the plastic tablecloth and tried to think of something witty to say but it was Jesse who kept up the conversation.

'My mother plays in a band.' Jesse told the pizza man.

'Really! You must be very proud of her then.'

'Yep,' Jesse grinned. 'She's making a record.'

The pizza-man looked genuinely surprised. 'A record? I am in good company tonight. When's it going to be released?'

'Oh, we're only at the demo stage at the moment,' I answered. 'The record's a long way off.'

'My mum plays electric guitar. She's got a Stratocaster,' Jesse added.

'A Stratocaster? That's good, is it?'

'They're the best.' Jesse enjoyed sounding knowledgeable. 'They're American.'

When the pizza was ready, Jesse grabbed some straight away but the pizza-man stopped him. 'Hey, wait for your mother.'

Jesse grinned at me. 'Mum doesn't mind. Do you Mum?'

I picked up a piece and ate it slowly while Jesse stuffed his into his mouth, juices running down his chin.

119

JANIE CONWAY HERRON

'Growing boys get hungry, eh?' The pizza-man leaned in conspiratorially. 'I come from a family of five boys, I should know.'

'I haven't got any brothers or sisters.' Jesse grabbed another piece of pizza.

'Be thankful there's no one to fight over pizzas with. I fought with my brothers all the time.'

Jesse frowned. 'I wouldn't fight with my brother if I had one.'

'And what does your mother say about that?'

'She says she has to find a father first.'

'Oh, I see.' The pizza-man was sensitive enough to know the conversation had become too personal and retreated behind the counter.

When we'd finished eating, I gave Jesse the money to pay and stood beside him as he proudly handed over the twenty-dollar note. Standing on tiptoe, he strained over the counter, as the pizza-man counted the change into his hand

'You've got a good boy there,' he said.

'I know I have,' I replied and smiled down at Jesse.

6

ON THE BRINK

I WAS SIXTEEN WHEN I lost my virginity. After kissing for hours Sean's face was up close to mine. I'd been waiting for months to get this close to him and now we were in his bedroom, in his bed and there was no one else home. My body was in a kind of languor while my lips felt bruised and swollen. Sean turned out the light and my heart beat way too hard. He took his shirt off and lay down beside me. Apart from his guitar playing, I loved his eyes the most. They had a way of holding my attention. Up this close they were mesmerising.

'Why don't you get undressed, Lil'?' Sean's hand slipped inside my bra.

I hesitated.

Sean kissed me again. 'You do want to do this, don't you?'

'Yes, but...' I didn't want to say I wanted to have sex. I'd had some vision of being overwhelmed when I lost my virginity, of it all occurring in spite of myself.

'It's going to happen some time so it may as well be with me,' Sean coaxed, his pragmatism falling far short of the romance I had been envisaging.

I wriggled out of my tight jeans, embarrassed about the shape of my body, my full breasts and the fleshy rolls around my stomach. In the intimate moments that followed everything changed. When Sean entered me, the pain I had anticipated never happened. The moment of losing my virginity passed without the slightest twinge. When it was all over I was left wondering what all the fuss was about. I was sure there must be something more to making love. This had not been the life-changing experience I'd expected. It was only later, when I lay awake in Sean's arms, savouring the comfort of being held by my sleeping lover, that I felt something close to what I called love.

Over the next few months I spent lots of time over at Sean's house. Sometimes I stayed the night,

another song about love

pretending to sleep on the sofa. When the big house was dark and I was sure Sean's parents were asleep, I sneaked into his room where the narrow single bed was just big enough for us both.

'I hope you're being careful, Lillie. You know you need to take precautions,' Mum cautioned as our conversation free ranged late into the night.

'We are, Mum,' I assured her, wanting to sound more in charge of things than I was. 'Sean knows about condoms. He's got a stack of them in his drawer.'

'Good darling, I'm glad. There are so many things that can happen, you know. Not just becoming pregnant but also getting sexually transmitted diseases.'

'Getting what?' This was something that hadn't been covered in my sex education classes at school. Wendy and I giggled at our biology teacher Miss Pearson's awkward, disembodied demonstrations. She pointed to charts of human bodies on the wall, showing the vital parts of a man and a woman needed for procreation. It sounded as if the sex part of things happened separately to emotions like the ones we'd read about in Wendy's romance comics. Miss Pearson never mentioned the possibility of anything other than a baby coming from this union of man and woman.

'A condom protects you from more than pregnancy, Lillie,' Mum said. 'Make sure you use one.'

JANIE CONWAY HERRON

'But Sean wouldn't have a disease. He's only young like me.'

Mum smiled. 'It's true you're young, but these kinds of things can happen to anyone.'

Although Sean did have condoms in the drawer beside his bed, we often became lost in passion and using them was the last thing on our minds. Besides, Sean had described using condoms as being like taking a shower in a raincoat. In an effort to please him, I never insisted on him using one. Consequences seemed a long way away, something that happened to others, not to us. When the day of reckoning did come, Sean and I were both unprepared.

'It's not your fault that I'm pregnant, Sean,' I explained. 'It was an accident.'

Sean nodded, gladly taking the line of least resistance that I offered him. 'What are you going to do, then?'

'I could have an abortion.'

'How? It's illegal.' Sean frowned. 'Paul told me he knew a girl who only had a local anaesthetic so she could jump off the table if the police raided the clinic where she had it done.'

I imagined myself naked, laid out on the table, gathering myself up to escape from the police, blood running down my legs. Sean could see it too; all of a sudden the line of least resistance was not so easy for either of us. 'I'll ask Wendy, she'll know what to do, or I could ask my mother,' I reassured.

'Your mother! You can't tell her!'

another song about love

Sean's startled expression amused me. 'I've already told her we've been sleeping together. She just advised me to take precautions.'

I knew Mum wouldn't make moral judgments. The only difficulty was finding the right moment of sobriety to tell her.

'We could always get married and have the baby.' Sean was beginning to see himself as a man instead of a boy, as a father instead of a son.

'I haven't finished school yet,' I answered quietly.

Sean held my hands. 'You could leave school. I could support you.'

I shook my head. Sean didn't understand. I wasn't about to leave school at sixteen. I had too much I wanted to do with my life to let that happen.

On a winter afternoon, Mum and I sought refuge in a cafe at the top end of Collins Street. We'd been waiting for a long time. As we drank coffee to pass the time away, the dimly lit café added to the intimacy between us. Outside, the grey sky had a bitter edge to it. The waitress must have wondered what we were doing as she brought sandwiches for Mum while I sipped my black coffee very slowly. Every now and then Mum went to the phone box across the road and made a phone call. Then she'd go to the toilet. I was sure she was going there to take a little nip of something to give her courage. When she returned I could tell she'd tidied her hair and touched up her lipstick. I watched her closely for telltale signs of drinking. I needed her too much to say anything, so I reached for her hand instead.

In the evening we took a tram to the doctor's surgery. We were the only passengers and after we'd paid for our tickets the conductor dozed up the other end of the carriage, leaving us alone. I hummed a nervous tune to the sounds of the wheels on the tracks as they clattered down the empty suburban streets. Cold, hungry and scared, I hadn't had a thing to eat or drink for hours. Mum was under the influence of the nips she'd been having, but still keeping herself together. I could smell whisky on her breath and knew she had some in her bag. It was the only deception between us. Mum had learnt, during the course of many inquisitions by both Dad and I, to deny her drinking. There was no use accusing her now.

The doctor was an old friend of Mum's from her nursing days. He'd agreed to do the abortion as a special favour. I had strict instructions not to give his name to anyone and to this day I can't remember what it was. As Mum stood close holding my hand the doctor administered the anaesthetic, his large smiling face looming over me. I looked up at Mum and felt her hand squeezing mine as darkness descended. What felt like seconds later, I woke to the sound of a voice saying, 'Thank you, thank you,' and was surprised to realise it was my own.

another song about love

The red-faced doctor was still leaning over me, smiling. 'Your mother is waiting outside. Shall I call her in?'

I nodded as a dull ache in my pelvis throbbed in time with my heartbeat.

In the early hours of the morning, we sped through the city streets in a taxi. I leant into my mother's shoulder, breathing in the musky smell of her coat as she kissed the top of my head. When the taxi pulled up outside our house Mum paid the driver, then helped me inside and put me to bed. Through the open door of my bedroom I watched Mum draw back the curtains in the lounge room. Dawn flickered out across the frosted lawns and the milkman's cart clip-clopped up the road. She lit a cigarette, inhaled and let the smoke out on a long sigh of relief.

Sean's arm circled my waist and he kissed the nape of my neck as we sat in his room. Over the months since my abortion we had learned to be more careful when making love. My shyness was disappearing as sex became increasingly enjoyable. Though I was becoming a woman, I still had young girl's problems.

'Jesus, Sean, I've failed my exams. I can't believe it. My dad'll kill me!'

'No, he won't. He probably expects it.' Sean stroked my hair.

JANIE CONWAY HERRON

With awful certainty, I realised that Sean was probably right. 'I've failed my exams, failed at dancing,' I said, sinking into gloom. 'Dad and you are right, I may as well have got married and had kids after all.'

'There's lots of other things you can do, Lil'.'

'Like what?'

'We could play music together, maybe even do a gig some time.' Sean looked at me with a steady, twinkling gaze.

'But I'm not nearly as good as you are.'

'I can teach you. You learn fast.'

I smiled. 'Maybe I can still make Dad proud of me.'

'Why don't you do something for yourself for a change? Forget about whether your father approves or not.'

'Sometimes it's hard to know what I want for myself.'

'You want to play music, don't you?'

'More than anything,' I replied.

The bus ambled through the evening traffic on the way to our first gig. I didn't mind how long it took, I was too nervous about playing to worry about being late. I thought about the bus crashing and a tragic scenario of being killed captured my imagination. But if the bus crashed now I'd die before my first performance. I had to face it. There was no escape. We were well rehearsed. I had been practising every day. But, when

another song about love

I planted my feet on the bus floor my knees shook. What about my hands on the guitar? I was sure I'd play a wrong chord, or sing a wrong note. When the bus wheezed to a stop and the doors flapped open, I stepped hesitantly onto the pavement, gripping the handle of my guitar case.

Sean put an arm around my shoulders. 'You're nervous aren't you?'

'That's the understatement of the year,' I replied as we walked towards a small neon light flickering in the distance. People milling about under the half-light in the doorway stared at us as we made our way through the queue and the doorman let us pass. As we climbed the steep stairs to the dark room above, excitement transformed my nervousness into something more positive. A low stage was tucked into one corner of the room, almost apologetically, and a yellow spotlight threw a weak circle of light onto the stage. As I looked around at the people trickling in, a small wiry man walked towards us, hands extended towards Sean. Winking at me, he pulled Sean into a big hug as a grin travelled through the many wrinkles on his face. Sean introduced me as the best rhythm guitarist and harmony singer he'd ever worked with.

Out in the backroom, Frank pointed out a mirror behind the door. 'In case you want to fix your makeup or something.' I'd spent hours putting my makeup on, painting fine lines around my eyes and tiny lashes underneath my natural ones. When I checked myself in the mirror my dark eyes stared back at me.

JANIE CONWAY HERRON

'Black-eyed Susan,' my father called me as a prelude to asking what was wrong with looking natural. But tonight dark eyes were an essential part of the act.

Sean tuned our guitars while Joe poked his head around the door then brought an enormous array of instruments into the room. His eyes, framed by a pair of thick-lensed glasses, gave him an innocent, bright-eyed stare. Tonight Joe was playing with Terry, a songwriter whose crystal-clear guitar picking irritated Sean. I knew there was a great deal of competition between them. When the rest of his entourage crowded into the room Terry pulled out a shiny Gibson. It was the kind of guitar Sean wanted to buy but couldn't afford.

Joe sat down next to me and introduced himself. His short sight made him sit right up close, while his big eyes blinked through the thick lenses of his glasses. He had beautiful skin, like a young boy's and a curly mouth that made all sorts of shapes as he spoke.

Someone rolled a joint and then handed it to Terry. He took a long and flamboyant drag then passed it to Joe. Joe handed it straight to me. 'I don't smoke,' he said without apology. 'Do you?'

'Sometimes,' I replied. I'd never encountered marijuana before but I was afraid of appearing uncool. I took a tentative drag. The smoke burned my throat and tears started into my eyes. I handed the joint to Sean and rushed into the toilet. Tears streaming down my cheeks made black rivers of my eye make-up. After

another song about love

several big gulps of water the coughing stopped. I wiped away the black streaks with wet toilet paper then patted my skin with my sleeve. Those long hours of intricate face painting had ended in a mass of patches under my eyes. Black-eyed Susan had turned into a forlorn panda bear. I splashed more water on my face and cleaned away the patches, as lightly as the rough paper allowed.

By the time I was ready to face the boys in the back room, Frank was calling us on stage. I looked over at Sean and his warm smile comforted me. The room was a mass of shadowy heads and every corner was filled with people. A hush descended as the audience waited for the first note. I spied Wendy and Paul in the middle of the crowd and they both gave me the thumbs up as Sean counted me in. Our two guitars wove in and out of each other in the intro to the first song. As my voice flew out over the top of Sean's, I sensed the gentle pull of the thread holding our voices together and felt the music in my feet, stomach and throat. The audience listened reverently to the quiet songs then clapped along to the more up-tempo ones. When we sang our last number, they yelled for more. Sean leant in close and suggested we do, a song we hadn't rehearsed but Sean thought it suited my voice more than the high fluting soprano tones of the songs I'd been used to singing.

I shook my head. I'd only just graduated to singing the warm honey tones that the song required of me.

JANIE CONWAY HERRON

'Come on,' Sean insisted. When he started up a standard blues intro, the notes fell commandingly and I was forced to follow suit. We played a few twelve bar rounds on guitars before I took a deep breath and sang. From the depths of my body came another voice, different from the high-pitched folky one that had harmonised with Sean all evening. This voice was husky and low, weaving around the guitar runs rather than soaring over the top of them. When the song came to an end, I looked up and the audience applauded.

In the back room Terry and his friends were busy partying, but Joe had seen our bracket. 'That was great, man,' he patted Sean on the back then turned to me. 'You should do more numbers like that last one. I just love those old blues songs. Those black women sure can sing, can't they?'

'I hadn't heard that song before Sean taught it to me,' I answered.

'What? You can sing like that and you've never heard the original?'

I was flattered by Joe's surprise. 'Nope. Sean found it in a copy of *Sing Out* magazine. He thought I'd like it because it was a woman's song.'

'Well, I'll be damned. You'll have to bring Sean over sometime and I'll play you the original.'

'That'd be nice. I'd like that,' I replied.

7

NUMBER ONE

VINCENT'S STUDIO WAS FINALLY READY for recording. Scarlet Sisters was the first band to use it. Once the band had put down the instrumental tracks we were ready to record my vocals. I adjusted my headphones, closed my eyes and took a deep breath. Waiting for the drum roll that heralded the beginning of the first verse, I missed the intro. When the song started again, I counted the bars. This time I got the intro right but my voice, caught between the two headphones, was too loud in my head.

JANIE CONWAY HERRON

I could hear every breath I took, every little crack in my tone. Distracted, I dropped a line in the verse and waited for Vincent to wind the tape back again.

'Take one headphone off and put your finger in your ear,' Anna advised. 'It will feel more like a gig.'

I pushed the headphone off my left ear, put my finger in and listened carefully for Ali's drum roll. Anna was right, the music was slightly muffled but my voice still stood out. This time I got right through the song and as the last refrain repeated itself, I played around with a few different ways of singing it. I was pleased with the results, but Vincent wanted to do another take.

'I think you can do better than that, Lillie. I'll add some studio atmosphere. Hope it helps.' Vincent turned the lights down and I waited for the track to play but nothing happened. Anna and Stevie were talking animatedly to one another. Then Vincent nodded his head as Anna gesticulated furiously.

'Hey you guys, what's going on?' I yelled into the microphone but they couldn't hear me. I tried jumping up and down and waving my arms. 'Remember me? I'm the singer.' Still nothing happened. Vincent disappeared below the mixing desk and out of my line of sight. Anna waved and her mouth moved while she made signs through the window. Stevie did the same thing but I couldn't understand anything they were saying. Vincent's face appeared

another song about love

again but his voice was so loud that I had to pull the headphones off. Tentatively I put them on again.

'Sorry, Lillie, everything dropped out but we've fixed the problem. You ready for another take?'

I nodded.

'Okay, we're rolling.' Vincent raised his hand.

I tensed and missed the beginning again. 'Hey, you guys, I think I need something to relax me,' I yelled. 'Anyone bring any alcohol?'

'Try some port, it loosens the vocal chords,' Anna said, pressing against the window and making stupid faces. Her humour was lost on me. I felt like asking her to do the vocals instead but that was an open admission of my insecurities.

Vincent's voice boomed through the headphones again. 'Take a break, Lillie. Stevie's going for supplies.'

Exasperated, I flopped down on the couch in the control booth with Ali. 'Relax Lillie,' Ali advised. 'You wrote the song? You're the one in control.'

'Am I? I feel like everyone else is, not me.'

Ali stretched his arms out into a leisurely yawn. 'Don't take it so seriously. These things should be fun. You're not responsible for everything that happens.'

'But it's so nerve-wracking in there. I can hear every little mistake I make.'

'The art of recording has a very Zen aspect to it, you know,' Ali advised. 'Unless you let go of your desire for perfection, you're bound to make a mess of it.'

JANIE CONWAY HERRON

'Easier said than done,' I sighed.

When Stevie returned, I drank port straight from the bottle. The sweet liquid made my limbs feel heavy and my anxiety disappeared. With the headphones on again, I was ready and waiting for the music to start. At a gig we often let an intro go on for a long time. Jamming for a while, we'd take Ali's drum roll or Stevie's guitar line as a cue. If I started singing a verse before they were ready, the band followed me but in the studio the length of the intro was fixed and I had to be precise. The song began again. Feeling for the slight build that heralded the drum roll at the beginning of the verse, I let my voice fly.

'*Everybody wants to be a number one, a special one. Climb the top of the tree, a number one, a special one.*' When the bass and guitars began a steady wind up towards the middle of the verse, I knew I'd got it right and kept on singing. '*Well you know it don't matter when you're dead and gone. Thrive on competition just to keep on keeping on now. A number one, a special one.*' A row of smiling faces looked out from the mixing booth. By the time the second verse began I was confident enough to play around with the melody. When the final chorus came round I felt my throat open up as I reached for higher and higher notes, '*A number one, a special one. A number one, a special one.*' When the song ended, I let out a whoop. 'Is that a take or what?' But when Vincent played the song through without the backing track I could hardly bear to listen. The vulnerability of my disembodied voice

another song about love

was excruciating. I concentrated with every fibre of my body, sensitive to any little catch in my voice or out of tune note. Vincent played around with the sound, making it dry and thin, then echo off into the distance until he settled on a sound that he liked. He looked across at me.

'Like it, Lillie?

'I'm not sure,' I answered as I listened to my naked voice. Vincent flicked a few switches, the band came pumping through underneath. It sounded better. I smiled at Vincent. As the song moved into the second verse, I sang a harmony while Anna added a third part above that.

'Hey you two, that's just what this song needs. Try putting it down.' Vincent pushed us back out into the studio.

As I waited for the cue to come in, I looked at Anna closing her eyes in concentration. With her left finger pushed firmly in her ear, Anna slapped the rhythm out on her thigh, her body moving with the music. I closed my eyes and listened too, then pitched a harmony above my original melody. Anna found another line above that. After a few takes the sound was so full that I had trouble distinguishing which line I was singing. When we reached the chorus, the sound of our multitracked harmonies exploded in my ears.

The session finished with Stevie's guitar overdubs. Stevie was a natural in the studio. He had myriad musical effects that he could draw out of his guitar.

JANIE CONWAY HERRON

This time he used a slide to make the sound of seagulls fly across the surface of the verses. While he wove intricate musical phrases in between the vocal lines, Vincent built a fine multi-layered texture into the song. But it was Stevie's solos that had us all galvanised. The stillness of his body belied the wildness of the soaring notes he elicited from the guitar, his feet rock solid on the floor, his body erect, only his head indicating any emotion. He leaned affectionately towards the neck of the guitar, almost caressing it with his cheek, as he played the wild and bent solos that would become his trademark.

Ali leant over and nudged me. 'That guy's unbelievable.'

I grinned. Words seemed inadequate with the room so full of Stevie's music.

On the way home, my head swum as *Number One* repeated in my head. I sang the chorus and Anna joined in. The car filled with the sound of our harmonies as Anna wound through a network of side streets to my place.

The house was in darkness except for a flickering light under the door to the loungeroom. Wendy was asleep on the couch and the light was coming from the television. I turned it off and Wendy sat up, her shocked expression exaggerated by the tousled hair sticking out all over her head.

'It's only us,' I laughed.

another song about love

'Jesus, you frightened me.' Wendy rubbed her head furiously, making her hair stick up even more. 'I put the kids to bed in Jesse's room. Jesse was so thrilled to have Sam and Ant staying over at his place that he's forgiven me for the other day. What time is it?'

'Late,' Anna answered. 'It's been a long day.'

I sat down beside Wendy and threw my arms around her neck. 'Thanks for looking after the kids.'

'No trouble, Lil', I rather like being a surrogate auntie.'

We sat around my big teapot while conversation continued into the early hours of the morning. Smoke, tea and biscuits were imbibed as endless words were exchanged. The ashtray piled high with cigarette butts and joint filters, until the last drop of milk had been dripped into thick, stewed tea.

'Want to smoke the last one?' I croaked, handing a freshly rolled joint to Anna.

'You must have an endless supply, Lillie,' Anna observed. 'You gave Vincent about half an ounce before we left the studio.'

'I grew it to be smoked,' I replied, smiling at my own benevolence.

Wendy grimaced as she swallowed the last bitter dregs of the tea. 'Why don't you sell some of it? It must be worth quite a bit on the street.'

'No, I couldn't do that,' I said, passing the joint to her and laughing. 'It's against my religion. I'm not putting any monetary value on it.'

'You're making Vincent pretty happy, giving him smoko all the time.' Anna insisted.

'He's done us a big favour,' I said. 'We couldn't have afforded the studio time he's given us under normal circumstances.'

'But you don't have to be so generous with him. You never know, he might be selling some of it on the sly.'

'I wouldn't mind if he did. That's his karma, not mine,' I replied.

'What are you going to do with the tapes when you've finished, Lillie?' Wendy asked.

'Hawk them around various record companies and agencies. Geoff Short is running a big agency now. He's always been interested in Anna and me.'

Wendy let out a snort of disgust. 'Geoff Short's a sexist pig. You wouldn't work for him, would you?'

'I might. Look what he did for Frankie.'

'But Frankie's a bloke. Geoff doesn't understand women like you.'

'So?'

'You're an idiot, Lillie. You should find yourself a woman manager.'

'Find me one that can open doors like Geoff can.'

'I don't like letting men open doors for me,' Wendy's cheeks flushed red.

another song about love

'Hey you two, it's too late for arguments,' Anna intervened. 'I need some sleep. Can I stay the night, Lillie? It's too late to put the boys in the car now.'

'Sure, both of you may as well stay,' I invited. 'Then we can continue this conversation tomorrow.'

Morning sunlight streamed in through the front window as we prepared for bed. I pulled down the blind but the sun was already warming the room. Our sweaty skins touched momentarily as we stretched out in my bed.

'Thank God it's Saturday morning and we don't have to get the kids to school.' Anna moved over to the edge of the bed while Wendy cuddled up to me, curling her body around my back and kissing my shoulder. 'I can't believe I'm in bed with my two favourite women,' she whispered, stroking my leg. I grabbed Wendy's hand, holding it tightly. As we lay silently next to each other, I feigned sleep to avoid explaining that this was not the time for the experiment Wendy had so often exhorted me to try. Her small breasts and tight belly pressing into my back reminded me of the soft generous curve of my mother's stomach in the small of my back when I was a child. I longed to feel like that again, but Wendy was my close friend and what I really wanted was sleep.

JANIE CONWAY HERRON

Gently easing myself out of bed later that morning, I wound a sarong around me and headed towards the kitchen. The three kids were sprawled on the lounge room floor, watching, *Hey, Hey it's Saturday*. Empty cereal bowls, spoons and glasses strewn around the floor were proof of the breakfast they'd already had.

'Morning, Mum.' Jesse moved a car across the carpet and parked it in a garage made from a cardboard box.

'Good morning,' I replied, picking my way around the litter of cars and cereal bowls on the floor. 'I see you've already had breakfast. Who bought the milk?'

Jesse beamed at Sam. 'Sam did, with his pocket money.'

'You're a good boy, Sam, I'd better get some money to pay you back.' As I turned to pick up my purse, something soft and furry ran over my foot then rushed under the couch. When I screamed with fright, Jesse pulled out a dusty lump of fur that clung on to his wrist as he stroked it.

'I found him out in the back lane,' Jesse explained as the kitten clawed and scratched at him. 'Can I keep it, Mum, please?' Jesse kept his eyes fixed on me without grimacing even though the cat's claws were firmly embedded in his shoulder.

'It probably belongs to someone,' I replied.

'No, it doesn't, I'm sure,' Jesse insisted.

'He was hungry. That's why we bought the milk, so we could feed it,' Antonia chimed in.

142

another song about love

'He ate a whole bowl of cornflakes and milk.' Jesse added.

Sam stood behind him, tickling the kitten under the chin. 'It might not be a he, it might be a she and grow to have babies,' he added.

'We could give the kittens away, couldn't we, Mum?' Jesse was desperate.

'We have to find out if the kitten belongs to someone. I want you to knock on all the people's doors in the street. If no-one claims it, you can keep the cat.'

'Okay, Mum.' Jesse pulled the cat off his shoulder and put it down.

'You're going to have to feed it and look after it too.'

'Sure, Mum.'

'You promise?'

'I promise.'

'No piking and leaving it up to me.'

'No piking.' Jesse let out an exasperated sigh.

'Okay, that's a deal then.' I offered my hand.

Jesse put his arms around me his head fitting neatly into the curve of my waist. 'I love you, Mum.'

'I love you too, Jesse.' I leaned down to kiss the top of his head.

After cleaning up I took the kids to the park, leaving a note for Anna explaining where we'd gone, as well as the reason for the cat's presence. While the three children played in the old train, I lay down under some tall trees and watched a group of men and women playing volleyball, struggling back and forth with the ball and leaping up as high as they could to catch it. The sun was at its zenith and all the physical activity made me tired. Leaning my head on my arms, I buried my nose in the earthy-smelling grass as the sound of the kids and the volleyball players blended with buzzing cicadas in a thrumming mantra.

Sitting up to check where the kids were I squinted into the bright sunlight. Someone in a bright red shirt was walking straight towards me, waving. I waved back but it wasn't until Matt had passed the volleyball players that I recognised him.

He sat down beside me, grinning the mischievous grin that always made me think he was plotting something. 'The girls told me you were here.'

I picked at the grass. 'I've been wondering when you'd get in touch.'

'You could always get in touch with me.'

I smiled. 'I don't want to seem too keen.'

'Why not? At least it's honest.'

'I'd be too vulnerable.'

'I thought you were a liberated woman.'

'I am,' I replied, looking away and picking at the grass again.

Matt leaned towards me. 'I didn't come here to give you the third degree on the modern etiquette of male-female relationships. I wanted to ask you out.'

'When?'

'This afternoon.'

another song about love

'You didn't give me much warning, I've got the kids.'

'They can come too. I thought we might go to the beach or something.'

Without hesitation, I cupped my hands round my mouth and yelled. 'Hey, you guys! Wanna come to the beach?'

'Ooh yes!' was the chorused reply.

As we walked back to the house Matt slipped his hand into mine and squeezed it. Anna and Wendy were sitting at the kitchen table. The big teapot and the cups were out again, ready for another session.

'Matt's invited the kids and I to the beach for the day. Is that all right, Anna?' I asked. 'Sam and Antonia can borrow towels and stuff from us.' I could see by the look on her face that Anna wasn't too pleased with the idea of her two children spending time with Matt. I got two cups out and poured some tea. 'Milk?' I asked Matt as casually as I could.

'And two sugars.' Bemused, Matt leaned against the sink.

'Here, have a seat.' I tried to draw him into the circle but Matt declined. Leaning against the kitchen cupboard, he sipped his tea slowly.

I looked across at Anna with eyebrows raised but she didn't react at all. With Matt standing there, I guess she didn't know how to say no.

JANIE CONWAY HERRON

Antonia, Sam and Jesse sat quietly in the back seat of the car. As we drove out to the coast with a reggae tape blaring, I propped my feet up on the dashboard, stretched out and nodded off.

Matt prodded me. 'Wake up, little mother, we're nearly there.'

I tried to shake myself awake. 'I'm so tired. I stayed up till dawn talking to Wendy and Anna.'

'I know. The other two were still in bed when I arrived.'

I wondered what Matt thought when he found two women in my bed.

'How did the recording session go?' Matt asked and I was grateful for the change in conversation.

'We recorded a new song of mine yesterday. It ended up sounding great.'

'So what happens next?'

'We record some more songs and then do the rounds of the record companies. I've been thinking about taking a trip to Sydney to see what could happen there.'

'Mind if I come along for the ride? I've got some business of my own in Sydney. We could drive up in my car.'

'That'd be great.' I replied as my excitement rose and my vague plans began to take on a more certain shape.

another song about love

At the beach we parked at the end of a long line of cars and made our way over the hot asphalt towards the shore. The kids ran down between the brightly painted bathing sheds while Matt and I found a place close to the water's edge. When I took out the sun cream, ready to slather it on the bodies of the three children, Sam and Antonia submitted easily but Jesse pushed me away.

'I hate that stuff. It makes my skin feel all greasy.' He ran towards the water. Diving in, he splashed around then stood up, flipping his hair back from his face.

I stood at the water's edge beckoning Jesse back out.

Matt put his arms around my waist. 'Want to put some on me?' He sat down at my feet. When I squirted a long line of white cream across Matt's olive-skinned shoulders and rubbed it in, he leant into my hands coaxing me to rub harder.

Jesse dived under the water and seconds later he was standing beside me, dripping wet. 'You can put some of it on me now,' he said, offering his shoulders as Matt moved respectfully away.

Gently lapping waves cooled the soles of my feet. I watched as Jesse played around in the shallows with Sam and Antonia, then waded in up to my waist and dived under. Searching out Jesse's legs in the shallows I grabbed hold of his ankle. Jesse kicked out furiously, trying to free himself. When I let go, he jumped on my back and clung to my shoulders, growling and laughing. The other two jumped on as well and I became a whale carrying the three of them around on my back. Antonia clung onto my neck so hard I almost choked. I carefully pulled at her tiny hands trying to free myself, but the more I tried the harder she clung. Realising how frightened Antonia was, I headed for the shallows. As soon as she could put her feet down she scrambled to sit in the sand. The two boys hovered in the background.

'Hey Ant, cheer up, you're safe now,' Sam comforted, tugging at her foot.

Antonia tried to smile, but her sobs kept coming in great hiccoughing gulps.

I pulled her closer, rocking her. When she fell asleep, I put her down on a towel in the shade of the bathing shed and covered her with my T-shirt. Jesse and Sam were engrossed in burying each other up to their necks in the sand, so I walked to the water's edge and looked for Matt amongst the furthest line of heads in the deep water.

'Looking for me?' Matt stood behind me, his wet thigh rubbing against mine. 'I thought you were coming in.'

'I have to stay close to the kids in the shallow water. Now Antonia's fallen asleep, I need to stay and watch over her.'

'You could ask Sam and Jesse.' Matt picked up a handful of sand and poured it over my toes.

'Ant got scared when I took her out of her depth. I'm a bit worried about leaving her right now.'

another song about love

Matt let the last grains of sand slip through his hand. 'She'll be all right. There's no need to be so protective.'

I brushed the sand off my feet. 'I'll see what the other two say.'

Jesse was absorbed in building an elaborate castle around Sam, whose disembodied head stuck out of the sand. 'I'm building an Egyptian tomb, Mum. Do you like it?'

'It's great, Jesse.' I stood at a respectful distance from the sculpture. When Sam looked up, the surface cracked.

'Don't move, Sam!' Jesse commanded, as he smoothed the sand back. 'You nearly spoiled it.'

I knelt down so I was eye-to-eye with Jesse. 'Will you watch out for Antonia, while I go for a swim with Matt?'

Jesse frowned. 'But we're playing a game, Mum.'

I pulled him close. 'Listen, Jesse, I need to have some fun too. You're only here because of Matt and me. It doesn't take much to keep an eye on Ant while we have a swim.'

Jesse looked down at his feet while Sam looked up helplessly from the Egyptian tomb. 'Alright, we'll watch out for her.'

Out in the ocean I swam hard to catch up with Matt then floated beyond the furthest swimmers for a while, feeling the motion of the sea underneath me. When

JANIE CONWAY HERRON

Matt pulled me towards him I clung to his waist with my legs. Water flowed around us in a soft caress. He pulled me closer and my legs opened wider, pressing my clitoris against the hardness of his cock. Waves of pleasure moved through my body. When his hand slipped under the leg of my bathers I jumped. 'Relax,' he whispered as he pulled the crutch of my bathers to one side and carefully guided me onto him. I gave myself over to the delicious feeling inside me. Distilled desire threatened to erupt. I tried to bring myself to orgasm but Matt stopped me. 'We've got all night to make love. Let's save the fucking for later.' He withdrew slowly, lifting me upwards and kissing me. Lying on my back again, I closed my eyes and let myself drift as waves of unrequited desire coursed through me.

When we returned to shore, Sam was still buried up to his neck. Jesse had built an extraordinary castle around him but Sam looked bored. I looked over to check on Antonia. The towel and T-shirt were lying on the ground, with no Ant in sight.

'Where is she?' I screamed, pointing at the empty towel.

Sam was out of his sandcastle tomb within seconds, leaving Jesse distraught beside the destroyed monument. 'She was here a minute ago, we checked,' his voice trembled. 'She was still asleep then.'

I ran along the foreshore screaming Antonia's name while Sam and Jesse asked people if they had seen her. Nobody had. When half the people on the

another song about love

beach started looking for Antonia and there was still no sign of her, I imagined all the terrible things that could have happened. Sam and Jesse were white-faced with fear too. Only Matt was calm.

'Don't worry, Lillie, we'll find her,' he reassured me.

'Maybe we should try the police,' I said.

'Only as a last resort. I'll go for a drive, see if I can find her.'

Immobilised by fear, I watched Matt disappear between the boat sheds and head towards the car park. Within minutes he returned, holding Antonia by the hand.

'She was up sitting by the car waiting for us,' Matt explained, pleased to be the one who'd rescued the situation.

'I went looking for you,' Antonia said innocently, grinning up at the circle of concerned people standing around her.

I scooped her up into my arms and kissed her. When I turned to scold Sam and Jesse, the looks on their faces were proof they'd been punished enough.

As we drove back down the coast road towards the city, the kids slept on the back seat. Adrenalin kept me on high alert as darkness fell and the city lights panned out in front of us.

JANIE CONWAY HERRON

Vincent and Stevie set up for the mix. As they played each track, I was lost in the many nuances of sound available. My guitar sounded excruciatingly thin and trebly, as if it was coming out of the small transistor radio my father had given me as a child. When I complained, Vincent explained. 'We want the sound of it to cut through more, it won't sound so thin when it's mixed in with the rest of the band.' When he brought up the other instruments around the guitar I could hear the way it cut through without being louder than anything else. It was easy to visualise myself standing centre stage playing the rhythm.

When we listened to the final mix, Vincent turned the music up loud and it filled the studio. Stevie listened intently as the first track started and his seagull sounds wound up into the first of his wild solos. His enjoyment was obvious when he was involved in anything to do with music. Most other times he kept his emotions hidden behind a quiet, complacent facade.

At the end of the session, Vincent gave me the final mix on cassette.

I handed him some ganja in exchange. 'These are some of my best heads,' I announced proudly.

Vincent turned them over in the palm of his hand then took an old tobacco tin from his jeans pocket and added them to the stash he already had. 'I'll see you at the gig,' he said laconically. 'I'll have some dubs ready for the others by then. In the meantime, play this to the rest of the band and see if they like it.'

another song about love

As soon as Jesse saw me, he ran over and hugged me, entwining his skinny arms around my neck. Lifting him up I swung him round in the air. Anna and Wendy were lying together on a thin mattress in the shade. Anna sat up. A nervous look travelled across her face then disappeared into a smile. When Anna went inside, Wendy rolled over, propping herself up on her elbows. The corners of her mouth refused to sit straight.

'What's going on?' I asked. 'Since when have you two been an item?'

'Since we stayed at your place,' Wendy chuckled.

'What?'

'While you were at the beach we played around for a while.' Wendy shrugged as if it was inevitable.

'Well, you old devil, I didn't think that…'

'Didn't think what?'

I knew I was on dangerous ground. 'I didn't think Anna was into women.'

Wendy's face darkened. 'Fuck you, Lillie! Of course Anna's into women. She is one!'

'I meant sexually.'

Wendy leant towards me. 'You just don't like it up too close do you, Lillie? It makes you nervous.'

Wendy was right about my nervousness but not the reasons for it. 'Maybe I'm just scared of losing you both.'

'After all these years you're worried about something like that?' Wendy turned my face towards her. 'You ought to have more faith in our friendship, Lil'.'

The opening bars of the first song on the demo tape blared out from Anna's lounge room. In the cool dark, Wendy and I sat together listening to the final mix. Anna lay on the couch and closed her eyes, locked in intense concentration.

'She's beautiful, isn't she?' Wendy whispered.

'She sure is,' I agreed.

The cat rubbed against me, purring as I packed a bag for Jesse to take to Anna's place. We'd named the cat Pushka, but it made her sound more exotic than she was. She spent most of her time asleep on Jesse's bed or sitting in the window watching birds, her bottom jaw trembling with excitement.

'And these.' Jesse handed me a handful of his favourite cars. 'Don't forget my *Marvel* comics.' He pulled down a stack from on top of his cupboard. 'Can I take Pushka with me?' he asked, trying to catch me off guard.

'No you can't. Cats don't like to travel.'

'But Pushka will be lonely and hungry,' Jesse implored.

'Jonathon said he'd feed her and keep her company while we're away. I'm sure she'll be alright.' I zipped the bag closed. 'You finish packing any other

another song about love

things you want to take with you, while I get ready for the gig tonight.'

Hot water from the shower streamed down my back as I rubbed soap over my belly. I pushed my stomach out before pulling it in quickly, not wanting to dwell on the size of it. In my bedroom, I tried on one outfit after another. Nothing felt right. Within minutes I was standing in a mess of discarded clothes. I settled on some black tights and a large red shirt, black sneakers and bright red socks. The outfit was bright and big enough for me feel comfortable. I put kohl round my eyes, bright red lipstick on my mouth and teased my hair so that it stood out all over my head. This had to do. I didn't have time to fuss.

Jesse lay on his bed stroking the cat and looking mournful.

'Come on Jesse, leave Pushka alone and hurry up!' I said.

'But I don't want to leave her behind.'

'We're not taking her. You can feed her before we leave though. Hurry up.'

Jesse scampered down the hall with Pushka in his arms. I found an old silk scarf and spread it out on my bed, wrapped a generous supply of ganja in it and put it in my bag. While we waited for the taxi, Jesse hung on to Pushka, staring at me with imploring eyes. When the taxi arrived he solemnly put her back on his bed.

'I hope Pushka won't be lonely,' he murmured.

JANIE CONWAY HERRON

I took Jesse's hand. 'I'm sure she won't be. We're only away for a few days.'

Wendy and Anna were already packing the car, ready for our regular Thursday night gig at the Punters Club on Brunswick Street. Lifting Anna's bass amp, they angled it carefully into the back seat of the car then squeezed my amp in beside it. The guitars and the lighting gear fitted into the boot.

'Thank God for bench seats,' Wendy slammed the boot shut. 'If it weren't for the old EH we'd never get to gigs. I can't wait till we have our own road crew and truck.'

'Won't be long now. Just wait until I get back from Sydney,' I joked as I handed Anna the ganja. 'It's a thank you present for looking after Jesse. I want you and Wendy to smoke it all while I'm away.' As Anna opened the silk scarf, I added, 'My mother gave me that scarf when I was sixteen. I want you to have it.'

Anna quickly wrapped the ganja in the scarf again and tried to give it back to me. 'Lillie, this is too generous.'

'Nothing's too generous between friends, is it?' I laughed, pushing her hand away.

Jesse melted into my arms as I hugged him goodbye. Since my parents moved back to the coast I hadn't left him for more than an overnight stay anywhere. I knelt so that my face was up close to his. Tonight we were

another song about love

leaving the three boys alone together while we went to the gig.

'Jesse, you both need to be big boys now and look after Antonia this evening.'

Jesse nodded and smiled, then waved as Anna quickly steered me out the back door and up the side path towards the car. The three of us squeezed into the front seat and I sat in the middle, staring straight ahead while Anna drove.

'It must be hard saying goodbye to children.' Wendy patted me on the shoulder. 'Don't worry though. We'll ring your friend Claude and let you know if anything untoward happens. I'm sure everything will be alright.'

'Leaving Jesse was harder than I thought,' I sighed. 'But I'd better get used to it. If the band is successful, we'll be on tour all the time.'

'I don't want to leave Sam and Antonia alone too often,' Anna countered.

'We could always take the kids on tour with us,' I replied.

'They'd miss too much school.'

'Then we'll have to employ private tutors for the kids,' Wendy added.

'They'd still miss their friends,' Anna persisted, making my fragile hopes seem like faraway dreams.

We had been lucky to score a regular gig at the Punters Club. Bands played at the popular innercity hotel seven nights a week. Thursday night was an especially good night because it was payday for workers who'd go there cashed up. Tonight the hotel was packed and we struggled to carry the gear through the crowd. I dumped my amp on stage and climbed up, dragging my guitar with me. 'So many people and we haven't started playing yet.'

'Word's getting out, man. They've heard we're good.' Ali hit the snare drum. The sound rang out and he made a downward sign to Vincent and hit it again.

When I got my guitar out, Vincent jumped on stage and adjusted the levels on my amp. 'I thought we might boost the treble a bit tonight, go for that sound we got in the studio.'

'But I like the sound I already get on stage. It suits me,' I protested.

'Yeah, but it doesn't cut through enough. Here, try this.'

I strummed a chord and winced at the trebly sound.

Vincent adjusted the levels on my amp again. 'How does that sound?'

'It's still a bit thin.'

'It'll sound great once your guitar is combined with the other instruments. You'll be able to hear yourself better on stage too.'

I screwed up my face.

'Trust me, Lillie. I know what it should sound like out front. You can't hear it because you're on stage.'

another song about love

I looked away pretending to fiddle with the volume knob on the guitar. 'Alright, I'll try.'

By the time we were ready to play, people were pressing up against the stage and there was a sea of people going back as far as I could see. From the intro to the first song the audience was up and dancing and the band danced with them throughout the night. When the last song came round the audience yelled for more, ensuring it was time for me to announce the encore.

'We're going to do a song we've just recorded and hope to release sometime soon. It's all about the terrible things we do to ourselves in order to become successful. It's called '*Number One,*' and I hope it is one day.'

When the song finished, the crowd kept yelling for more. But the hotel manager turned the lights on. 'Sorry, folks, we've run out of time.'

As the audience drifted away I could see Matt sitting at the bar, talking earnestly to one of the barmaids. I walked over and tapped him on the shoulder.

'Hi.' I tried to make my voice sound as bright as possible.

'Lillie, this is my sister Selina,' Matt grinned.

Selina offered her hand. 'Matt's told me so much about you. I was really stoked when I found out you were playing here tonight. You should get good money. We've made a stack behind the bar. Come and I'll introduce you to the manager.'

JANIE CONWAY HERRON

In a musty room covered in band posters, Rob handed me a pile of cash. 'There's six hundred dollars there. You'd better count it.' In disbelief I fumbled through the pile of notes while Rob watched. 'It's been a good night. I hope the band can keep it up, then we'll all be happy.'

I finished counting the money, dividing it into equal shares, after Vincent's fee, and headed back to the stage to hand it out.

'I told you, you'd start making money if you stopped doing supports,' Vincent said as he counted the money and put it in his wallet. Then he added, 'I was thinking about ways you could pay for the recordings. I know the band hasn't got much money, but you could pay me in smoko instead of cash. An ounce of heads should square things off.' Vincent's mouth twitched nervously as he pulled at his hair.

I wanted to say something about all the ganja I'd already given him but that was putting a price on it. Lying, I told him I didn't have any on me. 'Can we sort it out when I get back from Sydney?'

'Okay.' Vincent put his wallet back in his pocket. 'It was a good gig tonight. Could you hear your guitar?'

'Yes I could, thanks.' I smiled. 'I'll see you next Thursday after I get back from Sydney.' I turned back to the bar hoping Matt was still waiting for me.

8

SUBWAY BLUES

I TRAVELLED BETWEEN SYDNEY AND Melbourne with my parents many times. I loved the sense of adventure as we headed north towards the smell of frangipanis in summer. My first trip to Sydney without my parents was also a mission to rescue my mother. It happened after a conversation with my father.

'What do you mean you've failed?' Dad cornered me.

JANIE CONWAY HERRON

'I've failed my exams, that's all.' I stared at the carpet.

'And what do you think you're going to do now?'

'I'll get a job.'

Dad snorted with disgust. 'If you'd studied hard and gone to school instead of wagging it, you could have reached your full potential.'

I had no idea what my potential was. At seventeen I believed a job meant economic independence.

Then Dad told me what was happening to Mum and his sharp words cut like a knife.

'She'll be in hospital for at least six months this time.'

I remembered standing helplessly on the shiny lino floor of the hospital corridor while Mum was dragged through double glass doors that muted her protests.

'Better call for an ambulance,' Wendy said as we stood over Mum's unconscious body. I'd meant to put her in a safe place, away from alcohol. A week was too long in that horrible place, reeking of pain and sorrow. Now Dad was talking about her being there for six months. I desperately wanted Mum to come home. Heaviness settled in the leaden air and the tightness in my chest remained locked inside. A scream needed to escape, like the cry of my mother as she was silenced by the thick hospital doors.

another song about love

In the middle of the night, I packed a small bag and put two pillows under the covers. At a glance it looked as if I was still in bed asleep. Quietly, I opened the window and leaned out before carefully dropping my bag and guitar onto the soft earth below. When I slid down the wall into the garden, Sean was waiting for me. We hugged quickly and started walking, keeping close to the night shadows. Once we were far enough away from my house, we relaxed, but I still jumped at the sound of an engine or the flash of oncoming headlights.

I hoped that if I could appeal to Mum's family in Sydney they'd put pressure on Dad to get her out of hospital. Sean decided to come with me for protection. That's what he said, but I knew a big part of him was also drawn to the adventure. We took the Princes Highway, winding up through all the coastal towns of Victoria and southern New South Wales. Though it was longer, we thought the police were less likely to look for us there once my father reported me missing.

White lines on black bitumen. The highway disappeared into the dark night horizon as we stood on the side of the road, shuffling our feet and waiting to flag down our first ride. An engine roared in the distance, changing gears as a flash of headlights revealed a truck weaving round the curves and crests of the road. It grew closer and we were almost swallowed up by the brilliance of the lights as a giant truck descended on us. With a change of gears the roaring engine wheezed and gasped. The driver braked then came to a stop and beckoned us up into his towering truck.

'Where're you two going? I can take you as far as Lakes Entrance.'

We climbed into the cabin, dragging our bags and guitars with us.

'Going to Sydney are you? At least I can get you off to a good start.' He helped us stash our things in behind the seat, then put the engine into gear.

Sean chatted amiably with the driver. Lulled by the sound of the engine, I slept, stirred only by the flash of lights when we passed through a town. The sound of the truck labouring up a steep incline woke me. The first rays of morning light had brightened the sky to pale grey. At the crest of a hill a panoramic view broke wide open and miles of ocean stretched right to the horizon. A long sand bank held back the surf from a maze of still water lakes where small boats added reds, whites and greens to the blueness of the waters.

The driver glided down the hill into town. 'Beautiful, isn't it?' he observed. 'I see this four times a week fifty weeks of the year and never get sick of it. I'll have to let you two off here, but I'm going to have breakfast first. You two hungry?'

The three of us sat together in a small roadside café, eating a greasy breakfast and discussing the frequency of accidents on the road. When I asked if most of the accidents involved cars and not trucks, the driver threw his hands in the air. 'Oh no,' he exclaimed. 'The trucks are the worst! Young drivers take all sorts of drugs so they can keep going straight through. They're supposed to take a rest after a certain amount of hours but they rig the logbooks so the inspectors don't pick it up. They're the ones causing the accidents!'

These words echoed certain doom when the next truck picked us up. The driver's dark, skinny face jutted forward over the steering wheel as he fixed his eyes on the horizon. Cigarette hanging from his bottom lip, he urged the truck onward. He was in a real hurry and yes he was going all the way to Sydney. I gripped Sean's arm as we flew along the road straight towards narrow bridges, horn blowing at oncoming cars. Most of the time I kept my eyes shut so as not to see the accident I was certain we would have. Unaware of my discomfort, the driver chatted on. He didn't need our conversation, he had a monologue of his own that toppled out of his mouth as fast as his driving. 'I've been driving for five years now, never had an accident. Good money if you can get enough work. You have to do a bit of cheating though. Rig the logbooks a bit. Why, last week I did a run to Sydney in ten hours. Then I turned around and took a load straight back! I had to stop on the way back, though.'

As the day wore on, the driver told us his life story in minute detail. The sound of his voice and the roar of his truck pummelled Sean and I into a stupor. As we approached Sydney, he let us off at Strathfield station.

JANIE CONWAY HERRON

It was early evening and the Sydney sky was turning orange-yellow. Sean pulled me close as we huddled together waiting for a train to take us to Sydney.

'I think I'd better ring home and let my father know I'm all right,' I said, searching through my purse for coins for the payphone. Sean was about to protest so I told him Dad would probably have contacted his mother by now and I should let him know we were both okay.

Unable to dig up enough coins, I rang reverse charges. While I waited for the connection I rehearsed what I was going to say to my father. To my surprise Mum answered. My plan had worked, but not in the way I thought it would. Mum was at home and sober. She didn't reprimand me, just gave me advice about how to get to my grandparents' place. Dad must have been relieved, but it wasn't obvious as we made plans for my return home.

I came out of the phone booth smiling. 'Guess what? Mum's out of hospital,' I told Sean. 'Dad couldn't cope with me running away, so he got her out. I didn't think it'd be that easy.'

'What do you want to do now, Lillie?' he asked. 'Go back home? I've been really looking forward to spending time in Sydney.'

'I've got to make sure Mum is okay,' I answered as tight-wired anxiety took hold of my heart again. 'Dad's going to pay my airfare so I can come home soon, maybe even tomorrow. We can stay at my

another song about love

grandparents' place tonight. Mum's ringing them to let them know we're coming.'

'So you've got it all worked out, have you? Back on the plane tomorrow, back to Mummy and Daddy. What about me? I suppose I walk back, do I?'

My eyes filled with tears but it didn't move Sean. After giving me enough money for the taxi fare to my grandparents' place, he picked up his guitar and walked away. As Sean disappeared round the corner, I stared at the piece of night air which moments before had been filled with his body. My heart called out as I waited for him to come back. After a while I gave up hope. When the taxi pulled out of Central Station I looked back, trying to catch sight of him. The streets of Sydney were alive with people and somewhere amongst them Sean was walking around, but I had no way of finding him.

Turning into a narrow street in the innercity suburb of Woollahra, the taxi wound down the hill to the block of red brick flats where Gran and Pop lived. When I was a small girl I'd spent hours there, drawing pictures with my grandmother or walking with my grandfather in the park nearby.

The front door opened before I had time to knock and I was whisked up into the arms of my grandmother. 'Oh my dear, she's quite grown up, isn't she?' she said to my grandfather.

JANIE CONWAY HERRON

'Yes, she's quite a young lady.' Pop drew me to him and I felt the deep resonance of his voice as I nestled my head on his chest.

In the little room out the back where I had stayed as a small child, I pulled the clean crisp sheet up round my neck and pictured my mother lying in the same bed. I imagined Dad coming to visit in the days just after the war and wondered if they'd ever made love there. Perhaps I had been conceived in this narrow bed. A breeze blew the lace curtains in the window, making a light swishing sound. I nestled further under the bed covers, breathing in the fresh night air. Drifting off to sleep, I dreamed of the salty sea.

The next morning, my grandmother made porridge, serving it up with brown sugar and lashings of cream in the red spotted bowls I remembered from my childhood.

Pop turned the teapot a ritual three times one way and then the other and poured hot strong tea into fine green teacups. 'I hear you're doing some singing with this new boyfriend of yours,' he announced as he pushed a jug of milk my way.

'Yes I am,' I answered.

'If you're doing a show up here I might come and see if you're any good.'

'Now Pop,' Gran cautioned, 'you know full well why Lillie's here.'

'Yes I do but I thought Lillie might have planned to do a few shows, seeing as she's brought her guitar with her and all.'

another song about love

'That's what Sean thought too,' I said, pushing back hot tears. 'He's decided to stay in Sydney but I want to go home and make sure Mum's okay.'

'Good for you,' Pop answered. 'And if Sean isn't man enough to stay by your side at this time of need, then I'd give him the flick. You could always do some gigs with me when you're next in town.'

Gran put her hand on my arm. 'This must be a very hard time for you. I can understand why you want to get home. Your dad needs you too. He's been distraught wondering where you might be. It's been hard for him having your Mum in hospital and trying to look after you too.'

I wanted to tell them everything. How Mum and Dad fought all the time and about Dad's affairs, but they were Mum's parents. They didn't know about the possibility of Mum being in hospital for months. I lacked the courage to tell them, even though that was the main reason I'd come to Sydney. Now Mum was home I was eager to make sure she stayed there.

After breakfast Pop put me in a taxi and pushed some money into my hand. 'This is to pay for the taxi but buy a little something for yourself while you're at the airport,' he said.

'Pop, this is way too much,' I protested.

'You're well worth it,' Pop answered. 'And don't you go forgetting that and giving yourself away to the first bloke who pays you attention, my girl.'

JANIE CONWAY HERRON

'I'll try not to,' I answered and Pop winked as he shut the door. As we drove away I looked back and watched him waving until the taxi rounded the corner.

After returning home, I waited for weeks for word from Sean. The weeks turned into months and still there was no news. None of our friends had heard from him either. A delicate emotional balance was being kept between my mother and father. Though they tried their best not to argue, the atmosphere was filled with tension. I became more fine-tuned to it than ever. Riding a tide of apprehension, I watched closely for any sign that the fragile cordiality between them might break down. Mum looked frail. I tried my best to gauge her sobriety, always alert to any signs of her drinking.

Eating kept my complex emotions at bay. When I played the guitar it distracted me from my vigil, but I was too uninspired to enjoy playing. Every tune I played reminded me of Sean. When I sang the songs we performed together I could hear every missing note he used to play. I took up smoking to stop myself over-eating. Smoking gave my voice a husky edge. I liked it better than the high-pitched purity of my folky style, but it didn't stop me eating. When I couldn't fit into my jeans I started wearing long skirts and outsized shirts to compensate. My room reflected the chaotic state of my emotions. Clothes, books and ashtrays piled high with butts all competed for floor space.

another song about love

If I was keeping watch over my mother, my father was keeping watch on me. I enjoyed shocking him with thick black make up round my eyes and unconventional clothes. Having promised Mum he'd stop being so critical, Dad retreated into silence, lengthy sighs indicating his disapproval. We moved into a world of innuendo where looks conveyed more than words and much remained unsaid. Fighting might have been better than the intensity of our shared silence.

'Let her make her own decisions,' I heard Mum advise Dad one night. 'You never know, she might even go back to school. It's a crucial time for her and she needs to work it out for herself. Music seems to be the thing she's most passionate about. She might make a go of that.'

Every now and then Dad looked into my room and sighed. He'd promised Mum he wouldn't say anything as I hunkered down in my room day after day, night after night, waiting for word from Sean. One evening, he dropped an envelope on my bed and waited for me to open it. It was a letter from Sean. My heart beat hard but I kept a straight face as Dad lingered in the doorway. I glared at him and he went away.

I tore the letter open. Inside was a picture postcard of the Sydney Harbour Bridge with 'wish you were here' written on the back and a letter. I read it over and over until the jumble of Sean's thoughts made sense to me. He was not coming back to Melbourne.

JANIE CONWAY HERRON

He'd found a band to play with in Sydney and they had a manager who'd signed them up for a recording deal. It was too big a chance for him to miss. If I wanted to come to Sydney, we might be able to do some gigs together. The letter was signed 'with all my love,' but I knew I'd lost Sean's love. I could feel the distance between us. The realisation brought clarity to my feelings. I looked around my room and noticed the way it reflected the disarray that had become an integral part of my life. It was time to make some changes.

The next weekend I chose a long black velvet skirt and a big black jumper, piled my hair on top of my head and added beads, earrings and bracelets that tinkled as I walked. It was as close as I could get to being pleased with my appearance. Lighting a cigarette, I inhaled long and deep and stared at the mirror. The face staring back at me wasn't quite my own, but it reflected a sense of mystery that pleased me. I passed by the lounge room door where Dad was sitting. The only words he could find were short sharp ones that rolled off his tongue like a command.

'You be home early,' he ordered.

'Okay Dad,' I clicked the door shut. I knew he'd be watching me out the window as I walked past. Our unhappiness had made us both tongue-tied. I longed to talk with him like we used to but I was too proud to show it.

another song about love

Frank's Place was already crowded when I arrived. When I offered to pay, the woman on the door waved me through. 'Musicians don't have to pay. It's Frank's policy,' she said and I was flattered by the recognition. Before receiving the postcard from Sean, I'd fantasised about us going back to our regular gig there, but after I received Sean's note this place had been off-limits. It was Wendy who talked me into coming down just to listen to the music. 'You don't have to play or anything. Just come and check it out; see how you feel. I'll meet you there after I've finish work at Hilliard's, then we can go home together. Terry's playing with that great guitarist Joe and he's got a really cool bass player with him too. A woman called Anna. You two would get on real well, I reckon.'

Most of the array of instruments standing on the stage belonged to Joe but the clean-looking Gibson had to be Terry's. As I stood immobilised by memories of Sean and I up on that same stage, a light tap on my shoulder drew me out of my reverie. When I looked around Joe was towering over me.

'Hey Lillie, where've you been? It's ages since we've seen you here.'

'I've been hibernating for winter,' I grinned, 'but Wendy talked me into coming tonight.'

Joe smiled his lovely crooked smile. 'Wendy's out the back if you want to go see her. I'll see you afterwards, eh?'

JANIE CONWAY HERRON

I watched Joe move over to the stage and studiously check the tuning of his instruments. He looked like some strange insect as he crouched over the guitars, his long delicate fingers moving lightly over the fret board. Off stage he was awkward and shy, but as a musician Joe had the grace of a well-trained dancer.

Out the back Wendy was in fine storytelling form, her loud voice filling the room. It was sometimes hard to believe the truthfulness of her stories. She was one of those people who had a gift for making an ordinary event sound astonishing.

I stood behind her, not wanting to draw attention to my presence. As soon as Terry saw me, his raised eyebrows made Wendy turn around.

'Hey, kiddo, you made it!' Wendy embraced me. 'And about time too, it's been ages since we've been out together.'

I sank into my friend's embrace. 'I've been trying to hibernate for the winter,' I replied, holding onto the excuse like a mantra.

'You've just been pining for that boyfriend of yours who left you and went to Sydney,' Terry announced.

'Shut up Terry, don't be such an arsehole,' Wendy snapped.

I took a deep breath and picked up the gauntlet. 'No, man, you're wrong there. I left him in Sydney. I've been polishing up my solo act so that I can go out on my own.' Terry's dismissive snorts in reply only

another song about love

strengthened my determination. 'I thought I might ask Frank for a solo spot one night.'

'Good on you, Lil',' Wendy encouraged me. 'I'm sure Frank'll give you a go.'

My bravado faltered. I didn't even have the courage to ask Frank, let alone get up on stage by myself.

Terry sensed my uncertainty. 'Frank doesn't usually have solo singers. He prefers a duo or a group, that's why I've got Joe playing with me. He's my backing band. The guy's so talented, it's as good as having a whole band and half the price.'

'Watch it, Terry. If you praise me up too much I might start tripling my fee.' Joe leant towards me.

I wished I could evaporate into thin air. I turned to leave the room but Joe grabbed me by the arm.

'If you get a gig, I'd be happy to play with you,' he said loud enough for Terry to hear. 'Stick around after our bracket and we'll talk about it.' Joe kept hold of my arm and stared at me with those enormous eyes, his mouth breaking into a curly grin. I fell for him in that instant.

'Okay, I'll do that.' I smiled back. 'Have a good gig.' When Joe let go of my arm I headed out into the audience with Wendy bouncing along beside me.

'Joe's in love with you, you know,' she announced.

'Do you think so?'

'I know so.'

'How do you know, Wendy? That old crystal ball again?'

'Well kind of,' Wendy hesitated. 'He kept asking about you every time I came here, so I asked him.'

'You what?'

'I asked him if he was in love with you.'

I felt my face going bright red. 'Oh God, Wendy, how could you?'

'It was easy, especially when he said yes. He reckons he fell in love with you that first night he heard you sing.'

My heart beat with an odd mixture of elation and disbelief. 'How come guys talk to you so easily?'

'Most blokes think of me as their best friend.'

'Come on Wendy, when the right man comes along, they'll fall for you.'

'Sometimes I think it's easier to be friends.'

'Do you?'

'Was being in love with Sean worth it?'

'Yeah,' I confirmed as my emotions shifted. 'Now I'm feeling better, yes.'

As the band came on stage, a tiny dark-haired woman appeared out of nowhere with an acoustic double bass. When she started playing I was awestruck. Her fiddle playing was equally proficient.

Later Joe introduced me to Anna. 'Wow, you're a great player,' I exclaimed.

another song about love

'You're a pretty good musician yourself,' Anna replied, 'I've seen you and Sean play here a few times.'

'Really?' I was both flattered and surprised.

'I've always admired Sean's playing but you added something else, a real human element that kept Sean honest and stopped him from trying to be too flash. If you ask me, it's a common flaw in male musos. They can be all style and no content, if you get my drift.'

I didn't know what to say but I liked this tiny opinionated woman who seemed so much more self-assured than I was.

Over the ensuing weeks I became a regular at Frank's Place and practised hard at home to extend my repertoire. When Frank gave me a spot, I invited Joe and Anna to accompany me. The gig went well and I was invited back again. Before long I became a regular performer at this popular folk venue.

By the time I'd turned eighteen, Joe and I were a couple, spending most of our time together. I frequented secondhand clothing stores and transformed the clothes I found into exotic outfits. Lots of jewellery combined with long velvet skirts and lace tops became my signature style. Old ladies' lace-up shoes became elegant footwear, while hats of different sorts were added to my collection. When Joe started dressing up as well, I found him some velvet capes and encouraged him to wear high-heeled boots that accentuated his height. On the street people turned to look at us. We fostered their attention, pleased to be the subjects of their gaze. Joe and I went everywhere together and often performed as a duo or with Anna when she could take time out from her other musical commitments. If Joe played with someone else, I was always in the audience.

When Dad went away on overseas trips, Mum gave me the freedom to spend nights at Joe's place. When Dad came home, I had to be home before midnight. At eighteen years of age, I could legally do what I liked, but Dad's need to keep a tight control on me increased. If I was late, he waited up for me. When he questioned me about where I'd been, our old animosities started up all over again. Life at home became almost unbearable but, being protective of my mother, I felt unable to leave. When I told Joe what was happening, he suggested we try living together.

'What if I spoke to your dad about it?' he asked.

I shook my head. 'Even if I left home, Dad would blame Mum for being too permissive. They'd start fighting again and then Mum might start drinking.'

'You're not responsible for your parents' happiness, Lillie,' Joe advised. 'At least we could give it a try. Anything would be better than the way things are now.'

'Anything?' I asked.

another song about love

'Anything except losing you.'

'Really?'

'Yes really. Now are we going to front your father or not?'

I waited with Mum while Dad and Joe had a long discussion in Dad's office.

'Shall I see if they want a cup of tea?' I asked, desperate to interrupt after an hour had gone by.

'Let's give them another half hour,' Mum counselled.

After another hour, I knocked on the door then opened it before there was a chance of being turned away. My father's face told me things weren't going well. When I looked at Joe, I could see the tension in his eyes, the thin-lipped strain of his usually curly mouth.

Dad turned to me. 'While I appreciate Joe coming to ask my permission, I think you'll both understand when I say that no daughter of mine is going to live with a man and that's that. You can still do it if you're determined to, that's your legal right, but it won't be with my approval. You know what that means, don't you, Lillie?' Dad gave me a look that challenged me to defy him.

I tried to think of something clever to say but nothing seemed adequate. It was crazy to think about asking Dad if we could live together, especially now when things between Mum and Dad were fragile.

JANIE CONWAY HERRON

Joe's answer was so unexpected, it rendered both Dad and I speechless.

'Why don't we get married?' he proclaimed cheerfully, his big eyes gleaming through his thick-rimmed glasses. 'Then everyone will be happy.'

9

FOOL MYSELF

WHILE MATT WAS STILL ASLEEP, I got up early to prepare for the drive to Sydney. It was a clear crisp morning heralding the exit of that ferocious summer. I put the demo tapes and band photos in my briefcase alongside a list of record companies to play the demo-tapes to.

When I climbed the back fence, I could see Jonathon making breakfast in the kitchen next door. I called out, then climbed over the fence and dropped onto the sweet-smelling earth in his garden. In the row of semidetached federation houses where we lived Jonathon's house mirrored mine in design. My house was cluttered, filled with pieces of secondhand furniture I'd managed to score, the walls covered in posters and photos. Each piece in Jonathon's sparsely furnished house was carefully chosen. If you didn't look too carefully you might have thought you were in Japan rather than an Australian suburb.

He looked up when I came inside and directed me to a low table in his lounge-room. Sitting cross-legged he continued eating his breakfast, but not before offering me a small, fine china cup of green tea.

'Here's the key to my place,' I said, placing it on the table. 'Thanks for feeding the cat while I'm away.'

Jonathon slowly turned the mouthful of food he was eating over and swallowed before drinking his tea. In one graceful movement, from sitting to standing, he picked up the key and put it inside a small brass container. 'I'll feed her in the mornings after my run,' he said, and sat down at the low table again. Jonathon's grace reminded me of the dancer I once was; the consciousness in every movement he made, the ability to feel his own centre of gravity and move, straight-backed, through a room. I'd lost that self-assurance, though sometimes I could still feel it in my bones. When I climbed back over the fence, I felt clumsy.

'I'm really out of condition,' I panted as I balanced precariously on the narrow wooden ledge and hung by my armpits.

another song about love

'Some exercise might help,' Jonathon advised.

'I don't seem to get the time for exercise,' I replied.

'You can always make time.'

'I will one day.' I hung for a few more seconds, waiting for Jonathon to say something else. Then I noticed that all his plants had disappeared from the backyard. 'So you've harvested yours too,' I observed. 'I've got mine in my wardrobe, drying out.'

'I've decided to give up smoking weed. It's bad for your psychic energy.' Jonathon looked at me as if the conversation was below him.

'Oh really? I've not heard that,' I answered. 'When you're on a good thing why give it up?' I had an urge to pull funny faces, walk across the top of the fence or do a sudden handstand to impress him. 'I'd better go then,' I muttered, as I balanced my weight between my toes and armpits. 'Thanks again for your help.'

I took a cup of coffee in to Matt and tapped him on the shoulder. He was lying so still I thought he might be dead. When his shoulders moved I whispered his name, softly at first, then more loudly.

Matt woke in fright, protecting his face with his arms.

He looked so defenceless I couldn't help laughing. 'Sorry, I didn't mean to scare you, but you're so hard to wake up.'

Matt looked around with fear still in his eyes. 'I thought it was a raid.'

'A raid?'

'When the cops arrive in the middle of the night and you wake up with their guns pointing at your head.'

'I can't say I've ever experienced that.'

'Well, I hope you never do.'

I pulled clothes out of the wardrobe and put them in an old suitcase. Carefully wrapping one of my dried plants, I lay it over the tapes in the briefcase.

'That should really impress the record companies,' Matt commented.

'Yep, nothing wrong with getting into a bit of payola early in the piece.'

'Are you serious?'

'Of course not,' I laughed. 'It just seems like the best place to put it. I want to take some to Sydney, to make sure we have a good time.'

For someone not used to waking before midday, eight o'clock in the morning was far too early for Matt. He stood in front of the bathroom mirror and ran his wet hands through his hair, trying to get it to sit flat. 'Have you organised somewhere for us to stay?' he asked.

'My friend Claude said we can stay with him. You'll like him, he's a kindred spirit.'

'He won't mind me being there?'

another song about love

'Claude loves meeting new people. By the time he's finished with you, you'll think you're the most interesting person on God's earth.'

Matt stared into the mirror again, stuck his head under the tap and combed his hair down flat. 'I'm ready for anything now,' he said grinning. 'Let's get this show on the road, shall we?'

By nine-thirty we were out on the Hume Highway and just after midday we crossed the border into New South Wales. As the miles passed, Matt and I fell into increasingly intimate conversation.

'My sister put a pillow over my face when I was a baby and I nearly suffocated. My mother stopped her just in time.' Matt looked over to check my reaction. 'Another time she made me put my hand in the toaster and then turned it on. I nearly lost the top of this finger. Look, I've still got the scar.'

I took his hand. The top of his middle finger was scarred and stunted.

'I had a girlfriend who dropped me because she couldn't stand the thought of me touching her with it,' he added.

'I didn't even notice it until you showed me,' I reassured him.

'Are you shocked?' Matt asked.

'I'm more shocked that your sister did such a thing to you.'

'She was really jealous when we were young. We only became friends when we got older.'

185

'How old was she when they brought you home?'

'Five.'

'Plenty of kids have to get used to having a younger brother or sister. It isn't that dramatic. I wish I'd had a brother or a sister to share things with. Was she adopted too?'

'No. After Selina's birth my mother couldn't have any more children, so my parents adopted me. Right from the start I was a compromise.'

'But they must have really wanted you. They chose you.'

'I don't know why. I don't even look like them.'

'Maybe that wasn't important to them.'

'It's important to me.' Matt offered his hand once again, sliding it along the seat, palm up. When I took hold of it, he kissed my fingertips. 'I've never met anyone like you, Lillie.'

I'd been longing to hear something like this. I had all the time in the world to listen as long as Matt made me feel special.

More stories and secrets unfolded as we drove down the long straight inland highway, bitumen and white lines before us. By evening we'd reached the outskirts of Goulburn, driving past the forbidding razor-wired walls and lit up observational towers of the prison. At the Paragon Cafe, we sat in high-backed Laminex booths, while a wispy-haired waitress waited for us to decide what we wanted. I asked for chips and salad with a milkshake while Matt ordered sausages, fried eggs and coffee. When the waitress left he apologised. 'I always feel compelled to eat things like this in these places, just to prove I'm Australian.'

'My mother was brought up near here. She was only fifteen years old when she was sent to Goulburn to do nursing.' I explained, remembering Mum's stories of how the family was bankrupted during the depression and she was sent to do nursing there. Her sadness and sense of loss were intrinsically linked to Goulburn for me.

'The only memories I have of my birth mother are buried deep in my subconscious,' Matt confided. 'I think about her a lot and wonder if she ever thinks about me.'

I sucked at the milkshake the waitress brought. Long cold gulps gurgled at the end of the straw. 'I'm sure your mother thinks about you. I would, if I was her.'

Matt smiled. 'You wouldn't give up a child in the first place.'

I took in more large gulps of the milkshake. 'I had an abortion when I was sixteen. That child would be a teenager now. I think about that a lot. Whether the baby was a boy or girl. What he or she might have been like. How different my life would be if I'd had that baby.'

'Do you ever feel guilty about it?'

'I think I grieve for the person I didn't get to know, but I don't feel guilty. I didn't really have a

JANIE CONWAY HERRON

choice. My father couldn't have handled his one and only daughter pregnant so young. What shame! My mother organised the abortion. She didn't want me to have the baby either.'

'I wish my mother had an abortion instead of adopting me out like she did.' Matt took hold of my hand. 'When we get to Sydney I'm going to try to make contact with her. I've got some papers with me and I'm going to get some information from the agency that arranged the adoption.'

'That's a big step to take.'

'I've been thinking about it for years.' Matt looked away. 'There must be some record of the moment I made it into this world and I'm going to find it.' Matt let go of my hand, pulled out his wallet and went to pay the bill. As he joked with the waitress I could see him carefully building a fortress around his heart once more.

We arrived on the outskirts of Sydney and headed towards Newtown. As we drove down King Street, I pointed excitedly at everything I saw, while Matt negotiated the traffic.

'There's the street, over there. Quick, turn right.' I pointed toward the opposite side of the road and Matt turned into Claude's street. 'It's number thirty-seven,' I said, trying to read the street numbers in the dark.

'There it is. That big old house there.' Matt pointed to a terrace on the other side of the road. 'Why

another song about love

don't you rustle up your friend Claude, while I park the car.'

I knocked on the front door of the house and waited. It still felt like summer in Sydney and there was optimism in the warmth of the balmy evening.

'You must be Lillie,' the old man who answered broke into a broad, toothless smile. 'Claude told me he was expecting you. My name's Harold but people call me Harry.' Wrapping my hand in his thin bony fingers, Harry shook it vigorously. 'Come on in. Claude's waiting for you.'

I hesitated. 'My friend is parking the car. I'd better wait for him.'

'Don't worry I'll direct him.' Harry pointed up the stairs. 'Two flights up, you'll see the door to his flat.'

The house smelled musky and the olive-green walls had faded over the years, giving the place a sombre feel. The wooden banister had been polished by many generations of hands sliding along it, while the once floral carpet was worn so thin only a trace of the flower pattern was visible at the edges.

I climbed the stairs to the landing and knocked on one of the two doors in front of me. When it flew open I was swept up in the whirl of Claude's welcome and the distinct aroma of the patchouli oil he'd been wearing since the early hippie years when I first met him. The walls of his apartment were painted orange and blue. Mattresses scattered with a vast array of

189

patterned cushions lined all the available wall space. Claude was a picture of brightness too, with his purple shirt and loose red pants tied at the waist. His long grey hair was tied back in a ponytail and his still youthful body evident in the ripple of muscle in his stomach.

'I couldn't leave this apartment the way it was when I moved in,' he explained. 'It used to be a boarding house for old men, but they divided it into flats. I livened my part of it up a bit. Come, I will show you the rest.'

In Claude's bedroom an elevated platform bed was covered in a rainbow mosquito net, the dark blue roof above it painted like a night sky with luminous stars. By the window, a hammock stretched from one wall to the other. As Claude went to let Matt in, I lay back in it and let the flickering lights of the Sydney night skyline dance before my eyes.

Claude put our bags in a corner and pointed at the mattresses on the floor. 'There's plenty of space, I often sleep here myself.' When Matt and I sat down, Claude smiled. 'What a beautiful couple you two make. You always have had good taste in men, Lillie. Aesthetically speaking that is.' Reaching into a cupboard he pulled out an ornate wooden box. 'The best hash in Sydney,' he announced, taking out a smaller box, inlaid with mother of pearl. Inside was a small block that looked like a piece of chocolate.

I pulled out my briefcase. 'I've got something to show you too.' I opened the locks and pulled out the ganja. 'I grew it myself. It's practically all heads and smells just as strong as your hash.'

Claude ran his nose along one of the heads and took a deep breath in. 'Looks like we're going to have a good week,' he said as he handed the hash box to Matt. 'You seem like someone who can roll a good joint. Why don't we start with a mull to celebrate your safe journey to Sydney? I will make some coffee.'

I watched Matt choose some sky-blue papers, carefully break off a head from my plant and crumble it up into a ceramic bowl, before mixing a small amount of Claude's hash in with it. By the time Claude returned with the coffee, Matt had rolled a masterpiece.

'This looks almost too good to smoke.' Claude held the joint up to the light then handed it to Matt. Flicking the lid on his silver lighter he held the flame out.

Matt took a long toke on the joint, sank into the cushions behind him and fell into an exhausted sleep.

'So, you are going to be a big star at last, Lillie,' Claude proclaimed.

'I hope so. I've brought some demos up to take round to the record companies.'

'Why don't you play them for me?' Claude put the tape I gave him in a rusty old tape deck with paint splattered all over it. 'When I sell my next painting I will buy a new tape deck but until then, I make do with this. If it sounds good on this, it will sound good anywhere.'

JANIE CONWAY HERRON

The first drum roll sounded more like Jesse practising on cardboard boxes and the strength of the bass rattled the speakers, but Claude didn't seem to notice. He listened attentively, nodding his head in time to the music. 'You have always been good, Lillie,' he commented. 'I remember when I first saw you playing with Sean. I was riveted. I thought to myself, now here's another like-minded soul. I can always tell. Like René, he's another one.'

It was excruciating to listen to this distorted version of my song, so I seized on the opportunity to make René the centre of conversation. 'You're a scoundrel trying to pass René on to me. He's so in love with Jemma.'

Claude sighed. 'I knew she'd leave me sooner or later. We were too different. She is so young whereas I am an old man.'

'You! An old man,' I scoffed.

'Lillie, I'm nearly fifty years old. I've seen a lot of life. Jemma is still in her twenties. I knew she would leave me but I didn't think she'd go back to René.'

'Why not?'

'I misjudged her. I thought she was young and frivolous. Like a butterfly always going on to the next thing. I was greedy and René reminded me so much of myself as a younger man. I worked hard at taking Jemma away from him just to prove to myself I could. All the time I was arrogant enough to think I was doing it for René's good. But really, it was my own vanity.'

another song about love

'Did you love her?'

'I felt as if I did. I was infatuated with her because she represented my lost youth. I thought I was beyond jealousy and competitiveness, beyond falling in love. In the end I felt guilty. When I saw the look of betrayal on René's face, I couldn't stand it. But instead of being honest, I still played a game. I suggested he visit Melbourne and sent him to you on the pretext that he should get away for a while. The three of us had this 'all is fair in love' conversation, but I was playing with them both. I could see them trying to reason it out, attempting to make their heads rule over their hearts. Now I realise, that's what makes you grow old.'

'You always see yourself at the centre of things, Claude,' I counselled. 'You don't give René or Jemma enough credit for having their own feelings. René wasn't interested in me romantically but I'm thankful that we met. He's been a very good friend. Jesse adores him.'

Claude checked to see if Matt was still asleep, then whispered. 'What about you, Lillie? Does this beautiful boy satisfy you?'

'It's early days yet.' I looked over at Matt's sleeping face.

'You are in love with him, no?'

'I'm trying not to be but I do like him a lot.' I fiddled with the bracelets on my arm as the next track began and my voice filled the room with another love song.

JANIE CONWAY HERRON

'Don't you know what love is, Lillie?' Claude asked as he took my hand.

'I'm not sure I do any more,' I replied.

'It is the thing that makes the world go round, is it not?' Claude laughed. 'Don't be so scared of it, my friend. It is at the very heart of everything you do, believe me.'

In a dress shop on King Street I tried on one dress after another. After half an hour, I'd tried on almost every dress in the place.

'What about this one?' Matt handed me a bright red dress.

I held it up in front of me. 'No, it's too small.'

'It stretches, and with a nice jacket it will look great. Try it on,' Matt insisted.

The salesgirl ushered me into the changing room once more.

I came out frowning. 'It's too tight. You can see my stomach sticking out.'

'It looks great. That's the one, alright.'

'Are you sure?'

Claude turned me around. 'It's good, Lillie. Very rock and roll.'

I stood sideways and looked at myself in the mirror. Running my hand over my stomach I held it in as much as I could.

another song about love

Claude looked over my shoulder. 'A woman should not be ashamed of her curves, Lillie. You are a woman are you not? You have had a child. You are not a teenager anymore. Grown women have curves.'

Never comfortable with the shape of my body, I mostly tried to ignore it. The redness of this dress captivated me, but the tightness made me very self-conscious.

The salesgirl, adept at manipulating these moments, pulled out a black satin jacket from the window and held it up. 'This would be perfect with it.'

When I tried it on it fitted well and gave a visual impression of slimness. I tried to calculate whether there was a way I could afford both the dress and the jacket.

As if he'd read my mind, Matt pulled out his wallet. 'I can pay for the dress, if you can afford the jacket, Lillie.'

I hesitated, not knowing how to accept Matt's generosity.

'I'd like to buy it for you,' Matt persisted. 'I like that dress on you.'

Claude and the salesgirl nodded their approval.

When I went to put my old clothes back on, Matt stopped me. 'Keep wearing it. I want to walk down King Street with you in that dress.'

We sat in the window seat of the Cafe Lupa, watching the parade of Saturday morning shoppers out on King Street.

Numerous coffees later, as we walked back down King Street, I slipped in between Matt and Claude, hugging them both.

'How does it feel to have such a beautiful girlfriend?' Claude asked Matt.

'Claude, you are such a flatterer,' I laughed.

'Why shrug off a genuine compliment as flattery?' Claude persisted. 'You must believe in yourself, Lillie. Otherwise you wouldn't be trying to be a musician.'

'I just don't know how to do anything else,' I answered.

'What about you, Matt? Don't you agree with what I am saying?'

'Yes,' was all Matt could muster.

'See, Lillie, we are in agreement. You will have to accept that you are both talented and beautiful.'

Back at Claude's place, Harry informed us that we had visitor. 'I told him you were out, but he said you were expecting him.' Harry winked at Claude. I sensed mischief ahead but I wasn't prepared for who was waiting for me at the top of the stairs. As my eyes adjusted to the darkness, I recognised the figure sitting on the top of the landing and leapt into Sean's arms.

'Oh my God, how did you end up here? I didn't know you knew Claude. Wow, it's good to see you.'

'I've known Claude for ages,' Sean explained. 'My band has a regular gig down the road and he often comes down for a drink. We got talking one time and

196

discovered we both knew a lot of the same people. He told me you were coming a couple of weeks ago, so I thought I'd surprise you with a visit.'

'I can hardly believe it,' I exclaimed. 'The last time we met up here must be at least eight years ago now. God, I was so pregnant then it's lucky I made it through the tour without giving birth on stage. I have a son now, Jesse, but Joe and I split up after he was born.'

'I know. Claude's kept me up to date with what's been happening to you. You wouldn't want to know how many kids Claire and I have now. Way too many if you ask me, but we're all happy and healthy and that's all you can ask.'

Behind me I could hear Claude ushering Matt up the stairs with a stream of explanations. 'I didn't tell Lillie he was coming. They knew each other as teenagers. Sean helped Lillie when she first started singing.'

We talked most of the afternoon. As I played the tapes, I couldn't help trying to impress Sean, with the band I'd put together, with my knowledge of music and with my body in the bright red dress Matt bought me. When Sean had to leave, we made arrangements to go and see him play that evening. It wasn't until we were sitting together waiting for Sean's band to go on that Matt gave any indication he was put out.

'Are you all right?' I squeezed his arm. 'You're not jealous, are you?'

Matt pulled his hand away. 'Nah, I'm okay.'

'Well, if you are feeling jealous, don't be,' I bristled. 'Sean is married with children. Whatever we had between us is well and truly over.'

Matt shrugged. 'Don't worry about me. I just get shy sometimes.'

The band sounded great and I was riveted, clapping enthusiastically after every song. At the end of the set, I bought a round of drinks and handed Matt a scotch. He sculled it quickly, then went to the bar and ordered more. By the time Sean came over to our table, Matt was leaning back in his chair, happily anaesthetised, watching Sean and I discuss record companies and contacts he had that I could use.

Suddenly, Sean stood up. 'I've got to go,' he explained. 'I promised I'd spend the day with the kids tomorrow.' He offered his hand to Matt. 'Nice meeting you. I'll probably see you again before you go back to Melbourne.' He gave me a polite kiss on the cheek and shook Claude's hand as he added. 'Thanks for letting me know Lillie was in town.'

On the way home Claude chatted to the cab driver, while Matt and I sat in the back. 'You look immensely fuckable in that dress,' Matt pulled me closer.

After Claude went to bed, Matt and I smoked a joint while lying in bed. Touching each other, we blew smoke into each other's mouths. Our caresses increased in intensity. When we made love, Matt moved hard and furious as if he needed to possess me.

another song about love

I put my hands on his hips and then climbed on top, staring into his eyes. I moved slowly over him savouring the delicious feeling of him inside me. When he came, he yelled so loudly I had to put my hand over his mouth.

'Sshh, you don't want old Harry to hear you, do you?' I laughed.

'I don't care if the whole world hears me,' Matt answered.

'Touch me,' I whispered, guiding Matt's hand between my legs and showing him the rhythm that I liked as I pushed myself against him. When my orgasm contracted around his fingers, Matt whispered something so softly I had to ask him what he'd said.

'I love you,' he yelled so loudly I was sure even Harry could hear him. I sensed Claude leaning back in his hammock, smiling.

The following Monday, I looked for the nearest phone box. I had a pile of coins and a list of contacts. There was a red pay phone in the Café Lupa and I asked the waitress if I could use it.

'Sure,' she answered.

'I've got quite a few calls to make,' I added.

'You can make as many calls as you like.'

I smoothed out the list of contacts on the table next to the phone and stacked a pile of coins in front of me. Several cappuccinos later I reached the end of the list with only two appointments and a number of people to call back. Despondent, I gathered up the remaining coins and paid for the coffees.

'How'd you go?' the waitress asked as the till rang open.

'Not very good, I'm not having much luck getting onto the record companies.'

The waitress' face broke into a broad grin. 'I thought you looked like a muso. You're a friend of that French fella, aren't you? Saw you in here the other day. That other bloke, is he your boyfriend?'

'Sort of,' I answered, reluctant to stake such a claim.

'You'd better make your mind up,' the waitress replied. 'A good-looking bloke like that'd have all the girls after him. I wouldn't let him out of my sight if I were you.' The waitress winked and handed me the change. 'Come back any time. I'll be able to tell everyone that you made your first record deal over the phone in the coffee lounge where I worked.'

As always, Harry was waiting to let me in. He stood at the bottom of the stairs watching as I made my way up to the flat. The smell of ganja seeped out from under the door and I heard Claude's loud laughter along with the muffled tones of Matt's voice as I stood outside. When I knocked on the door everything went quiet.

'It's me!' I yelled.

another song about love

Matt opened the door and pulled me inside, smothering me with hugs and kisses. When I struggled to pull away from him, he let go. 'Hey, what's wrong with you?' he asked.

'I didn't get through to very many people.' I flopped down on one of the mattresses. 'I've only got two appointments so far. I hope I can get a couple more before we have to go back to Melbourne.' Claude handed me the joint they'd been smoking and I shook my head. 'I need to keep my wits about me, otherwise I'll end up spending the whole time I'm here stoned and won't get anything done.'

Incredulous, Matt and Claude look at each other and then back at me.

'It's only a joint,' I said.

At the Family Records Department, Matt's heavy boots echoed loudly along the polished linoleum. He strode in like a cowboy with guns at the ready. A middle-aged woman stared across the counter at the dishevelled man who marched towards her. Matt pulled out a piece of paper from his wallet, carefully unfolded it and pushed it at the woman. 'I want to make contact with my real mother,' he said. It was more like a demand than a request.

The woman read the piece of paper, occasionally glancing at Matt over the top of the glasses she had attached to a chain around her neck. 'Just a minute, sir, I'll check our records,' she said, before disappearing behind a wooden screen.

Matt beckoned me over to him then pulled me close. I watched the stunted top of his middle finger moving up and down as he beat an impatient rhythm on the counter. When the woman came back, Matt stood up straight, eager to accept the information the woman had.

'I'm terribly sorry, sir,' the woman quavered. 'We can't give you the name of either of your parents, unless they have given express permission on the adoption papers. However, we can let you know that your mother was twenty years old and in good health when she gave birth to you. Your father was probably of Southern European extraction. Your parents were not married.' With her glasses perched precariously on the end of her nose, the woman looked like some strange bird about to catch a worm.

There was silence as Matt tried to comprehend, then he whispered, 'You mean you can't even tell me my own mother's name?'

'No sir, I cannot.'

'Do you know what it is?'

'I'm sorry sir, we are not allowed to divulge that information.'

Matt leaned over and the woman flinched. He banged the counter then spoke through clenched teeth. 'Well, that's all right, because what I really wanted to know is whether my mother breast-fed me or not!'

another song about love

Matt snatched the piece of paper from her hand and strode out through the double glass doors.

I followed Matt outside and found him staring out at the thick city traffic. When I put my arm around him, his shoulders were heavy with the weight of his sorrow, his body rigid and unresponsive.

'I should have known it'd be like that,' he said. 'Joyce warned me they wouldn't let me know who my real parents were, but I thought it was just sour grapes on her part. I thought she didn't want me to find my real mother.'

The city traffic clanged and hooted.

That evening we all got stoned. I laughed and talked, trying to make up for Matt's mournful silence, while attempting to prepare an evening meal. When the rice burned, I turned the gas off.

'What is wrong with you?' Claude asked as he methodically sliced carrots into long sharp slivers that sat neatly in a row on the chopping board. 'You are so nervous you talk like a chatterbox while Matt has turned into a block of wood. He's a moody boy, that one. I think you will have to get used to silence between the two of you.'

'Matt had some bad news today,' I replied. 'He tried to find out who his real parents are, but they wouldn't tell him.'

Claude's tongue clicked between his teeth as the carrots hissed in the hot oil. 'That is very sad for him, don't you agree? He must have a big hole in his heart right now. What are you being so nervous about, Lillie? He is not angry with you. He is just hurting, that's all. Take him in your arms and hold him like his mother never did.' Claude tipped the rice into the wok, stirred it in with the vegetables and turned the gas off. 'We will start by warming his heart with a little food.' Claude handed me some bowls and chopsticks before carrying the wok to Matt. 'Smoked rice and vegetables.' Claude announced. We both laughed but Matt did not join in. The rest of the evening passed slowly as we ate together in silence.

When we went to bed, Matt lay with his back to me, the broad expanse of his shoulders making an imposing wall between us. When I wrapped my arms around Matt's waist, he turned and curled up like a baby with his head on my stomach. His tears trickled down the sides of my belly.

In the morning Matt was his old self again but I was a bundle of nerves as I got ready for my first appointment. I still felt uncomfortable in my tight red dress and wearing the black silk jacket didn't help as much as I would have liked. Matt drove towards Strathfield station, while I silently rehearsed my sales pitch. Strathfield was the gateway to the Western Suburbs now. It had changed a lot since I'd sat with Sean that evening waiting for the train that would take us into Sydney.

I strained to catch a glimpse of the station as we pulled into a parking space. The towering glass

another song about love

buildings of the shopping plaza made me feel very small. I caught sight of my reflection in the glassed-in entrance to the shopping mall and a familiar feeling of being both too big and too small undermined my confidence. Willpower and the knowledge of how much was at stake in the meeting got me inside the door, into the lift, and propelled my feet towards AM Records. At the end of a long passageway, a receptionist smiled at me from behind a blue-grey desk.

'Can I help you?' The receptionist's gaze was unflinchingly direct. Up close, the woman's flawless skin and perfect pink lipstick made me conscious of the loudness of the red and black colours I was wearing.

'I have an appointment with Michael Griffin.'

'What's your name, please?'

'Lillie, Lillie Bloom.'

The receptionist's long pink fingernails clicked against the telephone. 'Michael, there's a Lillie Bloom here who says she has an appointment with you.' She smiled then nodded and let out a little laugh in appreciation of some private joke which I was sure was at my expense. 'Okay Michael, I'll pass the message on.' My heart sank with the certainty that he was going to make some excuse not to see me. 'Michael will be out in a few minutes, if you'd like to wait over there.'

I walked the short distance to the chairs the receptionist had indicated and tried to look relaxed.

JANIE CONWAY HERRON

After ten minutes I had crossed and uncrossed my legs so many times, it felt like I was dancing.

When Michael arrived I jumped to my feet and stood, hand outstretched, until Michael's large soft hand held mine.

'Glad to meet you.' His broad face broke into a puppy dog grin. 'So you've brought something in for us to hear.' He ushered me into his office and pointed to a large black leather couch. I sat on the edge to keep myself from disappearing into the huge expanse of leather.

Michael leaned back in a large swivel chair. 'So what's happening in Melbourne?'

I took a deep breath. 'Well, I'm in a band called Scarlet Sisters which is doing lots of gigs and getting pretty big audiences.'

'I heard the band's pretty hot.'

'You did? Who from?'

Michael leant back in his chair. 'Word gets around. I keep my ear to the ground.'

'I'm glad you've heard good things about us.'

'So let's hear the product, eh. Got the music with you?'

Balancing the briefcase on my knees I clicked the latches. The case sprung open tipping me off balance. Tapes and photos flew across the floor as I scrambled to rescue them. Mortified, I found myself face to face with Michael.

'Shall we dance?' He held out a handful of photos as I climbed back onto the leather lounge,

206

another song about love

pulled my dress back down, handed Michael the tape and tried to put my briefcase back in order.

The first song started up and Michael listened to the entire song with his eyes closed. So much of my sense of self was riding on that song, I felt as if every note was etched into my psyche. When it finished Michael pressed the stop button.

'That one of your songs?'

'Yes.'

'It's not bad. Is that you singing?'

'Yes, it is.'

'You got a publisher?'

'No, I haven't.'

'You should get one. Phil's not bad. If he likes you, he'll get right behind you. Phil Lucas, you heard of him?'

'No.'

'He's based in Melbourne. Go and see him when you get back. Tell him I told you to give him a call.'

I had been waiting to sell the band but Michael didn't leave any room for the sales pitch I'd rehearsed. He played the next two songs, one after the other, without comment. When all the songs had been played, I waited, in high anticipation, for his final verdict.

'I like that first song. It'd go well on the dance charts. It's got a strong feel.'

'So are you interested in signing the band?'

JANIE CONWAY HERRON

The frown on Michael's face made me realise I'd jumped in too soon, but it was too late to rescue myself.

'Not exactly,' he replied. 'Don't get me wrong. You've got some good material there, great potential. The band's got a long way to go, though. We've got a lot of big-name acts at the moment and I don't think we can give you the support you need. Why don't you try one of the smaller independent companies? Get yourself an agent or some young manager with a lot of energy.'

When Michael stood up, my hopes disappeared. This had been an exercise in keeping his ear to the ground, just in case.

I clicked my briefcase shut. 'Thanks for listening, anyway.'

'It's been a pleasure meeting you.' Michael's hand rested on my shoulder. 'Don't forget to go and see Phil in Melbourne. He's a good mate with Geoff Short. You know him, don't you?'

'I was going to see him when I got back to Melbourne.'

'Good girl. Geoff's got Melbourne sewn up. Get him on side and he'll get you signed in no time. He talked us into signing Frankie Brave. You like his album, Blue? We're releasing it in Germany next month. We think he should go well there.'

As he wound up his own sales-pitch I felt comforted by the fact that at least I could impress Michael with the company I kept. 'Frankie's an old

another song about love

friend of mine. We've done quite a few shows with him. Our bass player Anna used to play in his band until we formed Scarlet Sisters.'

'Really?' Michael seemed genuinely surprised.

'Anna and I both write songs for the band. She's a great bass player.'

Michael nodded in a non-committal way and guided me towards the door. As we waited for the lift, I kept my eyes focused on the numbers as they lit up, only turning to face Michael as the doors opened.

'Good luck, Lillie.' Michael ushered me inside. 'It's a long way to the top if you want to rock and roll.'

The lift doors muffled Michael's laughter as my spirits sank in tandem with the lift. By the time I reached Matt's car, my disappointment had turned to frustration. I slid into the front seat and slammed the door.

'Didn't it go too well?' Matt asked.

'I made such an idiot of myself,' I groaned. 'The first thing I did was drop everything out of my briefcase onto the floor. Then I got really tongue-tied. It was awful!'

'It's only the first. There's plenty more to go.'

'I couldn't stand too many more like that one. I let myself get so intimidated.'

'Perhaps you need someone else to do the selling.'

'That's what Michael said.'

'Maybe you should take his advice.'

JANIE CONWAY HERRON

On our way through Newtown, Matt pulled up in front of a pub. 'Feel like a drink?'

'Actually, I feel like getting roaring drunk,' I answered.

The hotel on King Street was small with rows of tables around a central bar and a pool table in the back. We made our way to a dark corner where a couple of lanky boys were playing pool with a stocky girl sporting a shaved head and a ring through her nose. The girl strode around the pool table looking for a shot, then stood leaning on her cue, as she waited for the boys to finish. Her voice boomed her triumph across the room every time she potted a ball. Her eyes were large, but her face, unframed by hair, seemed small and vulnerable. When she grinned across the pool table at me, she had a mouth full of broken teeth.

'Want a game?' she asked.

I shook my head.

'What about your boyfriend? He looks like he enjoys the odd game.'

Matt stood up. 'Don't mind if I do.'

'My name's Patsy and this here's Horse and Tony.' Patsy handed Matt a cue. 'What's your name, sweetheart?'

'Matt.'

'And your girlfriend's?'

'Lillie.'

'Pleased to meet you.' Patsy offered us her hand.

another song about love

While Matt became involved in a serious pool game with Patsy, Horse and Tony, I drank steadily. Rounds of drinks were bought and pool games played. A backslapping bravado built up between Matt and the other players. Each time he won, he put another drink in front of me and by the end of the evening we were all drunk. Closing time found us standing on King Street, hanging on to each other to keep from falling over.

'Why don't you both come to our place?' Patsy said as she stuck her head under Matt's arm. 'We live just round the corner.'

Matt swayed towards the street. 'What about my car?'

Patsy grabbed hold of his jacket. 'You're too drunk to drive. Leave it here.'

We staggered down the street until Patsy stopped and opened a gate in an iron fence before leading the way across a tiny cement yard. It took her a while to get her key into the door and usher us inside. A fluorescent tube flickered furiously then a blinding white light made Patsy's face look even paler than before. There was a strange smell in the kitchen, somewhere between a tip and a doctor's surgery, as if rotting food was well on its way to becoming penicillin.

No longer able to remain upright, I slid down the wall onto the floor.

'You all right?' Patsy's broken-toothed smile beamed through my blurred vision. Someone threw me a couple of cushions and I sank gratefully into them. Matt sat on the floor beside me. As Patsy's sharp nasal voice cut through Matt's round mellow tones, their voices echoed down the tunnel of my drunkenness. I concentrated hard, trying to keep from passing out but in the end, I lost the struggle.

Next morning, bright sunlight streamed in through the window. When I sat up, a sharp pain screamed in my head and black dots formed in front of my eyes. Matt was nowhere in sight and the strange rotting stench from the night before was overbearing. Splashing cold water on my face, I gulped down several mouthfuls, took a deep breath and tried to make sense of where I was. Quietly making my way down a passageway off the kitchen, I looked into the first room where the morning light was obliterated by heavy curtains. I could just make out the fully clothed body of Horse lying on top of the covers. The door to the next room was closed. I carefully turned the knob and opened the door. There were Matt and Patsy in bed together. Patsy's naked body lay face down. Her left arm hung over the edge of the bed, exposing the spider's web tattoo that spread up her arm and over her shoulder. Matt was asleep on his back, a dirty grey sheet covering him to the waist. His smooth, hairless chest moved gently with the rhythm of his breathing. I moved closer. Standing right by the bed, I saw the bowl and a blackened piece of foil with an empty syringe beside it. Backing out of the room, I walked quickly down the hall to the kitchen and out into the

another song about love

blinding morning light. I flipped the latch on the steel gate, stopped to get my bearings then turned towards King Street. As I passed Café Lupa, the waitress waved at me. I looked away, staring into the shop windows. My red eyes, swimming in black mascara, stared back at me.

In order to get Claude's attention without having to endure Harry's scrutiny, I picked up a stone and hurled it as hard as I could at one of his windows. It fell clattering into the gutter. The second stone bounced off the window and into the bushes. Moments later, Claude's face peered round the curtain. When I waved, he opened the window.

'What happened to you?'

'Let me in and I'll tell you.'

Sitting beside me, Claude listened as I stammered out the story. The telling helped clear my confusion. I ended up laughing at the sight of myself standing on the nature strip with mascara streaming down my face, my brand-new red dress and jacket all crumpled with sleep.

'What am I going to do?' I asked. 'I stink of alcohol and cigarette smoke and I have to be at Desert Records by two o'clock this afternoon.'

'Take your dress and jacket off and we'll wash them. We've got at least three hours before you have to leave.'

'Maybe I won't go.'

'Lillie, are you serious about your music?' Claude said. 'If you are, you'll have to be tougher than this. Get in the shower and I'll wash your clothes.'

I let rivers of soapy water run freely over my body and by the time I had dried myself, I was almost in control.

When Claude hung my dress and jacket in the window, the tiny red and black garments flapped in the breeze and drops of water sounded a steady rhythm on the kitchen floor. He pushed a large mug of coffee across the table. 'You are beginning to look better, Lillie. 'Have a little rest now. I will wake you in plenty of time.' I closed my eyes and pictured Patsy and Matt in bed together. The sight of the syringe was just as disturbing as Matt's presence in another woman's bed. As these images looped around in my mind, I drifted into an exhausted sleep.

Claude gently woke me. He held up the dress and the jacket. 'I pressed them while they were still damp. They look as good as new.'

When I was ready, Claude walked with me to King Street. I was glad to be armed with my heart-shaped sunglasses. 'That feels better,' I sighed. 'Now it doesn't matter what my eyes look like.'

Claude opened the taxi door for me. 'Take care, Lillie. Remember sometimes you've just got to fake it to make it.'

'You're too kind to me, Claude.'

Claude grinned. 'You'd do the same for me, I know.'

another song about love

Desert Records was situated in an old terrace house in Surry Hills. It wasn't far from Cleveland Street where the constant traffic set up a mantra, humming in the background as I walked. The record company was located in a quiet tree-lined street, their name painted in red on a bright orange door. I knocked.

Derrick's muffled voice yelled, 'The door's open.' He motioned for me to sit while he continued talking on the phone. 'Na, I haven't got it here, George. I'm sure I gave you a copy of the schedule. Give Nerrida a ring at the agency; see if she can fax a copy to you. No, mate, you'll just have to cut your losses and hire a van. I know the cost cuts into the band's wages. Put it down to promotion. Everyone in the band's on the dole anyway. They'll get by. Tell them it's an investment in the future. We're all losing money on this one. Christ, when I think of the hours I've put in. I know, George, you'll just have to give 'em a pep talk. It's hard times for everyone okay? Right, George, I'll call you back later; I've got someone with me right now.' Derrick slammed down the phone and offered me his hand. 'Sorry to keep you waiting. It's Lillie, isn't it?'

'Lillie Bloom from Scarlet Sisters.'

'The band from Melbourne; you're looking for some sort of deal, eh? Times are pretty tough at the moment, especially for a small independent concern like this one. We can't afford to float the sort of costs

215

that a big company can. Have you been to any of the big ones?

'I was at AM Records yesterday.'

Derrick's eyebrows lifted but I wasn't sure whether he was surprised or impressed. 'What did Michael Griffin think of it?'

'Oh, he liked it,' I lied.

'That's good. You're doing well to get a big company like that interested. So why did you come and see us?'

'I prefer the artistic freedom of a smaller company. I've got a tape of some songs we recorded in Melbourne, if you'd like to hear them.'

'I'd love to. There's a player right behind you. Put it on.'

This time I didn't drop a thing as I opened the briefcase and handed Derrick the band photos. When I put the tape on, the music filled the room. As the sound bounced off the walls, Derrick sifted through the photos.

'Interesting looking band.' He pointed to Ali. 'Good drummer you've got there. Where's he from?'

'Malaysia.'

'What does he think of playing in Australia?'

'He likes it. He really likes doing original material.'

Derrick frowned. 'I bet he's used to getting more money than we pay over here. Have you ever thought of going solo?'

another song about love

'No, I haven't. The bass player and I started the band. We're a team.'

Derrick was unmoved by my loyalty. 'It's easier to promote a solo artist from a recording and management point of view, especially a female artist like yourself.'

'I'd rather be part of a band. It gives you more musical scope.'

'You could have top session guys playing with you,' Derrick persisted and his insistence on session musos all being guys annoyed me.

'Anna's an excellent bass player,' I replied proudly.

'I can see you fronting a band of young punks. Give your music a tougher edge, make use of the fact that you play guitar. I know some young session guys up here; they're looking for a singer with some original material. You want me to speak to them?'

'No, I'd rather stick with the band I've got.'

'Hmm, pity.' Derrick stood up and moved round the desk. 'Leave the demos with me. I'll get my partner George to have a listen. He manages a few bands around Sydney. We might organise a tour up here, see how the band goes, then talk about recording.' Derrick's firm handshake implied that he meant what he said.

I walked away from Surry Hills towards Central Station, my body aching with the simple effort of putting one foot in front of the other. Longing for home, I wandered down the dank cement subway underneath Central Station with trains rumbling overhead. I looked for the phone boxes and rang Melbourne.

'What's wrong, Lil'? Sydney a bit too rough for you, is it?' Wendy teased.

'Not just Sydney.'

'Don't tell me, your boyfriend's done a bunk on you.'

'Sort of.'

'Bastard,' Wendy hissed through her teeth. 'What about the demos?'

'I haven't managed to see a lot of record companies. Things don't seem to be happening very quickly.'

'You weren't expecting to come back with a contract, were you?'

I felt too foolish to answer.

'You silly bitch, you always expect too much,' Wendy chuckled. 'No one gets a contract straight away. It takes months of negotiation. I thought you knew that.' I wanted to defend myself but, before I could reply, Wendy added, 'I've got a small boy here dying to get on the phone to you.'

'Mum!' Jesse yelled excitedly. 'When are you coming home?'

'Tomorrow, Jesse, but I might have to go straight to the gig, so I'll see you the day after, okay?'

'Alright.' Jesse sounded disappointed.

'It won't be long, Jesse, only two more sleeps.'

another song about love

There was a long silence and then Wendy came back on the line. 'Jesse has been fine the whole time you've been away. I don't think he realised he missed you until he heard your voice.'

I fed the last of the coins into the phone. 'I don't know what's happening with Matt but I'll get back, one way or another. Take my guitar and amp to the Punters Club and I'll meet you at the gig.'

'Okay, Lil'. Don't let that bastard get to you. He doesn't deserve you.'

'I don't know about that, Wendy.'

'Lil'!'

The red light flashed as I yelled, 'Love to everyone,' and the phone went dead.

I stood in the aisle as the bus headed west towards the huge red sun hanging low over the Newtown sky. When I saw Matt's car parked outside Claude's apartment, my first impulse was to run away, but Harry was already standing at the front door.

'There you are! Your boyfriend is upstairs with Claude, making dinner. It smells real good.' Harry followed me to the foot of the stairs. 'Boy, you modern women have got the men well trained. In my day a man wouldn't be caught dead making a meal for his missus.' Harry's laughter followed me up the stairs to Claude's apartment. The smell of curry wafted towards my nostrils and hunger helped me reconnect with my physical self.

I put my head round the kitchen door to find Claude and Matt standing together at the stove. 'Hi,' I said softly and they both turned round.

Matt grinned. 'We're making a gourmet meal to celebrate our last night in Sydney,' he exclaimed. 'We've even bought a bottle of French champagne. Shall I crack it now?' Matt put his arm around me.

I pulled away from him and sat down. When I looked up, Claude was standing behind Matt pulling up the corners of his mouth in such a grotesque grin that I couldn't help laughing. As Matt popped the champagne cork and poured the first glass for me, I tried to find some trace of regret in his face.

'To your success,' he said, clinking his glass against mine.

During the meal, I tried hard to bring the conversation around to the previous evening, but Matt skilfully eluded my questions. It wasn't until we were in bed and my head was swimming with champagne that we talked.

'Look, I'm sorry about last night,' Matt said.

'What are you sorry for?' I feigned indifference.

'For ending up in bed with Patsy. Nothing happened, we were too out of it.'

'But something might have happened if you hadn't been?'

'If I hadn't been what?'

'Out of it.'

another song about love

'If I hadn't been out of it, I wouldn't have been in bed with her.'

'Sounds like an excuse to me.'

'An excuse for what?'

'For getting out of it.'

'Christ, Lillie, I'm trying to apologise.'

'I don't trust apologies,' I explained. 'People think they can do the same thing over and over again then, if they apologise, everything will be alright.'

'Okay, I won't apologise but I will promise not to do it again.'

'I don't mind if you sleep with other people, so long as you're honest about it.'

'Now I'm really confused.'

'So am I. I'm not against either of us having relationships with other people, but it hurt to see you lying next to Patsy.'

'Would it help if I promised not to sleep with anyone else?'

'No. That's not what I meant. You could promise not to hit up again though. At least then I'd know you didn't sleep with someone because you were too out of it to know any better.'

Matt rolled away from me. 'I can't promise that, Lillie.'

'Why?'

'Because as soon as I made a promise like that I'd be sure to break it.'

'Can't you just pretend you're going to stop using?' I pleaded.

JANIE CONWAY HERRON

'So you want me to fool myself into going straight?'

'Can't you at least try?'

'If only it were that easy,' Matt sighed.

'I'm so scared,' I said, turning away and curling myself into a tight ball.

'That makes two of us,' Matt whispered as he wrapped his arms around me.

10

HAPPILY EVER AFTER

AFTER FIVE YEARS OF MARRIAGE I put a scrapbook of newspaper cuttings together, tracing the important moments of our musical career. A headline above the first cutting read, MELBOURNE'S FIRST HIPPIE WEDDING. Below it was a photo of me in a lace dress holding a bouquet of flowers, with Joe standing next to me in a burgundy velvet suit and high-heeled boots. A crowd of people all dressed in an array of colourful clothes surrounded us. Wendy was in the photo, too, frozen in the moment

JANIE CONWAY HERRON

of handing me a daffodil on a long stem. Mum and Dad were standing behind us, bewildered by the fact that their daughter's marriage was newsworthy. I don't think they'd ever considered me to be a hippie before this and neither had I. The caption underneath the photo described us as if we were members of some religious sect.

I'd been treating the presence of reporters at our wedding as a crazy joke until one of them asked me what I did for a living. I was about to describe the part time job I had in a secondhand clothing shop, when Joe kicked my ankle.

'We're musicians,' he answered quickly.

I realised Joe had turned our wedding into a publicity event, the first of many in our career together. Up until then I'd been playing music but hadn't seen myself as a musician. That day I became a musician, a hippie, as well as Mrs Penman. Over the next five years we were a production team, planning recordings, performances and tours, eating, sleeping, playing, writing, recording, touring, doing interviews plus radio and television appearances.

We'd planned a tour for our first album. At the bottom of an interview in *Go Set* our tour dates were listed. But I was pregnant. I'd been dreaming of being pregnant for a while, holding on to this inner knowledge tightly, afraid to share it with Joe until proven correct by the medical profession. In the mornings I threw up and in the afternoons satisfied my

another song about love

cravings for custard tarts with relish. In the second-hand shop where I worked I found an old wicker pram like the one I'd seen in pictures of myself as a baby. I put a deposit down, then as I paid it off, began daydreaming about wheeling the baby round in it. As my nipples grew dark and my breasts swelled, the feeling of new life inside me grew too. Speaking softly, I shared secrets with the baby, rubbing the thick centre of my belly as I did.

When I told Joe, he did nothing to hide his disappointment. We were just about to promote our first album and needed to do gigs. We'd never be able to manage touring with a baby in tow. Why didn't I have an abortion? I'd had one before, couldn't I have another one? Exasperated by my insistence on keeping the baby his indifference verged on cruelty. It was a side of him I hadn't encountered before and I didn't understand.

When I started bleeding, the doctor warned me I'd lose the baby unless I stayed in bed for a week. Joe wanted me to walk around so I'd have a miscarriage. I determinedly stayed in bed, retreating under the covers until the bleeding stopped, just in time for the first of our Victorian tour dates.

In a park in a country town, three young women stopped to congratulate me on my pregnancy. Talking and laughing with these warm friendly women made me feel good about it. With a feeling of pride in the small swell of my belly, I walked back to the motel where we were staying.

Joe's stubborn gloominess had hung over us both for weeks, pulling at our shoulders and the corners of our mouths all day. Every night we got up and performed our loving couple act. Trying to fight the gloomy atmosphere, I laughingly told Joe about the women in the park. When Joe looked at me and said nothing, I yelled, 'What the hell is wrong with that?'

With dagger-like precision Joe's words went straight to my heart. 'I don't want anyone to notice you're pregnant, that's all. It's bad for our image.'

My reply came out in a furious tide of anger, triggered by all the hurtful words and actions I'd endured over the last few months. 'How the hell do you expect me to hide my pregnancy? My tits are bursting out of my clothes. I can't get my jeans on. Look at me, Joe. I'm pregnant. I'm a ripe plum about to fall from the tree. I can't hide it!'

Joe stared at the floor. 'I don't expect you to, but I don't have to like it either.'

'And what am *I* supposed to feel about that?' I stabbed at my heart with my finger until Joe lifted his eyes to meet mine.

'I don't know how you feel,' he said. 'I only know how I feel. I've never had a father so how can I know how to be one?'

My anger ebbed and died with Joe's words. As I lifted my dress and guided Joe's hands over my tight

another song about love

shiny belly, a shudder ran through my body. 'That's our baby in there,' I whispered.

As my belly grew, Joe built a public image around the three of us. Instinct told me that if Joe was going to feel okay about having this baby, I needed to allay his many fears. Spinning a cocoon of safety around us both, I built a picture for him that I thought he wanted to hear.

'Do you think you can keep playing music after the baby's born?' Joe was going through his list of things that might go wrong. But I was resolute. I would be a super mum. We could have the best of both worlds: parenthood and a music career. The two directions might be diametrically opposed, but together we would be able to bridge that gap. I kept on playing until my stomach was so large I could hardly reach the guitar strings. When I was seven months pregnant, an offer of a big gig in Sydney came through.

Joe looked crestfallen. 'We can't do it.'

'Why not?'

'You're too pregnant. You can't travel the distance.'

'I could go by plane.'

'They don't let people fly when they're as pregnant as you are.'

'I'll lie to them.'

'You, lie?' Joe looked at me in disbelief.

'Joe, just let me take care of it, please.'

JANIE CONWAY HERRON

When I went in to pick up my flight ticket, I put on the embroidered mauve smock Mum had made me, plaited my hair in two long braids and tied them with matching mauve ribbons. Satisfied that I looked too young to be pregnant, I took a bus into town.

The tour agent beamed a friendly smile, then asked me a strange question.

'Pardon?' I asked, though I'd heard him quite clearly.

'Half or full fare?'

'Oh, full fare.' Stunned, I handed over the money, then walked out of the office as fast as my burgeoning belly allowed.

Back home I flopped down on the lounge and stretched my legs out. Everything was quiet, the only sound a tree brushing the window as a warm northerly whipped around its leaves. 'We did it, little one,' I whispered as I patted my stomach and the baby moved inside me. 'Don't come too early,' I whispered. 'I don't want you to be born while we're in Sydney.'

When the phone rang I relaxed into the familiarity of my mother's warm voice. She had been sober for a long time by then and I no longer looked for signs of her drinking.

'I've just had a phone call from Uncle Jim and it looks like Gran and Pop need to go into a nursing home.'

'What?' Alarmed, I listened attentively as Mum explained.

another song about love

'They're both in agreement. We wouldn't move them unless they wanted to. It's just that they're no longer able to look after themselves.'

'I was planning on seeing them when we got to Sydney.'

'That's why I'm ringing you, dear. I know you need a place to stay, and Uncle Jim says we need someone in the flat when the removalists come to pick up the few bits and pieces that can be sold. What do you think?'

A picture of the little flat without my grandparents was difficult to imagine, but the cocoon of my pregnancy helped me stay calm. 'Okay, that'd be great Mum,' I replied. 'Joe can help me clean the place up. It'd be great to be able to stay there.' After a long conversation with Mum I hung up. When the baby moved I was reminded of all the generations that had led to this tiny being coming into the world.

As the plane flew over Sydney, I thought about Sean and how old our baby would have been if it had been born. I imagined a cute six-year-old – probably a girl, I decided – and a lot of suppressed love flowed through me. Every time I had driven down the Hume highway into Sydney since Sean had disappeared from my life, I had expected to see him. I had often scoured the Sydney rock magazines for his name or a photo of him, without success. Sometimes I still missed him terribly; missed his laughter and uncomplicated way of seeing things.

JANIE CONWAY HERRON

The taxi wound its way from the airport, through the back streets of Sydney to Woollahra. We passed the tobacconist, where I used to buy my grandfather tins of Four Square tobacco, continuing down the hill to the red brick flats where my grandparents had lived ever since I'd been born. From outside, everything looked the same. I stood on the neatly cut square of front lawn for a moment waiting for my grandmother to peer through the venetian blinds before remembering they weren't there. The front door key Mum gave me, fitted easily and the door swung open. Inside everything looked and smelled the same, as if in waiting for my grandparents' return.

It was easy to imagine my grandfather sitting listening to the races on the radio, rocking back and forth in his chair, pressing the ends of his fingers against one another in spider-like motion. The big wooden table where I used to have porridge with brown sugar and cream for breakfast was still in the kitchen with the familiar pewter sugar bowl sitting in the middle. When I opened the cupboards all the green crockery and the red and white spotted bowls were exactly where they had always been. In the lounge room the baby grand stood black and shining in the corner. Lifting the lid I pressed a key, listening as the note sang into the room. I pictured Pop playing, those same jewelled fingers dancing over the keys as he grinned and beckoned me to come dancing with him.

My grandparents' bed was made and turned down with a vase of flowers on the bedside table. A

another song about love

note from my uncle welcomed Joe and me to the apartment. I tiptoed out to the back room where my mother used to sleep and opened the window. Lying down on the old single bed I let my memories drift in on the summer air.

When my uncle tapped on the front door I rushed to open it.

'I didn't expect you to be so pregnant.' He chuckled as he looked me up and down. 'Are you sure you should be performing at this late stage?'

'Well, that's show biz, Uncle Jim, you know how it is.'

He nodded. He knew what it was like. He'd been singing since he was a small boy. 'I thought I might take you over to visit the oldies. You got time?'

The two of us became engrossed in family stories as we drove north over the Harbour Bridge. I particularly loved it when Uncle Jim described Mum as a happy hopeful young woman and told me about all the antics they'd get up to.

We turned down a wide, leafy street into the driveway of a huge old house, but as we walked down the highly polished linoleum floors of the corridors, I realised the place was more like a hospital than a home. Uncle Jim ushered me into a light airy room. In one corner a frail old woman, tied into a chair, muttered to herself. I searched for the familiar faces of my grandparents amongst the people in the room. A nurse, leaning over someone at the far end of the room, pointed towards us. My grandmother peered around the nurse's skirt. My grandfather sat next to her, gazing out the window, his hands pressed together. His still-jewelled fingertips moved in and out in their old familiar pattern.

Uncle Jim strode towards them, arms outstretched, his warm voice bellowing across the room. 'Darlings, I've brought a visitor to see you.' He took his mother's hands in his.

She laughed and looked towards her husband. 'Len, look who's here to see us.' Gran's usually strong voice was high and quavering. 'Now who's this?' She looked at me curiously.

'It's Lillie, your granddaughter,' Uncle Jim answered.

'Lillie?' There was a question mark in Gran's voice and then relief on her face as she recognised me. 'Oh yes, how silly of me, so it is. It's just my eyesight isn't what it used to be and you look so different.'

'She's pregnant, that's why.' The gruff strength of my grandfather's voice put me at ease. Rising from his chair he offered it to me. 'Here, have a seat dear, get all that weight off your feet. You look tired.'

I shook my head. 'No Pop, I'm okay. I don't need a seat.'

'Hey Dad, why don't we go for a walk in the garden? Leave these two women to talk for a bit?' Uncle Jim rescued.

another song about love

Pop grunted then nodded and winked at me. As his grin broadened, the familiar gold tooth flashed. 'They've got a piano here, maybe you could do a dance for us all later, while I accompany you.'

'Sure, Pop, I'll do the dance of the sugar plum fairies, just for you.'

We all laughed. Gran wasn't quite sure why, but out of politeness she laughed with us too. I sat down beside her and stroked the dry skin on the back of her hand. Turning both our hands over, Gran looked at her own palms, then at mine. 'Our hands are exactly the same, aren't they dear?' She looked straight into my eyes and the strength of her look took my breath away. My grandmother was drinking me in, savouring the look of me. She knew I was family but I wasn't sure she knew exactly who I was.

'Tell me dear, are you still singing?' she asked.

There she did remember me. 'That's why I'm here in Sydney. I'm singing in a concert.'

'A concert, that's nice. I always enjoy concerts. Will you be the only one singing?'

'No, Gran, it's a concert where there'll be lots of other singers, poets and artists, that kind of thing.'

'We used to do that in my day too. I loved it. Sometimes I'd sing while my sister played the piano. I met your grandfather at one of those evenings. He was so handsome and played the piano divinely. I didn't think he'd notice me, but he did.'

I knew this story well, but I was content to hear it as many times as my grandmother wanted to tell it. I took Gran's hand and held it against my stomach so she could feel the baby kicking. 'That's your great-grandchild in there.'

'Oh?' Gran kept her hand on my stomach. 'When are you due?'

'In about six weeks.'

'Oh, you must be impatient for it by now.'

I had to think about that. 'I'd like to get back to Melbourne first.'

'You don't live in Sydney, then?'

'I went to Melbourne when I was a little girl, remember?'

'Oh yes, I remember now. I do miss your mother a lot, especially now that the only young female company I have are nurses. They're kind, but they're not family.'

I felt like crying but I didn't want either of my grandparents to see how upset I was. When the tea bell rang, Pop and Uncle Jim returned and we said goodbye. Gran and Pop stood in the driveway hugging each other and waving as we drove away.

Uncle Jim squeezed my hand. 'We all have to get old some time. Those two have had a long and happy life together.'

'What will happen if one of them dies first?'

'The other one will die very soon after.'

'Do you think so?'

'I know so.'

After Uncle Jim left, I sat by myself and watched the sun go down. I had a strong sense this could be the last time I'd see either of my grandparents. In the semi darkness, my tears fell unchecked. I'd been unprepared for my grandparents' aging and the vulnerability that went with it. Since we'd moved to Melbourne, we hadn't visited them every second weekend like we'd done when I was a little girl. Although Dad travelled by plane for business trips, it had been out of the question for the three of us to fly too often. During school holidays we'd drive down the Hume highway with Dad at the helm. I loved those trips. My parents seemed happy when we were on the road and the sense of adventure we shared was wonderful. Over the years those visits had become less frequent, especially when Mum was in and out of hospital. Since my hitchhiking adventure with Sean I hadn't visited them at all. Now their fragility made it obvious that they were not long for this earth.

When the baby moved I stroked the taut skin on my belly and kissed it. Curling into myself, I waited for Joe to arrive from Melbourne. It was after midnight when I heard his car pull up outside. I opened the door and beckoned him into the room where my grandparents had slept together for decades. Comforted by his arms around me, I drifted off to sleep.

The next evening Joe drove slowly through the streets of Kings Cross and pulled up outside a large yellow terrace house.

JANIE CONWAY HERRON

'Take a look at this place, it's cool!' Joe chuckled as he got out of the car. We were ushered inside the building by a white-faced clown who mimed directions while blowing bubbles in the direction of a room on the right. As I followed Joe in, we were surrounded by blue sky and white clouds floating round the walls, floor and ceiling while cherubs flew through the sky. The air in the room was laden with the heavy scent of incense. People drifted in and out through various exits, including a hole in the wall that disappeared off into another part of the house.

I sat on the edge of the stage while Joe set up. A woman with bright red hair and a flowing skirt sat next to me. Smiling a toothy smile, she patted my stomach. 'Your baby's due soon,' she observed.

'Yeah.' I smiled back, glad of the woman's interest.

'Just needs to drop, then it doesn't take long.'

'I hope it doesn't drop before I get back to Melbourne.'

'You can will it not to, you know. I've had three children. By the third I realised, it's all in the mind.' She nodded at Joe. 'Is your boyfriend performing here tonight?'

'We're both performing. We came up from Melbourne on a week's tour.'

'No shit, far out!' The woman shook her head. 'You must be Lillie Bloom. My name's Claire, I believe you know my man, Sean. He knew you were performing tonight. That's why we're here. He told me you're a pretty good guitarist. He's tried to teach me but I'm not very good at it. I prefer photography.'

Laughing politely at everything Claire said I was distracted, waiting for Sean to appear.

'Why don't I go find Sean and tell him I've found you,' Claire beamed. 'He wanted to surprise you, but I guess I've spoiled it now.' With a flick of her bright red hair, Claire disappeared through the hole in the wall.

I put my head close to the baby. 'You still in there, little one?' My question was answered by the gentle push of a small foot against the wall of my womb.

'How're you doing, Lil'?' Sean sat down next to me, his long thin legs sticking out in front of him. 'You're getting mighty big. How long to go?'

'Six weeks, more or less. You've got some kids with Claire, I hear.'

'Yep,' Sean grinned. 'Claire wanted to. I just went along with it, really.'

'Come on now, I bet you wanted to have babies too.'

'Well, yes, but it wouldn't be cool to admit it, would it?' Sean's green eyes twinkled. He hadn't changed.

As we began our bracket, Sean sat with Claire in the front row. The clouds on the walls and ceiling disappeared into darkness as the spotlight fell. I sang an ancient folk ballad about a magic man who had been captured by a fairy queen. For the length of the song I kept my eyes closed and pretended Sean was the only one in the room. When we finished the song Sean was the first to applaud, hooting loudly as the rest of the audience followed suit.

At the end of the evening Claire and Sean said their goodbyes and we all promised we'd try to stay in touch with each other.

'Hope you have a wonderful birth,' Claire's mass of red curls brushed against my cheek as she kissed me. 'It's the most wonderful experience you can have.'

I didn't dare look up at either Sean or Joe.

Joe took Claire's hand. 'Hope you both have a good life up here in Sydney too. Perhaps we'll catch up with you when we're up this way again.'

'Yes, maybe our kids can play together,' Claire insisted. Something in her tone of voice convinced me that Sean had never said anything about our almost baby.

'Yeah, see you both again,' Joe added and I looked back to see Sean and Claire disappear like angels amongst the painted cherubs and clouds.

The removalists arrived at the flat early next day.

'You the granddaughter?' one of them asked.

I nodded.

another song about love

'We've already given your uncle a quote on what the furniture is worth. Can you check this list and sign here?' His nicotine-stained finger pointed to the end of the page and he stood close, looking over my shoulder as I read.

I had already packed the green dinner set, the red and white bowls and the pewter jug, plus all my grandparents' letters and photos, to give to Mum and Uncle Jim. I knew each piece of furniture on the removalist's list intimately. It was heartbreaking to think of it all being sold. Even my grandfather's baby grand was going to be packed onto the back of the truck. My finger hesitated at the last item. 'These lace curtains. I'd really like to take them with me, if you don't mind.'

Looking relieved that this was the only disputed item, the furniture man nodded assent.

I sat with Joe on the low fence outside my grandparents' flat and watched as everything was packed into the back of the truck.

'You okay?' Joe held my hand.

'Yep,' I replied as I watched the sum of my grandparents' life slowly climb the steep hill and vanish. When I went back inside, the empty rooms felt as if my grandparents had already died. I wondered how they could have left the flat knowing they'd never return. It was an ending, not only for them, but for the rest of the family too.

JANIE CONWAY HERRON

After we'd packed and finished the last of the cleaning, I shut the front door and got into the car. Joe was driving me to the airport before he headed back to Melbourne.

'Got everything?' Joe asked, revving the engine.

'Oh, I forgot one thing,' I answered, then grabbed the keys and entered the flat for the last time. The lace curtains fluttered in the half-open window of the back room, above the space where the bed had been. Three generations of family had slept in it. My baby-belly made it difficult to reach the curtain rail from the floor but I managed to take them down and fold them neatly. I closed the door and took the curtains out to the car.

'For the baby's room,' I said in answer to Joe's raised eyebrows. We drove up the hill away from the only home I could remember being in my family since my early childhood.

11

STONED

AS MATT AND I PREPARED for the trip back to Melbourne the first light of day filtered out over Sydney streets. I thought about the trip to Sydney with Joe and the loss of innocence after Jesse had been born. Driving back from that first tour I clung to the hope of happily-ever-after, only to have everything fall apart. Now I was struggling to keep another band together and it wasn't easy. We had only the daylight hours to get back for Scarlet Sisters' gig at the Punters Club and neither of us had slept well. I wrote Claude a thankyou note, wrapped it round some of my homegrown herb and left it on the kitchen table. Softly, I pulled the door closed and followed Matt to the car, thankful for his companionship and support.

As we drove south down King Street, he handed me a small envelope. 'I've brought a little bit of something to help us through the day.' Inside was some white powder. 'Compliments of Patsy.' Matt grinned as if this news should please me. 'It's speed, not smack, Lillie. You won't get addicted from one taste.'

I pushed the packet along the seat. 'I'm not into any white powders and I'm definitely not using needles.'

You can snort it, Lillie. You don't need needles. You'll need something to get through the day and do the gig tonight. I thought you'd be pleased.'

'And I thought you were trying to get off this stuff.'

'It's only a little bit of speed,' Matt insisted.

Reluctantly, I put the tiny envelope in my bag and watched it disappear amongst all the other bits and pieces that had collected there.

In a petrol station on the outskirts of Albury, a police car slowed down as it drove past and a young fresh-faced cop stared straight at me while Matt was checking the tires.

another song about love

'We'd better have a line soon, just in case those coppers pull us over on the highway,' Matt suggested as he got back into the car.

Down along a back road under some trees, Matt parked the car while I searched amongst the papers in the bottom of the bag and pulled out the speed. Matt carefully laid out two lines on a mirror then rolled up a ten-dollar bill and snorted the first line.

'This one's for you.' Matt held the mirror out.

I shook my head.

'Come on, Lil',' Matt held out the rolled-up bill, 'just once. It'll help you get through the trip and the gig. It'll be a long haul by the time tonight's finished.'

Matt's pleading expression made me laugh. A strong desire to please him overcame my reluctance to use powders. It'll be okay, I reasoned. Just this once won't hurt me. When I took the rolled-up note and inhaled, an electric shock shot up my nostril and a sharp chemical taste collected in my throat.

'You all right?' Matt asked. When I nodded, he cleaned up the last bits of powder with his finger then handed me the envelope.

I dropped it back into my bag then waited for the effects. It was the first time I had taken any sort of white powder and I was expecting some profound change to my consciousness. After a few minutes, nothing had happened so I pulled out a joint. 'Want to smoke this now?'

JANIE CONWAY HERRON

Matt nodded and the tension of our encounter with the police disappeared in a haze of smoke while the highway, cutting through dry undulating hills, stretched endlessly before us.

'I feel like the cat who's got the cream,' I laughed as a combination of speed and ganja hit my senses.

Just before Wangaratta, we smoked another joint. The smoke drifted away on the cool afternoon winds whistling past the windows, as words and laughter tumbled between us.

Matt handed me a tape. 'This one's from Africa. It's great music for travelling long distances.'

I closed my eyes and listened to a chorus of women singing and pictured myself in Africa singing with them. I could see their many colours, the graceful firm-footed way they danced and I imagined following their every movement, my hips swinging out as my feet pounded the dusty earth. My fantasy was brought to an abrupt halt when I felt Matt braking. A cop was flagging us over. The tires spun in the dry dirt as we came to a stop.

The cop stuck his head in the driver's window. 'Can I see your licence, sir?'

Matt's hands shook as he searched for his license. 'Oh, here it is,' he said almost too casually.

'Is this your car?' the cop asked, still smiling.

'Yes.'

another song about love

'Would you mind waiting while we do a check on your license?' Politeness hung in the air like a time bomb waiting to go off. The cop went back to the car to radio in Matt's particulars.

'This is it, mate.' Matt let out a long sigh. 'We're in for it now.'

'You've got a current license, haven't you?' I asked as nausea rose from the pit of my stomach.

Matt grimaced. 'They'll check a lot more than my license. It won't take them long to find out I've got previous drug offences. And here we both are, shit-faced.'

The cop was leaning on the bonnet, talking to a policewoman inside and nodding furiously. When he returned he asked Matt to get out of the car.

'I see you've been in trouble before, boy,' I heard him say.

Matt didn't reply.

'Not getting up to your old tricks, are you?'

'I've been clean for over a year now, sergeant,' Mat replied but the tremor in his voice said otherwise.

'You'd want to be, wouldn't you, son, or else you'd be breaking your parole,' the cop persisted.

I sat in the front seat, frozen with fear. My eyes darted around the inside of the car looking for a hiding place for the drugs in my bag. The policewoman walked straight towards my side of the car. She was young and attractive, with wavy, brown hair that stuck out under her hat.

JANIE CONWAY HERRON

'Can you get out of the car, please?' she asked. I tried to smile but my jaw was too stiff. 'May I look through your bag?'

I handed my bag over and prayed. Surely that little piece of paper looked like rubbish. But I was too optimistic. Within seconds the policewoman was opening the offending envelope.

I was so surprised I gave myself away. 'Yeah, that's it,' I blurted out.

This was the first and only time the policewoman became animated, 'Hey Sergeant, look what we've got here.' She held the folded paper between two fingers as if the contents were contagious. Within seconds, both cops were firing questions at me. I regained my senses enough to refuse to answer.

The sergeant set to work on Matt, who also refused to speak. 'Look, I'm asking you one more time. Do you have any more drugs?' The sergeant was rapidly dropping any signs of politeness. 'You may as well tell us now, because if you don't, we're going to take this car back to the station and tear it apart, piece by piece, until we find what we're looking for.'

I thought about the remainder of the plant I had in my briefcase and the joint in my jacket pocket but as Matt remained silent I decided to do the same.

After pushing Matt into the back of the police van and slamming it shut, the policewoman got into the driver's seat and pulled out onto the highway. The sergeant drove Matt's car with me in it. All I could think of was Matt being thrown into gaol for breaking parole. The only way to stop this was for me to take the rap. A strange calm came over me as I invented my story. The only hitch was Matt. My plan relied on him denying everything.

I smiled as sweetly as I could at the sergeant. 'Matt didn't know anything about those drugs you know.'

The sergeant looked amused. 'Pull the other one, sweetie. Your boyfriend's got a record a mile long. I'd be very surprised if he was the golden boy this time.'

'No, it's true. He didn't know anything,' I protested. 'He's been trying to go straight. I got the speed without him knowing about it.'

'Sure, and pigs can fly. Tell me all about it when I take your statement.'

I had a flash of having to give Claude's address and the cops raiding him so I asked, 'Can you tell me what my basic rights are?'

'You should have asked your boyfriend, sweetie. He knows all about it.' The sergeant was all smiles as he withdrew into smarmy politeness.

'I can't ask him Sergeant, so I'm asking you,' I answered, returning an equally courteous smile.

'What do you want to know?'

'Do I have to answer every question?'

'Not without a lawyer present.'

'So what do I say if I don't want to answer the question?'

'Just say, no comment.'

We arrived at the police station and the policewoman bustled Matt inside while the sergeant looked through the car. He started with the boot but didn't find anything so he pulled my suitcase out of the back seat and went through that. The sight of my clothes all over the back seat was embarrassing. I half expected the sergeant to pick up my underwear and smell it.

The briefcase sat innocently on the back seat with my clothing spread all over it. When the sergeant put my clothes back and went through Matt's bag, I hoped he might not search it. But my hopes were dashed when he clicked the latches and the briefcase flew open.

The sergeant pounced on the ganja, then frowned in disbelief. 'Why didn't you tell me about this before?'

'Because I thought I might get away with it,' I replied as everything settled into an eerie calm inside me. There was nothing left for the sergeant to discover now except for the joint hidden in the pocket of my jacket. I slung it casually over one shoulder and walked into the police station.

As they interviewed me, the two officers fell into role-playing, good cop versus bad cop. It might have been easier if the guy had been the bad cop – that was the way I'd seen it done in the movies. It was the woman who gave me the hard time. The sergeant seemed sweet by comparison.

another song about love

'Come on darling, stop protecting your boyfriend,' he drawled. 'You're a nice girl. What are you doing with a bad boy like that?'

The policewoman pointed out the window. 'I don't know what you're doing this for. He's not going to wait for you. Look, I can see him getting into his car now.'

I sighed with relief. They'd let Matt go.

The policewoman scowled and leaned towards me. 'We can charge you with associating with known criminals if you continue to see him.'

The sergeant stepped in with some fatherly advice. 'We couldn't stop you seeing him if you declared that you're living de facto.'

'We're not. I'm a single parent. I'm not living with anyone.'

The policewoman leaned over the desk again. 'So who's looking after your kids, while you're gallivanting around the country with known criminals?'

'My son is staying with friends.'

'Do these friends know about your drug running?'

'No.'

'So where did you get that speed?'

'No comment.'

A half-smile crept across the sergeant's face. 'Tell us how you managed to use it without your boyfriend knowing.'

249

'And what about the marijuana, where did you get that?' added the policewoman.

'From a friend.' I stared at the floor. There was no way I was going to admit that I had four more plants at home.

'Looks homegrown to me, plenty of stick and stem,' the sergeant said to the policewoman.

I was surprised by his use of smoker's jargon.

'So who's your friend?' the policewoman asked as if we were part of a mutual conspiracy rather than an interrogation.

'No comment,' I repeated.

'Let's stop pussy-footing around, shall we?' she snapped. 'If you don't give us some answers, we'll send a squad in to search your home.'

'I've got nothing to hide,' I lied.

'Why did you do it, Lillie?' the sergeant asked.

'I told you. I've been up in Sydney trying to get a record deal. I have to play in Melbourne tonight, after driving all day. I got the speed from a friend just to help me along a bit.'

'Who is this anonymous friend? It isn't your mate Matt, is it?'

'No! Why can't you believe he wants to go straight?'

'Guys like that never change,' the policewoman bellowed.

'If someone believed in him, he might have a chance.' I heard my own voice plead and almost believed it.

another song about love

'You really think you can help him stay on the straight and narrow, do you?' The policewoman's eyes had reduced to slits.

'Something like that.' I looked away in an effort to avoid her piercing gaze.

'That's why you travel round with a briefcase full of marijuana and packets of speed,' the policewoman hissed.

'No comment,' I whispered. She was really scaring me now.

'What kind of music do you play?' asked the sergeant. The blandness of his question disarmed me.

'Blues, reggae, funky stuff,' I answered.

'I like country music,' the sergeant replied warmly.

I smiled. 'I used to play in country rock bands.'

'I like Slim Dusty.'

'My ex-husband sometimes plays with him.'

'Was he a druggy too?'

'No, he doesn't touch alcohol or drugs.'

'You should have stuck with him,' the sergeant said.

'Maybe,' I answered, feeling more daring, 'but I believe marijuana should be legal. We'd all be better off if you guys had more time to catch the real criminals, the ones who harm other people. People who take drugs only harm themselves. And that's their prerogative, don't you think?'

The sergeant looked bemused. 'A lot of people get killed by drugs.'

'If marijuana was decriminalised it wouldn't be associated with harder drugs. It's less harmful than alcohol.' I was on firm ground now and was about to erupt into a long rave when the policewoman interrupted.

'Sergeant, can we get on with the charges?'

'Right, I'll get the papers.' The sergeant straightened his uniform then left the room, leaving the policewoman and I to sit in silence.

When I looked out the window I could see Matt leaning against the car, staring across at the police station.

The sergeant lined the charge sheet up and typed my statement. After what seemed like an eternity, he read the document out.

'We're charging you with possession of illegal drugs and granting you self-assured bail, that means you can go after you sign this document. You'll be summoned to appear in court at a later date.' He handed me the statement.

Relieved, I signed my name with a big flourish. 'This signature could be worth a fortune in a few years,' I quipped. The sergeant's laughter gave me the confidence to ask one more question. 'Tell me what's your opinion of marijuana? Do you think it should be legalised?'

'No comment,' the sergeant answered quickly. 'But I'd rather be in a room full of stoned people than a room full of drunks.'

another song about love

Outside, Matt was leaning across the roof of the car with his head buried in his arms. When I touched him on the shoulder, a look of relief spread across his face and he hugged me tightly.

'Are you okay?' Up close, Matt's eyes were wild and frightened.

'Sure,' I answered. 'The sergeant's a fan of mine now.'

'What did they charge you with?'

'Possession of prohibited drugs.'

'They didn't charge you with using or distribution?'

'Only possession. I told them you knew nothing about it.'

'You didn't have to do that.'

'I had less to lose than you. They'll probably give me a fine and a good behaviour bond.' Telling Matt what had happened, I saw myself as some kind of heroic survivor. 'They even threatened to search my house,' I said proudly.

'Do you think they would?' Matt asked.

'What do you think?' The reality of my house being invaded cut the vision of my heroism with paranoia.

'They might be on their way right now,' Matt replied.

'I'd better ring Jonathon then,' I said as my heroism turned to water.

'Can't it wait until we get back?'

JANIE CONWAY HERRON

'Not with all those plants stashed in my bedroom.' This was the first time I'd considered the sanctity of my house or the precarious situation I'd placed Jesse and I in.

By the time we reached the next town, my bravado had disappeared. I crossed the street to a phone box and looked around to see if I was being followed.

I dialled Jonathon's number. 'We just got busted in Wangaratta,' I said, my voice flat with fear. 'They've threatened to search my house. You know that stuff in the bedroom, hanging up between my clothes. Can you get it out of there as soon as possible?'

'What do you want me to do with it?' Jonathan's voice crackled down the line.

'Anything, just get it out of there.'

During the rest of the trip, my mind went wild with thoughts of going to gaol and Jesse being taken away from me. We passed through Seymour at sunset and a short while later Matt drove past the blue stone tower of Pentridge gaol, its barbed wire topped walls lit up against the night sky.

'We could have ended up in there,' I said.

'Not me, mate, I'm not ending up in there again.' Matt accelerated and overtook the car in front of him, revving the engine hard as he changed gears.

'But you could have if I hadn't...'

another song about love

'Look!' Matt interrupted. 'I don't want to think about it, all right?' He gave me such a long hard look that I retreated into silence.

The band was already playing when we arrived at the Punters Club.

Wendy spotted me first. 'We thought you weren't going to make it,' she yelled over the music. 'We were worried you'd had an accident.'

'Nearly as bad.' I picked up my guitar, which had been set up ready for me to play. 'Matt and I got busted. I took the rap and got charged with possession.'

'You what?' Wendy frowned. 'Jesus, Lillie!'

I picked up my guitar and began playing.

'What happened?' Anna hissed when the song came to an end. Before I had time to explain, Ali started up the rhythm for the next song.

Throughout the set, I looked for Matt in the audience but couldn't find him. When the bracket finished, the band descended on me.

'Where's Matt now?' asked Wendy.

'I don't know. He dropped me off, but hasn't come in yet.' I tried to sound nonchalant but his absence felt like a betrayal.

'He's probably worried he'll get a roasting from us,' Wendy hissed.'

'It wasn't his fault. If it wasn't for him, I might not have got back at all.'

'If it wasn't for him, you wouldn't have been busted.'

'Can I get you a drink, Lillie?' Stevie asked. 'You look like you need one.'

'Thanks,' I replied, grateful to avoid Wendy's questions.

At the end of the night I sat at the bar, watching Selina clean up.

'How'd your trip to Sydney go?' she asked breezily.

'Fine until the trip home.'

'What happened?'

'We got busted.'

'You're joking.' Selina almost dropped the glass she was wiping. 'Has Matt been arrested again?'

'No, I took the rap. Matt didn't get charged.'

Selina stared at me. 'You did what?'

'I took the rap. I told the cops Matt didn't know anything.'

'And they believed you!' Selina snorted.

'After a while they did,' I replied.

'Ungrateful bastard, he doesn't deserve you.'

I was pleased that somebody appreciated my actions.

On the way home, I told Wendy about my conversation with the sergeant. 'Next he'll be turning up at a gig and wanting to come home for a smoke,' she laughed and I was relieved to laugh with her.

When we pulled up outside my house, my bags were standing at the front door with a note folded into

another song about love

the handle of the briefcase. *Need some space. I'll call you in a few days. Love Matt.*

'Sounds like he's got a bit of soul searching to do,' Wendy observed.

I screwed the note up. 'I didn't feel like being alone tonight.'

'Do you want me to stay with you?'

I nodded gratefully.

'I'll just ring Anna and let her know I won't be home.'

'Home?' I queried. 'Are you two living together already?'

Wendy's face lit up. 'Anna's tired of bringing the boys up by herself. I've always wanted a family too.'

'But you hardly know each other.'

'Lillie,' Wendy frowned. 'We've been friends for more than fifteen years.'

I checked my wardrobe to see if my plants were still there and breathed a sigh of relief. They'd all gone. Out in the backyard I peeked over the back fence into Jonathon's kitchen. The curtains were pulled back but there was no sign of movement. I decided to wait until the next day to ask what had happened.

Back in the kitchen, Wendy was putting the kettle on. 'What were you doing out there?'

'Looking to see if Jonathon was up. I rang him after the bust and asked him to get rid of my plants, which he did. I wonder what he did with them?'

'You mean there's no ganja in the house.'

'Almost.' Fishing in the pocket of my jacket I pulled out the last joint. 'I had this in my pocket the whole time I was being questioned.'

'No kidding,' Wendy laughed. 'I'll smoke to that.' Wendy pulled out her lighter and held it under the joint as I inhaled.

I woke the next morning to the sound of soft knocking on the door. When I opened it, Jesse flew into my arms, wrapping his skinny legs around my waist. 'Where's Pushka?' he asked then disappeared down the hall.

Anna waved from the car. 'I think Jesse has his heart set on staying home today. Tell Wendy I'll come back after I've dropped Sam and Antonia off at school.'

As I waved goodbye, Jonathon opened his front door. Dressed in white, he looked like an ad for washing powder.

He greeted me with a broad smile. 'I got rid of that stuff for you.'

'So I noticed. What did you do with it?'

'I burnt it.'

'You what?'

'I burnt it. In your fireplace.'

I pictured the plants piled high, the first match sending flames shooting through the dried leaves, the smoke billowing out of the chimney.

'I thought the drug squad was due any minute. Burning it seemed the logical thing to do,' Jonathon

258

another song about love

explained. 'It's only drugs, Lillie. It might be good for you to stop smoking for a while.'

'You would say that, wouldn't you,' I said, as the events of the last few days bubbled into hysteria. 'Jesus, the whole neighbourhood must have got stoned. It's a wonder somebody didn't recognise the smell.'

'There's more important things in life than ganja,' Jonathon advised me.

I shut the door and slid down the wall to the floor, laughing, 'I don't believe it. I just don't believe it.'

Jesse came and sat between my legs. 'What's so funny, Mum?'

'I'm laughing at the irony of life, Jesse,' I replied.

'What's irony?'

'Irony shows you another meaning. A meaning that hides beneath the surface of things and helps you understand the way the world works.'

'Oh?' Jesse tried hard to understand what I'd said, then nestled closer. 'I missed you, Mum,' he said.

Days went by without hearing from Matt but pride stopped me from calling him. The next week when we played at the Punters Club I looked for him in the audience. The crowd was small so it was easy to see if Matt was there or not. At the end of the night I doled out the pittance of the door deal left over after the expense of lighting, PA hire and Vincent's fee. There wasn't much. A quiet depression settled over everybody.

Anna was the first to voice her dissatisfaction. 'I hate playing to such small audiences. It makes me feel self-conscious. If we have lots of people, I don't think about the audience. But on nights like tonight, I keep watching people to see if they like the music or not.'

Stevie drank the last of his scotch in one gulp. 'I remember seeing Cold Chisel on their first tour of the east coast. There were only five people at the Station Hotel but look how famous they are now.'

Ali played a quick drum roll on the edge of the table with his fingers. 'I think I know why the people didn't come to see us tonight. Frankie's got a regular Thursday night residency at the Albion and the same people who go to see him, like us. He's cutting into our audiences.'

'Bastard,' Wendy chipped in as she stacked the lights at the hotel entrance.

Only Anna came to his defence. 'It's not Frankie's fault if he's more popular than we are.'

'All is fair in rock and roll, eh?' I quipped.

'I'll drink to that.' Stevie slammed his glass on the table.

'Frankie doesn't owe us anything,' Anna continued. 'It's up to us to get more people to come to our shows. Maybe we should go back to doing supports.'

another song about love

'If you do, you'll be working for slave wages again,' Vincent interrupted her. 'At least with your own gigs you have a chance of building things up.'

'That's all very well for you to say,' Anna replied. 'You get paid no matter what we make.'

'That's my point.' Vincent wasn't at all fazed. 'You pay me the same, but the more people you get, you make the profit.'

Frustration sent a rippling frown across Anna's brow. 'We need to do supports so we get to play in front of more people. It'll get our profile up. Then we'll get more people to our own gigs.'

'You just like the sound of applause,' I joked.

'You can think what you like,' Anna answered. 'If I want to play to just a few people I can play in my own lounge room. I'm not proposing we don't do this gig, but we should do a few supports as well.'

'You could always organise some gigs yourself,' I answered.

Anna looked startled. 'Don't be stupid, Lillie. You know I'm hopeless at organising that sort of thing.'

Don't criticise me then.'

'I'm only making suggestions.' Anna pushed the chair over backwards and struggled out the door with her bass amp. When she came back to collect her bass, she'd calmed down a little. 'I'll see you all at rehearsal. We can talk about it then,' she announced as Wendy followed her out the door.

At the end of her shift, Selina sat next to me.

'So Matt's moved in with you, has he?' she asked.

'I haven't seen Matt for over a week,' I answered.

'He's done his disappearing act again. Mum and Dad assumed he was staying with you. I must admit, so did I.'

'Why did you assume that?'

'He usually disappears when he's getting into smack and then comes home to dry out. I thought he'd really kicked it this time. Besides, you saved his arse. If it weren't for you he'd be back in gaol again.'

'He got back into smack while we were in Sydney,' I replied. 'We met some people at a pub and went back to their place. I didn't have any, but he did.'

'Why didn't you stop him?' Selina asked.

'Why should I? It's his addiction, not mine.'

Selina looked puzzled. 'I thought you were a good influence on him.'

'I might be, but I'm not his guardian angel. Do you know where he might be?'

'Somewhere in St Kilda, I guess,' Selina replied. 'He'll turn up sooner or later. He always does.'

It was after midnight before I got home. Looking at Jesse asleep in my bed I felt relieved. I couldn't afford a baby-sitter after my trip to Sydney and didn't want to ask Anna after she'd had Jesse all week. I couldn't take him with me either. He'd beamed with excitement at

another song about love

the prospect of being at home on his own and watching television in my room. All night I had worried that the cops might search my house while I was at the gig. In my imagination, the scenario had gone from bad to worse, ending with Jesse being taken away from me. But here he was, in our house, safe and sound. I turned the television off and crawled into bed beside him, the loud ringing in my ears a reminder of my night playing in a rock band. In the morning, the alarm startled us both awake.

Jesse was cranky and tired. 'Do I have to go to school, Mum?'

'Yes,' I answered brusquely. 'They'll be asking questions soon if you don't start going to school more regularly.'

I walked Jesse to school, kissed him goodbye at the gate and waited as he walked despondently across the yard and in the front door.

The café underneath René's flat was open when I arrived. The regulars had already gathered for an early morning game of backgammon and the first of the day's coffees.

'You're back!' Jemma greeted me enthusiastically. 'How was your trip? Did you see Claude?'

'We stayed with Claude,' I said, hoping I wouldn't be forced into talking about him. All I wanted to do was talk to René about how awful I felt.

A frown flickered across Jemma's face, chased by a smile. 'How is he?'

'He's fine,' I answered, burying my tired head in my hands.

'Lillie, what's wrong?' René asked. 'Has something happened to Jesse?'

'No, Jesse is fine; it's me.' I looked up. 'Nothing feels worthwhile anymore.'

'You look like you could do with a week's sleep,' Jemma said. 'Have you thought of going to see a doctor? Maybe you need a tonic.'

'I need to do something,' I replied. 'I can't go on like this.'

René took my hand. 'We could look after Jesse for the weekend.'

I shook my head. 'Jesse won't even stay at Anna's at the moment.'

'What about your parents?' Jemma asked. 'Couldn't they take him?'

'Not while school's on. They live way up on the north coast of New South Wales. I'd have to put him on a plane. Same with Jesse's Dad, Joe. It'd be far too disruptive if Jesse went to Tamworth. Besides, I don't want to worry anyone.'

'I can lure Jesse with wonderful things like going to the movies, the zoo, or something like that,' Rene suggested and Jemma backed him up.

'We'll just pick him up after school this afternoon and spirit him off on a big adventure.

another song about love

Meanwhile you should get yourself to the doctor and go home to sleep.'

René put a mug of coffee in front of me. I held it in both hands, sipping it slowly, letting the warmth sink in. It was as if I'd caught the unhappiness I knew my mother must have felt all those years ago. If she saw me now, I wondered whether she'd understand like she used to. Would she still have the capacity to make me feel better with the simple wisdom of her words? I longed for her warm arms around me, the deep empathy of our connection, yet I was hesitant about confiding in her. I didn't want to upset the tender balance of her equilibrium with my own problems.

I watched the syringe draw blood from my arm. 'Just a precaution,' the doctor said amiably as she pulled the needle out and pressed a piece of cotton wool into the crook of my arm. 'There doesn't seem to be anything seriously wrong. It's probably just stress. Some multi-vitamins should help. Go get yourself a good brand from your local chemist, then go home and get some rest. Ring up next week for the results of the blood test.'

When I walked out of the doctor's office and into the sunshine I made a point of walking on the sunny side of the street all the way home. The warmth eased the ache in my body but lying down at home relieved it more. Pulling the covers up round my neck, I drifted off to sleep, then woke in the middle of the night with Pushka curled in the crook of my leg. When

JANIE CONWAY HERRON

I turned the television on she yawned and stretched, rubbing her body against me and purring. Re-runs of *Countdown* played recent Australian clips back-to-back. First up was Frankie Brave with the hit single from his debut album Blue, soon to be released in Europe. I lay back, hugging the purring cat to me, as Frankie walked across a blue-tinted, rain-swept street. What was it about men like Frankie that allowed them to be so successful when I had to struggle for every little bit of recognition? He had something ineffable, a laconic charisma that charmed his audience without him having to try. I listened to his lyrics about loneliness and heartbreak. As his mournful face stared at me from the screen I understood his attraction for women. Why couldn't I have the same appeal? When the song finished I turned the television off and pulled the covers up round my shoulders. Pushka crawled in closer, buffeting her head against my chin as I drifted off to sleep.

I woke to a soft knock on the door early next morning. As I pulled back the curtain, Matt's face grinned back at me. 'Can I come in?' He pressed his face against the window, a strange gleam in his wild blue eyes. When I opened the door, Matt's eyes distracted me so much that I didn't notice the budgie, with feathers the same colour as his eyes, sitting on his shoulder. 'It's a present for you,' he said as he took it from his shoulder and held it out. Behind me I could hear strangled choking noises coming from the cat. I quickly shut the bedroom door and locked the cat inside. Matt continued holding the bird out as it fluttered inside his hands, its tiny head peeking out between his fingers.

I backed away. 'I can't keep a bird; I own a killer cat. That bird won't last ten seconds with her around.'

Matt's hands were still outstretched. 'It flew onto my shoulder in the street.'

'Then it's yours, Matt. You look after it.'

'Can't you put it in a cage and keep it away from the cat?' he persisted. 'I thought you were a kind person, I thought you'd be pleased to have it.' Matt's eyes grew wilder by the second.

I wanted to scream at him to go away, but the part of me that was glad to see him opened the door to Jesse's room. 'Here, put it in there.' The bird flew out of Matt's hands and I shut the door.

'Where have you been?' I asked as we sat together on the couch. I noticed the slight tremble in his hands. The way his mouth moved when he spoke. The sad downward turn at the corners of the lips I loved kissing.

His crazy blue eyes turned to me. 'I can't do this anymore, Lillie. This just isn't my scene. You need someone who's going to be a father to Jesse, someone who can take care of you. I'm a junkie. I have a hard enough time taking care of myself, let alone anyone else. I don't expect you to understand, but it's the truth.'

A painful, tight feeling seized my chest. Deep inside, I knew he was right, but every fibre of my being struggled against his words. 'Maybe I could understand if you let me.'

Matt placed the coffee mug on the carpet and looked away. 'Christ, I knew it wasn't going to be easy, but this is impossible,' he said then gathered me in his arms. His lips were dry as paper as he kissed me. 'Can't we just be friends?'

I rubbed the skin peeking out from his shirt. 'Can't we be lovers too?'

Matt sighed. 'You're asking for it.'

'Asking for what?'

'A whole lot of trouble.'

I ran my fingers over his lips. 'Let me be the judge of that.'

'Don't say I didn't warn you.'

I undid the buttons on his shirt one by one, covering his chest in small kisses. Matt pulled me up so that my head was level with his. Lifting the T-shirt I'd been sleeping in I pressed against him, letting my breasts trail across his chest.

Holding on to my hips, Matt entered me and moved slowly inside me. 'Let me do it.' Matt closed his eyes and his face screwed up in concentration as he tried hard to make himself come. I watched his consciousness slip away from me as he fucked harder. Moving with him, I tried to help him along and the couch banged against the floor with the force of our fucking. As I was about to tell him to stop, Matt collapsed on top of me. His heart beat hard against my chest.

'It's no use. I can't do it. It's the smack. We can keep going for hours and I still won't come.' Breathless, he laughed, 'Some women like it.' Withdrawing slowly he curled himself around me. I could feel the hardness of his erection against my buttocks while his lips brushed against my shoulder. 'Why don't you get back into your bed? I'll make us something to eat.'

With the bedclothes tucked firmly around me, I listened to Matt cooking in the kitchen. It'd been more than twenty-four hours since I'd eaten when Matt put a plate full of pasta and vegetables on the bed. 'Aren't you going to eat some too?' I said, stuffing food into my mouth.

Matt shook his head. 'I'm not hungry.'

I put my fork down. 'Looks like I'm getting all the pleasure today.'

When Matt looked up and laughed, the wildness in his blue eyes reminded me of the bird in Jesse's bedroom. In a moment of panic I imagined a cloud of blue feathers on Jesse's bed and the body of the bird hanging out of the cat's mouth. I hurried out into the hall. Everything was quiet. Slowly turning the handle, I opened the door to Jesse's room. The budgie was quietly chirping, perched safely on top of the curtain rail.

I leant into Matt as he peered over my shoulder. 'I can't keep it, you know.'

'Not even for a little while?'

'The cat will eat it.'

'I'll buy her a cage then.' Matt put his arms round my shoulders. 'I promise to come and visit her.'

'That's one way of making sure I get to see you,' I laughed, clasping my hands around the back of his neck.

Matt pulled back, gently breaking the clasp of my hands. 'Got to go now, mate. I have to go see a friend.' He blew a kiss from the front door as guilt flickered in his eyes and his grin went crooked. The door clicked shut. I listened as Matt's car started up. The sound of the engine grew fainter as he drove away. Back in bed, I pulled the covers up to my chin. Pushka rubbed her face against my cheek, purring as I stroked her silky fur.

12

LOVING ISN'T
EASY

JESSE WAS A LATE BABY and I often joked
with him about how I've been hurrying him up
ever since his birth. All the baby things were ready
and the old wicker pram stood expectantly in the
bedroom, but still I hadn't given birth. Every
movement in my womb felt as if it could be the
beginning of labour and I was growing impatient. Joe
and I had spent months preparing for a natural birth but
when the doctor suggested that he induce it, I jumped
at the chance.

JANIE CONWAY HERRON

Early on the prescribed morning, I waited with Joe at St Vincent's maternity ward. There was something incongruous about sitting in the waiting room as if we'd made an appointment to have a baby. I smiled at Joe and he smiled back as we both sat in silent anticipation. When a nurse called me in Joe was left sitting outside.

This was now a medical procedure rather than a natural birth. I had to submit to the gruelling procedures of an enema and having my pubic hair shaved. As I lay prone on an operating table the doctor broke my waters and gave me hormone tablets to bring on contractions. Laughing at my clumsy gait I clung on to Joe and walked round the corridors of the hospital in order to hasten the contractions. After all the months of waiting and preparing, when the first painful spasm came I was totally unprepared. Later I told my friends that I hadn't had time to get into the rhythm of the birth because the induction brought on the labour so quickly. In truth, I wondered if I could to bear it.

Joe was there throughout the birth. Every time a contraction came on I steeled myself, tossing and turning while Joe held my hand and comforted me. With my huge belly all I had to cover me was a tiny square of sheet. One of the nuns in this Catholic hospital felt compelled to rescue my dignity. Leaning over me she suggested that I keep myself covered when my husband was in the room. Joe and I looked at each other in disbelief. I felt like screaming, 'How the

another song about love

fuck do you think I got like this?' But another contraction came and I found myself struggling to keep that damned bit of sheet over my huge belly and naked pubes.

By afternoon the baby still hadn't come and the doctor asked me if I was tired. He nodded to the nurse before I answered, saying: 'I think we'd better give her a help along.'

Sensing they'd ask him to leave if I had a forceps birth, Joe encouraged me to keep going. 'Come on,' he said, holding my gaze, 'keep pushing.'

I let go and gave over to the contractions, pushing as hard as I could with each one. The next time the nurse checked my cervix she rushed out of the room to get the doctor, who arrived just in time to catch the baby. There he was, our baby boy Jesse, lying on my stomach, purple and slimy with a pushed-in chin and a pushed-out forehead.

'We've done it,' Joe said with tears in his eyes.

In the magnificent stillness hovering around us after everyone left, I took a closer look at my son. After months of talking to a spirit, there he was in the flesh, a tiny body wrapped up in a pale-yellow blanket. Excitement and tenderness overwhelmed me as I unwrapped the covers and took a closer look at this new life. The little soul had finally arrived in human form.

In the months that followed, things changed in ways neither Joe nor I could have imagined. Before the birth

JANIE CONWAY HERRON

I went everywhere with Joe, now one of us had to be at home with Jesse. I'd sit waiting for Joe to come back from a gig. When he was late, a terrible depression crept over me. Sometimes I'd imagine Joe had been killed and the police coming to tell me. Standing there mournfully, caps in hand, they'd break the bad news. 'I'm sorry to have to tell you this, but …' I'd be heroic and take the news bravely. Sometimes in these horrible imaginings, my beautiful baby was killed too and I'd weep at my terrible thoughts as well as my capacity to imagine them.

When Joe's footsteps sounded on the floor, picking his way through the mass of baby things strewn everywhere, I'd fight back the tears. I knew the last thing he wanted was to find me weeping. Sometimes he'd stand in the doorway looking so angry I was sure he wanted to hit me or shake me, but he never did. This was nothing like the rosy vision I'd had of myself as a mother. I didn't know how to control my terrible imaginings or the awful lethargy that had become my permanent state of being. Nowadays I understand that I had postnatal depression and should have sought help. Back then I had no idea what was happening. Joe didn't have any answers either. We were losing each other in the chaos, but instead of asking for help we tried to solve it ourselves.

'What's happening to us?' I asked as we lay in bed one night with Jesse asleep beside us.

Joe shook his head.

another song about love

In the silence that followed I sensed the return of his early ambivalence about being a father. He was horrified at the truth of his own predictions. Then Jesse cried. As I watched Joe pick him up and cradle him in his arms, I understood how much he loved his son.

Months went by like this. At the same time Joe was trying to keep the threads of our music career going. We'd agreed that I should take some time out from performing until Jesse was old enough to be cared for. In the meantime, Joe looked for a back-up singer and started doing gigs without me. When Trish joined the band, I was happy that things were working out. I didn't realise that Joe, reluctant to come home, had started spending more time with her.

One evening after we'd talked for hours about what was wrong with our relationship, Joe suggested that perhaps we needed to have affairs with other people.

'Do you really think so?' I asked.

'If we trust each other we could try it.' He held me close.

'But I can't imagine making love to anyone else,' I whispered.

Joe hugged me close. 'After the first time, it'll be easy.'

'You sound like you're talking from experience, Joe.'

'I'm just guessing,' Joe replied, slipping a reassuring arm around my waist.

JANIE CONWAY HERRON

As he did, I felt a strong sense of desire for the first time since Jesse had been born. Turning towards Joe I caressed him gently, slowly stoking my own excitement at the same time. When Joe responded, our lovemaking was as strong and passionate as it had ever been. Afterwards, encouraged by the knowledge that things were already changing for the better, we fell asleep in each other's arms.

I woke early next morning to Jesse's cries. While Joe slept, Jesse fed. When comfort became sleep, I put Jesse to bed. I picked up nappies and clothes and took them down to the laundry, vowing I would never let myself get that low again.

It had been months since I'd seen Wendy. We spent the afternoon sitting in her backyard. Wendy lived in an old terrace, with a mass of rooms for people to rent. A huge kitchen and dining room and an even bigger lounge provided communal space for everyone. There were rosters on the wall for cooking and cleaning as well as childcare.

'Wow this is an amazing place.' I stretched out underneath the shade of the big old fig tree in the back garden and watched the sun filter down through the leaves.

When I told Wendy about the new arrangement Joe and I had discussed she reached over and gave me a hug. 'Relationships are hard, especially when kids come,' she advised.

another song about love

'Tell me about it,' I said, thinking about all the awful nights when Joe was out at gigs and I stayed at home, fighting desperation that reminded me too much of my mother's sadness.

'You should come and visit me more often. It'd do you good to get out and about a bit more,' Wendy advised.

'I know I should but it's easier to stay home,' I replied.

'I think kids benefit from being round more people. Rhonda's kids love living here. You could move in with all of us, if you wanted to.'

It was an attractive offer but I wondered how on earth I'd get Joe to agree to something like that. Living with other people might help me feel less isolated but I knew Joe wouldn't want to.

'Hey Lil', why don't you let me read your palm?' Wendy pulled out the new book on palmistry she'd been telling me about. 'People say I'm really accurate.' I reluctantly offered her my hand then watched as she studied it. 'Look at all those worry lines on your palm,' she exclaimed. 'No wonder you get so nervous all the time. You should do some meditation or something.' Wendy traced a line that ran down the middle of my palm. 'That's your heart line. All these others crossing it indicate how many lovers you're going to have. Christ, you're going to have lots of lovers by the look of it.'

I pulled my hand away. 'Come on Wendy, I'm a married woman with a child.'

JANIE CONWAY HERRON

'So? Who knows what the future holds?' Wendy replied. 'With this new arrangement you have with Joe, anything could happen.'

One Saturday afternoon not long after Joe and I agreed to our more open relationship, I played with the band again. For the first time since Jesse's birth, I was spending time without him. The gig at the Station Hotel was crowded and the audience applauded when I got up to sing. In the break I sat at a table with Joe. He was very attentive, despite the presence of Trish, our backup singer and Joe's new lover. Anything seemed possible to me at this moment. I smiled at Trish in spite of the hint of jealousy hovering at the edge of my heart. When Trish smiled back, I felt like the heroine in a warped romance movie. It was a ménage-a-trois without an injured party. Now it was my turn to have an affair with someone else. I looked around at the men in the room and could hardly bear to meet anyone's gaze.

'Hey, it's great to be singing again, I didn't think I could do it,' I said to Joe.

'It's something you'll never lose, Lil'.' Joe beamed at me.

'Trish is a good singer too.'

'Yes, but she isn't you.'

'You're just saying that to make me feel better about you two,' I replied.

'She's a good friend, that's all.' Joe's diffidence was not convincing.

another song about love

'We agreed, no comparisons,' I said.

'Don't you get on my case,' Joe declared. 'So long as everyone knows what's going on, no one gets hurt, right?'

In a flash of insight I could see it was Joe who might get hurt, not me. When I reached over to touch his hand, I caught a glimpse of Trish watching us. 'You'd better go make sure Trish is okay,' I whispered.

'You being my conscience now, are you?'

'No, it's just that you're cramping my style. It's my turn now.'

Grudgingly Joe stood up and walked away.

Alone and feeling shy, I stared into my drink, scared of making eye contact with anyone. A soft tap on my shoulder made me look up.

'Remember me?' Paul said.

'Yes of course I do.' I replied, as memories of the parties at Wendy's place came flooding back. 'Here, have a seat.'

Paul sat down. 'Good to hear you singing again.'

'I haven't sung since Jesse was born.'

'I heard you got married. I didn't think it'd last this long.'

'Why not?'

'Relationships just don't seem to last these days,' Paul replied.

'It hasn't been easy,' I admitted.

'I guess a baby adds to the pressure, eh?' Paul grinned.

'It does make you dependent on each other if you're not careful,' I answered, acutely aware that our talk wasn't as innocent as it seemed. Paul was an obliging listener. He asked all about Joe and added a few relationship stories of his own along the way. It felt nice to have someone else to talk to and he seemed interested in how I felt. After a couple more drinks, I let my heart go with my mouth, telling Paul about the decision Joe and I had made to take other lovers. I confided that Joe already had another lover and I was scared of taking that step myself. Perhaps, I confessed, I had forgotten how to make love with a stranger after seven years with Joe. Paul laughed and said he felt the same and that he had been having similar conversations with his girlfriend. As we arranged to meet for dinner at the end of the gig, both of us understood the real reason for our meeting had nothing to do with eating.

We decided to go straight to Paul's place. We only had two hours before the second gig the band had that evening.

'My place is quite close to Monash University,' Paul said as his car flew along a winding boulevard, close to the Caulfield racecourse. 'We've got plenty of time to get you to the gig.'

'Jesus, Paul, I haven't slept with anyone else but Joe for years.'

'And I've been with Leslie for five.'

'You've never slept with anyone else?'

'Nope.'

another song about love

'What will she think of this, then?'

'She doesn't have to know.'

'That's a bit dishonest, isn't it? I thought you two had talked about having other lovers.'

'We talked about it, that's all. We didn't agree to do it.' Paul shot me a sheepish grin as we pulled up outside a sprawling old house that had been divided into a number of flats. As Paul fumbled with his keys, I felt as if I was cheating on a woman I'd never met.

'Welcome to our abode.' Paul opened the door and turned on a light that lit up the entrance of the house.

I hesitated.

'Come on in.' Paul encouraged me. 'Leslie's not here, she's staying up in the mountains until Monday.'

Our footsteps sounded loudly on the old wooden floor as Paul guided me into a large room with a big old marble fireplace and enormous bay windows.

'This used to be the drawing room of the mansion before they divided it into flats.' Paul turned on a small lamp then took hold of my shoulders and turned me towards him. His moist lips pressed against my mouth as his tongue pushed inside. We stood by the fireplace for ages, kissing. Paul's lips travelled down my neck as he bent at the knees and gently pulled us both to the floor. 'I've been wanting to fuck you for years,' he croaked, 'but you only had eyes for Sean.'

Nights of passion filled my fantasies for weeks after Joe and I discussed having other lovers. Paul's caresses were gentle, but it felt as if we were both disconnected and our bodies were going through some well-rehearsed dance. I lay there watching Paul and wondering if his closed eyes meant I could be anyone. My body was an empty vessel sailing on the tide of his needs. I'd lost all comprehension of my own. When Paul stopped I wanted to ask if he had come, but decided against it. He didn't ask me if I'd had an orgasm either. When I shifted my weight underneath him in an attempt to make myself more comfortable, Paul got up.

'How about a cup of coffee and some cheese on toast? Then we'd better get you to the gig. Can't have you late for the show. Joe might never forgive me.'

'Okay.' I tried to make my voice cheery but my heart felt weak with regret. Placing my hand between my legs I felt the moistness between them. A tear of sperm slowly trickled down my thigh and I wiped it away with my underpants.

'Where'd you get to with Paul, then?' Joe whispered to me that evening.

'We went to his place for a while.'

'And?'

'You know the rest.' I felt irritated.

'How was it?'

'How was what?' My vagueness was designed to make Joe stop asking such personal questions but it didn't work.

another song about love

'Oh for Christ's sake, Lillie, did you fuck him or what?'

'Or what?' I didn't know why I was taunting Joe like that but something about his questions was annoying. 'Listen Joe, let's talk about it later.'

'No, I want to know now.' Joe tried to sound jolly.

'Alright Joe, you asked for it. Yes, we did. We had a whopping great fuck in the middle of the lounge room.'

Joe's grin was lopsided as he struggled to contain the information I had just given him. 'Oh okay, I just wanted to know, that's all.'

'I'd rather tell you about it later tonight, Joe.'

'I was going to go out with Trish after the gig, seeing we have a night off from Jesse,' Joe said and it was my turn to feel hurt.

'But I thought tonight was a good chance for us to spend some time together,' I answered.

'Well, I thought it was a good chance to spend some time apart.'

'Right, then.' I stomped out of the dressing room, headed for the bar and ordered myself a whisky.

Suddenly Paul was standing beside me his face screwed up with embarrassment. He explained why he'd come back inside. 'I was driving out of the car park when I got to thinking.'

'What were you thinking about?'

'Nothing profound, I just had the feeling that, well …'

'Yes?' I half closed my eyes.

'I have the feeling that things didn't go too well between us before.'

'What made you think that?'

'Well, I was, how can I put it?' Paul was blushing bright red. 'Taking you home like that wasn't something I planned to do. I think I was a bit hasty and I was wondering if there was any chance of trying again some other time?'

I just managed to control the giggle rising inside me. 'When?'

'I don't know. I wouldn't mind if it were soon, in fact.'

'You just want to get your end in again before Leslie gets back, don't you?'

This time Paul didn't allow me to get the better of him. 'Not at all, I'd like another chance to make a better impression on you.'

'What about tonight then?'

'Tonight? What about Joe? Don't you have to look after your son?'

'Joe's already got better things to do with his time tonight and my parents are dropping Jesse off tomorrow afternoon. I have the rest of the evening after the gig free.'

The look on Paul's face was genuinely endearing.

I downed the last of my whisky and ordered another two. 'Let's drink to another chance.' I handed Paul a whisky.

another song about love

'Your place or mine?' Paul raised his glass.

Backstage, Joe was sitting in the corner talking earnestly to Trish.

I walked straight over to them and slapped Joe on the back. 'How are you two going?'

Joe looked at me disapprovingly. 'You're drunk.'

'So what if I am!'

'Don't let it affect your performance, that's all.'

'Don't let it spoil your performance, that's all,' I mimicked him.

Trish moved away as Pete, the drummer, lit a joint. When he handed it to Trish, I moved over to be next in line.

'Hey Lil', take it easy,' Trish whispered.

'None of your fucking business!' I shouted, making sure Joe could hear. 'I haven't had this stuff for a long time, but as Joe says, we've got to broaden our horizons.' I took the joint and inhaled deeply, staring defiantly at Joe. When I started to cough, I handed it on, and took another toke on the next round. All the time I was checking Joe out of the corner of my eye. I knew he didn't approve and an echo of the past – my mother's drinking and my father's disapproval – called to me. The more I felt it, the more defiant I became. As we launched into the first song Paul gave me a smile from the audience and I grinned back. When I sang, my voice, husky with marijuana smoke and whisky, soared over the band and the crowd went wild.

After the show, the dressing room was crowded with people so I arranged to meet Paul outside.

'Can you put my things in the car?' I asked Joe.

'Sure, I always do.' Joe was pleased the gig had gone so well. 'You want me to drop you home?'

'No, that's all right. I'm spending the night with Paul.' I managed to keep a straight face but inside I was nearly hysterical.

Joe kept looking down at his guitar, wiping the neck with a cloth and carefully making sure everything was in place. When he looked up his face was rigid, attempting to hide the emotions written all over it.

I reached up and touched his face. 'I love you,' I whispered, then walked out the door.

When I shifted to Wendy's place, I rationalised the move as being good for my relationship with Joe. I blossomed in the gregarious atmosphere of a group household. But it scared Joe and he moved in closer, doing things I knew he hated himself for. He often visited late at night, creeping up the stairs to my room, his heart pounding with fear. Instinctively I remained discreet about what I was doing and who with. Often he stood in the middle of the room watching me as I pretended to be asleep in the narrow single bed I'd set up next to Jesse's cot. Sometimes I took him into bed with me. Lying up close, he fell asleep. On other nights, he lay awake alone in the house that used to be ours, tossing on the painful knife-edge of his incessant thoughts. The furrow on his forehead grew deeper and his shoulders hunched over. As Joe became sadder, my need to move away from him grew stronger.

When Joe told me he'd stopped seeing Trish, I sensed he wanted me to be pleased, but I wasn't.

'Why did you do that?' I asked.

'Because I can't stand the thought of you sleeping with anyone else and it seems hypocritical if I'm still sleeping with Trish.'

'I hope you don't expect me to stop seeing other people,' I answered. Pride was the only thing that stopped Joe from saying yes. But as time went by, Joe lost all sense of pride and begged me to come back and live with him.

'I can't, Joe. I need more time.'

A pained expression spread across his face. 'How much time?'

'I don't know.'

As I retreated, Joe's pain increased. My feelings for him were locked deep inside me, making me say things that were hurtful to him. He edged closer to breaking point. When he reached it, everything collapsed.

At Caulfield Town Hall we played to a concert audience who listened intently as we sang songs we'd written together. The entire set was made up of love songs that documented our relationship. One of them even counted the number of mornings we'd woken up beside each other. As I leant into the microphone to sing the chorus, Joe smiled across at me. When I smiled back, Joe reached out to take hold of my hand. I turned and picked up my guitar, leaving his hand reaching into the space where mine had just been.

After the gig, Joe refused to give me a lift home. He couldn't stand dropping me off at a place that wasn't ours, and insisted I come home with him.

'But I can't, Joe. Mum is looking after Jesse and she's expecting me back there tonight. You know that.'

'Then we'll go and pick him up together and take him back to our place.'

'He'll be asleep, Joe. Why don't we all spend the day together tomorrow?'

Joe struggled to hide the desperation engulfing him. 'Please, Lillie, I can't stand being by myself any longer. I need you to come home with me tonight.' He gripped my shoulders tightly.

I struggled free. 'I can't,' I pleaded.

'How long's it going to take, Lillie?'

'How long is what going to take?' I'd become adept at directing conversations like this around in convoluted circles.

'I want to know when you're going to come back to me.' Joe held my face in his hands and turned me towards him.

another song about love

I closed my eyes and took a deep breath before answering. 'I might have to sleep with lots of different men before I come back to you.'

As the words rang in Joe's ears, he grabbed me by the arm and pulled me towards his car. I tripped and fell, banging my head against the pavement. Joe stopped and turned on me, his hands closing around my throat.

A crowd gathered around us but no one came to my aid. All I could see were different pairs of shoes in a circle around my head and Joe's angry face above me as his hands tightened around my neck.

Suddenly, Joe let go and collapsed to the ground. 'Oh my God, what have I done?' he cried, holding his clenched fists over his head.

In a voice that was flat with shock I commanded Joe to, 'Bloody well pull yourself together.' As I turned away, everything went dead inside me. There was nothing left for us anymore. Our relationship was over.

'You be careful now Lillie. Make sure you stay out in a public place. You don't want him getting violent again,' Mum cautioned when I told her I was taking Jesse to meet Joe. 'And don't let Jesse go off with him, whatever you do.'

JANIE CONWAY HERRON

Mum and Dad had become regular babysitters for Jesse, enabling Joe and I to keep our musical career going. But after that awful night, I found it difficult to persuade my parents that Joe and Jesse's relationship with each other was important. It was difficult to convince anyone of the significance of Jesse having an ongoing relationship with his father.

'Everything will be alright, Mum, truly it will,' I assured her. 'Joe's okay now and he's really sorry for what happened. Besides, we need to build some trust between us so Jesse can see his dad on a regular basis.'

'Yes, I know, you're right, darling, but I'm concerned for you. He could have killed you, you know. He's damned lucky you didn't press charges.'

'He'd be the first one to say that too, Mum. Joe's one of those people who was born with a bad hand of cards. Right now he's hurt and he doesn't trust anyone, least of all himself. You never know, his relationship with Jesse might help him to trust people again. I'll call you afterwards Mum, and let you know how things went.'

I put Jesse in the pram and walked to the Edinburgh Gardens to meet Joe. It was a long walk. By the time I'd pushed the pram half way there Jesse had fallen asleep.

Joe and I sat on the park bench near the old train. We'd been there often in happier times. Now we were tearing down the edifices we'd built around the dream of our life together.

another song about love

Joe sat with his head in his hands, looking like he wished the earth would swallow him up. 'I can't stay in Melbourne, Lillie. It's just too hard. I'm so scared that I might lose it again and do something terrible to you or even to Jesse.'

'You wouldn't do that, surely.' We were venturing onto the thin ice of the recent past again.

'If I saw you with someone else, I'm scared I might.'

'But you promised it'd never happen again.' I could feel frustration rising. I'd had something else in mind, some sort of redemption through Joe being a father – the kind of civilised working-things-out that had gone on in the days when Joe was going out with Trish and I'd been seeing Paul. Now my dream of Joe finding some salve for his hurt through his relationship with Jesse was going up in smoke.

'It won't be forever. I'll visit Jesse when I come down to Melbourne. When he gets older he can come up and visit me too. I just need to go somewhere and start again; somewhere people don't associate me with you.'

'So you'd not only bust us up, you'd forfeit your relationship with your son just for that?'

'Jesus, Lillie, I didn't bust us up. You did. Besides, I'm not going to the end of the earth. There's a really good music scene in Tamworth. It's been steadily growing since they started having the festival there. I want to be part of that.'

'I didn't know you liked playing country songs.'

'I'll just be putting a different musical hat on. I can still keep playing other kinds of music as well.'

'What about our music, Joe? What's going to happen to that?'

Joe looked me straight in the eye. 'Our music's dead, Lillie, caput, end of story. You'll keep playing I know you will. You'll find your own kind of music to play too. You always come through with flying colours.'

As I struggled with Joe's heroic predictions for me, Jesse woke up. When he saw his father, he lifted his arms towards him. Joe picked Jesse up, hugging him tightly. They went over to the old train to play and I realised the bond between the two of them would never be broken. Nonetheless it would be a very long time before Jesse and I saw Joe again.

13

ANOTHER SONG
ABOUT LOVE

A T REHEARSAL, ANNA WAS UNHAPPY with the arrangement of her song.

'Can't you make the rhythm more funky?' she asked me as she picked up my guitar. 'Just hammer-on like this and it'll come out right.'

I played the rhythm as close to the way she'd shown me as I could.

Anna frowned. 'Push the first beat of the bar a bit more.'

When I did that it sounded better. Then I tried to sing and lost the rhythm. The band stumbled to a halt.

'I can't play that riff and sing at the same time,' I said.

'It's no harder than singing and playing bass,' Anna answered, her smile doing little to counter her frustration.

'But you wrote the song. I've never played it before,' I answered, feeling so inadequate I wished I could disappear.

'Okay, we'll play it through without the singing.' Anna counted the song in.

I took a deep breath and concentrated hard on playing the intro in time. When the band came in underneath my rhythm, it took all of my concentration, but I managed to stay in time for the duration of the song.

Anna beamed. 'There you are, I knew you could do it.'

'But I can't play *and* sing,' I said.

'You could try practising until you can.'

'Why don't you sing it, Anna?' I countered.

'I'm not the lead singer, you are,' Anna insisted.

Stevie suggested that he play the rhythm during the verses and when he played a solo I could pick it up.

'That's a good idea,' I agreed.

'Piker.' Anna frowned.

Ali tapped impatiently on the high hat. 'Why don't we try it at least?'

When Stevie played the rhythm it slipped out easily as the band came in behind him. When the solo began, I gritted my teeth and launched into the rhythm. The band faltered for a moment. When Stevie began his solo, it picked up again. With relief, I sang the last verse and chorus, letting Stevie take over. When we'd finished Ali and Stevie looked pleased but Anna was still unhappy.

'I don't like it. The rhythm still drops out in the solo.'

'Give it a chance, Anna. We're only just learning it,' Stevie advised.

'Maybe we should drop the song.'

'Don't give up on me that quickly,' I pleaded.

'I'm not.'

'But if I could play and sing the song at the same time, you'd be happy.'

'You can do it, Lillie, you just need to practise.' Anna put her bass down and turned her back on me.

A tight drum roll from Ali drew everyone's attention. 'Why don't we pack it in for this afternoon and try again next rehearsal when everyone is feeling fresh?' He winked at Stevie who began putting his guitar away.

After Ali and Stevie left, I tried talking to Anna.

'It's not the song that's really bothering you, is it?'

'What makes you think that?' Anna's body language suggested much more than her words.

'You seem to be unhappy with everything to do with the band at the moment,' I probed. When Anna maintained her stoic silence I plunged into the murky waters flowing between us. 'The other night you seemed annoyed with Vincent and pissed off with the gig too.'

'Vincent thinks he knows everything, just because he was successful in England.'

'He's a good mixer though.'

'What's the use of having a good mixer while the rest of the band starves?' A wave of angry red rolled up Anna's neck and into her cheeks.

'It's worth it if we sound good, isn't it?' I countered.

'We don't need Vincent to make us sound good. Anyone can do that. Why can't he be a member of the band just like Wendy is? She takes the hard times with us. Vincent is just using us until something better comes along.'

'I've known Wendy since I was a kid. We can't expect the same loyalty from Vincent.'

Anna kept her gaze steady. 'You'd better talk to Wendy about that. I think she sees it a bit differently.'

Frustration lifted the pitch of my voice. 'So now the two of you have decided to exclude me from decisions about the band.'

'Who said anything about excluding you? I'm just letting you know how we feel. We're both sick of having no money. Wendy makes more doing lights for theatre and she has more creative input.'

'Wendy doesn't have to do lights for us if she doesn't want to.'

'That's right Lil', she doesn't. She does it because she's loyal, as you so carefully pointed out. Vincent isn't.'

'So? By the time Vincent is well known, we will be too.' I wished I could sound more confident.

Anna's knuckles whitened as she tightened the grip on her coffee cup. 'I don't know if I can wait that long.'

'What do you mean?'

'I don't think I can wait around for the band to become successful.' Anna whispered, trying to diminish the destructive power of her words.

'You sound like you want to break the band up?'

'No, I just want to leave it,' Anna answered.

'But I can't keep the band going without you.'

'Yes, you can. It'll be easy to find another bass player.'

'Sure, you're easy to replace.' My sarcasm turned on the edge of my fears. 'What about all the songs you've written? The ones we've written together?'

'You can do them without me. Besides you've got enough songs of your own to keep a band going for years.'

'You can't stop playing altogether,' I said.

Anna smiled, the fine lines at the corners of her mouth dancing up into her cheeks. 'I'd be happy playing in a covers band for a while.'

I shook my head. 'I don't believe this.'

'It was you who made me think about it.'

'I've never said anything about you leaving the band, Anna. It's never even entered my head.'

'Those people in Sydney suggested you go solo. They're into *you*, Lillie. You're a marketable product on your own, but with me, forget it. I'm not really interested in the glamour side of things. I've got two kids so I can't go on tour. I'm better off playing in a local covers band and bringing home some regular money.' 'But I can't keep the band together by myself,' I answered. 'And I have to look after Jesse too.'

'But you don't have to. Wendy and I will still support you. I just won't be in the band that's all.'

'When do you want to leave?' I asked. 'Not before we find another bass player I hope.'

'I've been offered something I can't refuse; a regular gig with a three-piece at Romano's Restaurant. It's good money, cash in hand.' Now that the truth was out, Anna looked relieved.

I stared across the table. It was obvious Anna had been thinking about this for a while. 'We could still do Thursday nights at the Punters Club, ' I offered.

'They want me to play Thursdays through to Sundays.' As Anna laid her cards on the table, our partnership snapped in two.

another song about love

Faced with the blunt truth of the situation I waited for the pain of rejection to kick in but a strange calm came over me instead. I had known Anna for over a decade and she had never stayed in bands for long.

'I'll miss playing with you,' I said as a fickle dream of becoming a solo performer formed in my head.

'I'll miss it too.'

'Really?'

'You've got something really special. It's what puts you up front of the band.' Anna replied. 'Me, I'm better off being a player in someone else's band. I'm hopeless at all the schmoozing being successful requires. You're good at it. And you write excellent songs.'

'You're just saying that to make me feel better,' I joked.

'I'm serious,' Anna insisted. 'You should take those guys up on the idea of a solo career. You've got what it takes. I haven't.'

Back home, I stared out the window at the cold, bare cement of the backyard. The changing of summer into autumn connected with the coldness inside me. I'd moved here after Wendy decided to live with her previous girlfriend, Maggie. I thought it was also time for Jesse and I to live on our own for a while. This place was all that I could afford. Now the shabby old wooden bathroom shed leaning sideways, propped up by the back fence and the barbed wire running along the top of the gate, reflected my poverty back to me, turning on the hollowness of my feelings. I shivered as a cold draft crept under my door. With a cup of tea and several pieces of toast I wrapped myself up in a blanket. Heavy with toast and dripping butter, I stared at the television without registering anything.

In the middle of the night the hissing of the television roused me. The loneliness was overwhelming. I had one more night alone before Jesse returned. His companionship was the only constant in my life. Impulsively I reached for the phone to call René and ask how Jesse was, but crawled into bed instead. Pulling the blankets around me I piled the doona on top then stared into the darkness. The shadow play of the streetlight hypnotised me while a cool breeze coming in underneath the curtains lifted the material in a soft dance. When the shadow on the wall changed to the shape of a round head, my body stiffened with fear. I lay perfectly still, trying to make sense of the strange clinking sound I could hear.

As the shadow moved this way and that, a voice whispered, soft and urgent. 'Lillie! Are you there?'

I pulled back the curtain. 'Fuck, Matt, you scared the shit out of me.'

Matt was holding something up to the window that sent stripes of shadow across the opposite wall. 'I found a cage for the bird, so I brought it around.'

'It's a bit late to be thinking about bird cages now, Matt.'

another song about love

'Is it?'

'It's two o'clock in the morning.'

'Sorry. Do you want me to go away?'

'It's okay. I'm awake now. Besides, I could do with some company.' I pulled the blanket around me and opened the front door.

Matt's heavy boots crunched down the hallway straight to Jesse's room.

'Is the bird all right? The cat hasn't got it or anything?'

'I don't know, I haven't looked recently,' I teased.

Alarm flashed across Matt's face. He turned the door handle slowly and we squeezed inside. When Matt turned on the light, the budgie fluttered around the room then flew back to the curtain rail. Matt reached up but the budgie plumped its wings and moved away. Head cocked to one side, it kept an eye fixed on Matt. He enclosed the bird in his hands while I held the cage door open. When Matt released it, the bird fluttered around in the cage before settling on the perch.

'You're going to have to find someone else to look after it,' I said, hoping that Matt might take some responsibility.

'I don't know anyone else but you,' Matt replied.

'What about taking it to a kindergarten or something?'

'That's a good idea.' Matt had absolved himself from any more accountability.

'I'm going back to bed. I need more sleep.' I gathered the blanket around myself once more.

'Do you mind if I stay?'

My tired heart skipped a beat and I paused for a second without bothering to turn around. 'If you want to,' I answered flatly.

'Are you sure? I don't want to impose.'

'You've got to be kidding.'

The next morning, I sat up in an empty bed. The house was silent. In the bathroom I found Matt leaning over the sink, his arm outstretched. A syringe, half filled with blood, was sticking out of his arm and a few splatters of red dotted the white porcelain. My best leather belt was pulled tightly around Matt's upper arm and he was engrossed in loosening it. He pulled the needle out and blood squirted down the sink. It took him a long moment to turn around. When he did, the pale blue of his irises took up most of his eyes and his pupils had narrowed to pinpoints. Caught between panic and nausea, I watched Matt's mouth move into an idiot grin as he croaked out a greeting.

'How dare you bring this stuff into my house?' My hand shook as I pointed at the sink.

Matt stood up slowly, reached in his pocket and held out his hand. Something small and brown like a tiny turd, sat in the middle of his palm. 'Want to try some?' Matt's words crackled between us.

another song about love

'You've got to be kidding.' I backed out the door.

Matt followed me down the hall. 'You shouldn't make judgments about something you know nothing about.'

I turned around. 'You want me to be a junkie too, don't you?'

Matt leant towards me. 'No, I just want you to try some, that's all.'

'No. No way.'

'Just once,' Matt pleaded. 'You can't get addicted from one taste. Besides, the first one's always the best. It's never better than that.'

As Matt's crazy eyes held my gaze, I tried to look behind his pinpricked pupils for some kind of emotion. There was nothing there. I closed my eyes. My heart beat so hard I could feel it in my throat. I felt his breath on my cheek.

'Come on, babe. I'll look after you. Just once. I promise you won't get addicted. This is pure shit. The best rocks in town. You couldn't hope for better for your first taste. No use trying to get this high again, Babe. There's nothing as good as the first time.'

Matt's hip street talk sounded so comical, that it made me laugh. In spite of all my resistance, my resolve faltered. I liked this man so much I didn't want to lose his affection. Matt was right, I told myself, I needed to try this drug before I made judgements about others. Besides, it was only going to be this one time.

JANIE CONWAY HERRON

I watched Matt prepare. Tenderly, he pulled the belt tightly round my arm and tapped a vein. I shut my eyes tight as the needle poised, felt the prick and the cold rush of something. A sharp, pungent smell hit my nostrils. My heart stopped beating so hard and a strange calm came over me. I'd never felt so relaxed before. In that instant I understood why this drug was so addictive.

I looked up at Matt and smiled.

He beamed back. 'There you go, Babe. There's nothing better than feeling like this. Nothing.'

I believed him. As we lay in bed, doors of perception opened between us. We talked about anything and everything was important, down to the smallest detail. At times we lay in silence, staring at the ceiling, and the silence didn't make me nervous like it usually did. I'd forgotten how to care. It was so liberating I wished it could go on forever.

Matt told me stories from the other world he inhabited. A life I'd only glimpsed on that first night in St Kilda now tumbled out of him. We were even now. The gap between us had closed.

Later, we sat in the kitchen drinking coffee and I slowly shifted back into my old self.

'Matt,' I said softly. 'Do you always share needles with people?'

'Yeah' he answered. 'They're not that easy to get hold of.'

another song about love

'I was just thinking about you getting things,' I stammered. 'You know, blood mingling. It's a sure way to catch things.'

Matt laughed. 'Don't worry. I'm as clean as a whistle. Besides, you should have thought about that when we made love. Sex is a sure way to get things from bodily fluids.' Matt said these last two words sarcastically and I sensed he was moving away from me again.

'But when you put things straight into the blood stream, surely that's a way of catching things more easily,' I persisted. I tried to think of myself as clean too, but I felt soiled. What would Mum think about what I was doing? As a nurse she had always made sure I knew about safe sex. There was talk about all sorts of new diseases you could get from that too. Most of the men I knew complained about condoms. I knew I'd put myself at risk. There was no going back. The moment I had the hit had changed me. 'Maybe everyone should have their very own fit, Matt,' I ventured, 'then you could be sure that you stayed clean.'

When Matt laughed hard and long in reply, I felt small and stupid. Slowly, I shrank back into the real world.

JANIE CONWAY HERRON

On the tram heading for Northcote, Jesse snuggled into my jumper, his eyes glazing over with the pleasure of our closeness. I wondered whether I had fostered too much dependence in him. Wendy's previous girlfriend, Maggie, had said as much.

'That boy is going to be a heartbreaker when he grows up,' she'd warned. 'The way you indulge him is going to make him a nightmare for any woman to live with.'

'At least he's grown up knowing that he's loved,' I'd countered.

I tickled Jesse's palm as we walked down the hill towards Anna's house. A big smile spread across his face as I savoured the feeling of his small hand in mine.

'René says I've got to look after you, Mum.' Jesse looked at me with his big Marmite-coloured eyes. 'He says you're not very well.'

'I'm just tired, Jesse. There's nothing to worry about. You don't have to look after me.' I swung Jesse up into my arms and pushed Anna's gate open. When I put him down he disappeared around the side of the house, looking for Sam and Ant.

I paused for a moment trying to overcome a rising sense of dread then walked inside. Everybody was waiting for me. I tried to look happy but my smile felt false.

'So what are we going to do now that Anna's decided to leave?' Wendy asked.

another song about love

Stevie cleared his throat. 'The way I see it, either we get a new bass player or fold the band. I wouldn't mind trying to keep things together, myself.' He looked across at me and smiled.

Wendy nodded while Anna remained straight-faced and silent.

Ali patted a soft rhythm on his knees with his open hands. 'To me the essence of this band is Anna and Lillie. I really don't think it will be the same without Anna.'

I bit my lip and remained silent.

It was Stevie who voiced my feelings. 'Jesus Ali, the band might be different. That doesn't mean it won't be as good.'

Anna backed Ali up. 'There are plenty of bass players better than me.'

As the rest of us spluttered in disbelief Wendy's voice cut through. 'That's right there are plenty of other bass players out there.'

'I'm not talking about good, better, best,' Ali added and I could see he was being honest, however brutal it seemed. The pained look on his face showed he wasn't enjoying himself. 'What I'm talking about is the unique thing between Lillie and Anna. It's the chemistry between the two of you that makes this band stand out. The band's not called Scarlet Sisters for nothing.'

'We could change the name,' Stevie added.

'But I can't stand auditioning bass players.' Ali grinned awkwardly.

'It looks like the decision is made,' I said. 'I don't feel like trying to go on with only two of us. Do you, Stevie?'

Stevie shrugged his shoulders.

'You two could do a duo act until you get another band together.' Wendy added.

'Maybe,' Stevie replied. 'But I thought the band meant a lot more to everyone.'

A flush spread across Anna's face. 'Having kids and spending all my time on something that's not earning enough money for me to keep them is too much for me. Government assistance doesn't go far when you've got two kids. The gig at Romano's earns good money and I need it.'

'Yeah, but you have to play shit,' Stevie replied.

'Maybe, but that's my choice. There's no such thing as a perfect world.'

'Tell me about it,' I whispered.

After Stevie and Ali left, Anna, Wendy and I continued talking.

'After all that hard work, it's all over, just like that.' A ring of defeat echoed in the brittle edge of my laughter.

'On to the next chapter in your career, Lillie,' Wendy encouraged me. 'You're much more success-oriented than Anna. A solo career could be good for you.'

another song about love

'We'll have to have a party next week to celebrate the demise of the band,' I said, feigning light-heartedness. 'That'll make sure there are plenty of people at the next gig, at least. Maybe Anna will have such a good time she'll change her mind and stay with the band.'

'Maybe.' Anna put her hand on my shoulder. 'Give me a hug, will you?'

I stiffened as she pulled me close.

When I went to collect Jesse, he didn't want to leave. 'But we're making a cubby house.' Jesse put his hand on his hips, surveying the upturned furniture.

'It's okay if he stays, Lillie.' Anna reassured. 'I'm sure you could do with another night to yourself.'

'Yes!' Jesse exclaimed.

Back home, I tried playing guitar but nothing I played pleased me. When I strummed loud angry chords they sounded awful. When I played something mellow it seemed corny and clichéd. Frustrated, I put my guitar away and walked around aimlessly. I made myself a cup of coffee and didn't drink it, turned on the television and didn't watch it, made a meal and didn't feel like eating. Memories of Matt bending over my arm with the needle poised drifted into my consciousness. The feeling of no feeling that followed the hit, the wonderful freedom of not caring. I longed for it and tried not to long for it, confusing it with longing for Matt. On a whim I rang his house, rehearsing a casual line of questioning if his parents answered.

Matt answered the phone. 'Hi Lil', I've been thinking about you,' he said casually, as if it was the most natural thing in the world.

'Have you?' I answered, my cheeriness reeking with deception.

'I've got something for you. I was going to bring it round soon.'

'That'd be nice,' I answered, but what I really wanted to ask was, when. Then Matt suggested he come over in an hour or so. Two hours later when I opened the door to him I was wearing the red dress he'd bought me.

Grinning, he handed me a small box wrapped in brown paper. I unwrapped the paper slowly. 'Take the lid off,' Matt said eagerly. A brand-new syringe gleamed menacingly inside. Matt pulled out another one, saying proudly, 'One each.'

Speechless, I stared into the box as Matt steered me down the hall to the lounge room. 'Come on, I've got some more of those rocks too.'

Heart pounding, I watched Matt preparing a hit for me. 'It's just the rush before the taste. You'll get used to it,' Matt explained and I almost believed him. But my beating heart sounded a louder warning. I went out back to the bathroom as a way of stalling for time. Staring long and hard into the mirror I was amazed to see my face shrinking away from me. An image of an old woman appeared in its place. Like some warped

310

another song about love

Dorian Gray vision, I understood it to be a picture of myself as a junkie. Fear overwhelmed my desire for the blissful taste Matt was offering. I splashed cold water on my face, pressed it into a towel then carefully closed the bathroom door behind me.

'Ready, Babe?' Matt held the syringe up when I came in the door.

I shook my head. 'I can't do it, Matt.'

'What?' Matt was incredulous. 'But I've prepared it. You can't not use it.'

I continued shaking my head. I had no words, only fear. As silence prevailed, the gap between us appeared again.

'Oh well,' Matt said, 'I'll just have to have both myself.'

'Sorry,' I whispered and disappeared to the kitchen to make coffee. When I returned, Matt was lying back on the couch, eyes closed, mouth wide open – unconscious. Images of my mother lying comatose on the floor flooded my memory. Young as I was in those days, I knew what to do. This was different. I noticed the pulsing vein in his neck and the slight rise of his chest as he breathed. I tried to remember how to do mouth to mouth but I was too panicked. In frustration I shook him hard and he came round smiling. But his eyes were still vacant. A voice repeated in my head. Keep him awake. Keep him awake.

'Matt!' I yelled in his ear. 'Matt, wake up!' I slapped his face and he came round again, still smiling.

JANIE CONWAY HERRON

Over in the corner of the room the black curving shape of my guitar case gave me an idea. I snapped the case open and handed the guitar to Matt. He grabbed it clumsily, looking at it without comprehension.

'Play something for me,' I yelled.

'Don't know anything,' Matt mumbled.

'Yes, you do.' I grabbed an old nylon string guitar leaning against the wall and plunged into a simplified version of *Brown Sugar*. Matt's eyes flickered with a faint gleam of recognition. 'Play with me,' I coaxed and Matt's hands started forming the chords. We played the song for hours, loudly and energetically. Every time I tried something else, Matt nodded off. Returning to *Brown Sugar* woke him. The song became a violent mantra, capable of wakening the almost dead from their sleep. Grinning like an idiot and throwing his head back enthusiastically, Matt croaked out every chorus, while I played on. Scarlet Sisters' sweet, funky soul was insipid by comparison. Designed to seduce ganja smokers into dancing, it would never keep a junkie awake. As I kept playing, I enjoyed the angry chords and the dark, bleak sound of junkie aggression.

By five in the morning I was the one nodding off while Matt made coffee. At six thirty I kissed him goodbye. Huddled in the doorway, I looked out across the street, greeted by signs of early morning stirring in ordinary houses where people prepared for an ordinary day. I turned around and went back inside, ready to begin my own.

another song about love

Scarlet Sisters played their last gig to a packed house and as I looked out on the sea of faces in front of me I had an urge to yell, 'Why didn't you bastards come and see the band earlier!' Instead I greeted them with words that rang strangely true. 'It's great to see you all here tonight, thanks for coming.'

In the break, I mingled with the audience. A woman asked me why the band was breaking up.

'Because no-one came to see us,' I answered curtly.

'Really?' The woman looked incredulous. 'Such a great band. You shouldn't break up.'

'It's too late now.' As I said these words, I could feel tears banking up behind my eyes. I turned away and rushed towards the women's toilets but there was a queue. Brushing away tears, I headed to the stage. There was a secluded place behind the speakers where I could cry in peace. A sudden flurry of activity heralded the band getting ready for the last bracket. They'd been looking for me.

Anna knelt down in front of me. 'We've got to play the last bracket, Lillie.'

'I don't think I can.'

'You have to. You'll regret it if you don't. We all will.' Anna grabbed my hands and pulled me up to standing. 'Come on, we all need you to play.'

'It's only a band. Worse things can happen,' Stevie added, picking up his guitar and strumming a few loud chords. 'Come on Lil', let's play all the best songs.'

As Ali, Anna and Stevie launched into the intro of the first song, my feet moved to the rhythm. I closed my eyes, savouring the strength of the music we made. When I sang, the sound of my voice powering through the PA helped my strength return. I opened my eyes to see Vincent smiling behind the mixer. Beyond him was a déjà-vu vision of Matt, in his white suit coat and black T-shirt, just as I'd spotted him six months before. When a grin spread across his face I found it easy to smile back. I introduced the last song. 'This one's very close to my heart.'

'Yes folks,' Ali yelled through his microphone. 'Lillie will be releasing it as a solo single soon, so watch out for it in your local store.'

As I sang the first bars, the words I'd written only a few weeks ago seemed prophetic.

Everybody wants to be a number one.

Climb the top of the tree, a number one.

Well you know it don't matter when you're dead and gone.

Thrive on competition just to keep on keeping on.

When we finished, the audience kept on applauding and we played encores until the house lights were turned on.

another song about love

'I'm sorry folks, that's all we can do,' I yelled. In an impromptu rush of generosity, I added, 'But if you want to party on, we can all go back to my place. It's just round the corner.'

From across the stage Anna mouthed, 'What the fuck?' As we packed up our instruments, she asked. 'What on earth did you do that for? The boys will freak out if people get there before we do. It's bad enough that they've had to be there all night by themselves. Now we're going to foist a whole lot of drunken fans on them.'

'Yeah I know,' I answered as sheepish guilt crept over me. 'I just felt like celebrating an important occasion after such a good gig. I'll make sure I get there before anyone else.'

When Matt and I arrived home people were already there. When I rushed to the front door, Jesse flew out of his bedroom, closely followed by Sam and Antonia.

'Mum! What's happening?'

'They're from the pub, darling,' I placated him. 'We're having a bit of a party to celebrate the band breaking up.'

'But I thought you didn't want the band to break up.'

'I didn't, Jesse, but now that it has, I thought we may as well celebrate.'

'Can we come to the party too?'

'Of course, but if you want to go to sleep perhaps all three of you should hop into my bed. It's going to be really noisy in your room.'

'They're not going to be able sleep anywhere with so much racket going on,' Matt observed.

When Anna and Wendy arrived, Antonia ran into Anna's arms. 'We're having a party!' she announced gleefully, making me grateful for the small mercy her enthusiasm brought.

A group of women stood round the tape player in the lounge-room. As the opening bars of the song they'd put on began, the women danced and sang along in loud, out-of-tune voices.

I blocked my ears and headed for the kitchen.

'Who brought them?' Wendy asked.

'I don't know.'

I wish they'd turn that shit off. Can't we find something better to play?'

'The music's not that bad,' I answered. 'It's from my collection of sixties women singers. We grew up with this music remember? I used to love groups like The Chiffons and The Crystals and so did you, Wendy. These women were my first singing teachers.'

'Yeah and you still find the rebel men they sang about irresistible,' Wendy replied.

'You were a great fan of romance comics as well as the songs those women sang,' I replied. 'All those true confessions, all that awful sexual guilt.'

another song about love

'It never got any of us anywhere,' Wendy said and strode out of the room. Within seconds, the sixties music had stopped and the opening lines of a Bonnie Raitt song floated back into the kitchen.

Wendy returned, beaming. 'There you are, now that's pioneering music.'

'Much better,' Anna said as she danced towards Wendy. When the track ended, instead of another Bonnie Raitt song, the women's out-of-tune voices rose over the top of the sixties tape they'd put back on. This time it was Dusty Springfield singing *Wishing and Hoping.*

'This is outrageous.' Wendy headed towards the door again.

I blocked her. 'They'll stop soon, Wendy.'

'But I've spent a lifetime trying to get over that shit.'

'I'll drink to that.' Anna opened a beer before chorusing along with the girls in the lounge room.

When Ali and Stevie arrived, the band started its own party in the kitchen. As Stevie poured whiskies for everyone Ali announced Stevie had some news. Stevie downed his first whisky then told us that Frankie had asked him to join his band.

'Frankie's guitarist is going into the recording business with Vincent and giving up playing live.'

I downed my whisky and Stevie poured me another one. 'To the future, whatever it may bring,' I proclaimed and we clinked our glasses together. 'Congratulations Stevie, you deserve it.'

Stevie grinned. 'You deserve every success too, Lillie.'

'This calls for a change in the music,' Wendy said then strode into the lounge room. Soon, her loud, booming voice was singing along with Bonnie Raitt once more. Anna and I followed her out and started dancing. Then I noticed Jesse and Sam dragging sheets and blankets out of Jesse's room.

'Where are you guys going?' I yelled.

The boys stopped dead. 'We're going to sleep in your room like you said.'

'Okay,' I answered. 'If the music's still too loud we can turn it down.'

'No, it's not that,' Sam said. 'There're people in Jesse's room.'

'Well, ask them to leave.'

Jesse's face went bright red. 'But they're doing things.'

'They're kissing,' sniggered Antonia.

'Shut up!' Jesse yelled.

'Shall I ask them to leave?' I asked.

Jesse looked down at the floor. 'No, it's all right.'

'Come on, Jesse,' I insisted. 'It's your room. I'll tell them you don't want strangers in there.'

'But he asked me not to tell you.' Jesse crumbled to the floor.

'Who did?'

'Matt.'

another song about love

Cursing, I opened the door to Jesse's room with one swift movement. 'Hi, fancy meeting you here,' I greeted Matt as brightly as I could.

Matt and one of the sixties girls were sitting on the bed. The girl hurriedly adjusted her clothes as Matt spluttered, 'I was just showing Miriam the budgie.'

I watched the woman squirm as Matt tied himself in knots of explanation.

'We were deciding on a name, and you know what we decided to call her?' Matt chuckled. 'You'll like it, Lillie.'

'Try me,' I said.

'We thought Blue was a good name for her, after Frankie Brave's album. He's Miriam's favourite singer.'

I pointed to the front door, yelling, 'Out! Get out of my house, now!'

Miriam squeezed past me and quickly disappeared.

When Matt put his hand on my shoulder, I pulled away. 'Get out, will you!' I yelled. 'Get out of my life and don't ever come back!'

Matt headed toward the front door, nearly tripping over Jesse hiding under his blanket.

He turned to face me. 'You know I love you.' Matt looked like he might cry.

'You don't even know what love is,' I snapped, then slammed the door. When I turned around, a crowd of partygoers was staring at me. I picked Jesse up and held him close. 'End of the party, folks,' I announced. 'I'm going to put my son to bed.'

Next morning I surveyed the post-party disarray while Jesse was still asleep. Gathering empty bottles I stacked them outside then collected ashtrays overflowing with the butts of cigarettes and joints. What was I doing inviting so many people into my life and expecting Jesse to take it all in his stride? Why had I let Matt bring heroin into our lives when I'd vowed I'd never do such a thing? I'd always made a distinction between smoking ganja and white powders but out of a perverse need to please Matt, I had gone against my own judgment. I remembered my days with Joe. We had both been so pure back then, not smoking or drinking. How had all those ideals flown out the window? What Jesse really needed was someone he could look up to as a role model. All I'd done was bring a bunch of adolescents home. Things needed to change.

When that crazy budgie chirped loudly from Jesse's room, I knew exactly what the first change would be.

Early Monday morning I took the birdcage around the corner to Jesse's old kindergarten.

'Are you sure you don't want the cute little thing?' the head teacher asked, as she held the cage up and cooed.

'We already have a cat. It's too much of a risk.'

another song about love

'Yeah, cats and birds don't mix, do they? If you ever want to stop by and say hello...'

'Thanks. I will sometime,' I answered before hurrying home. With a bucket of soapy hot water and a scrubbing brush I cleaned the windowsill in Jesse's room. When every last drop of bird shit had gone, I felt satisfied.

14
LIFE GOES ON

WAITING FOR THE LIFT TO take me up to the hallowed sanctuary of the nineteenth floor, I saw my stunted reflection in its steel doors. I looked more like a circus freak than the heroine of the next big dance craze. In Geoff's office, I pressed my nose against the windowpane and watched the people below move along the pavement like a tribe of ants.

Geoff let his words out on a cloud of ganja. As he fired off the clichés he was so used to using, I found it hard to retrieve the moment of writing the actual song he was talking about. Smoke hung in the air as Geoff waved the joint in circles raving, 'It's wonderful, just marvellous! It could be a number one hit, just like the title. Ha, ha. Get it? I like it. I like it a lot. It's a real dance number. I think it would do well on the dance charts!' Geoff leant closer. 'But we've got to have a better angle to sell it. You got any ideas?'

I stared at Geoff's bloodshot eyes, trying to find an appropriate answer.

'I tell you what,' Geoff continued as he stubbed the roach out in an ashtray full to overflowing with butts. 'I'll send you out to Jules and she can make some appointments with publishers. If we get the dollars from them, we can present a record company with the finished product and get money to make the clip.' He ushered me out the door, yelling at Jules to make an appointment with Phil Lucas. 'You handle it, Jules,' he said. 'I don't think I'll have the time.' Jules nodded and continued talking on the phone while Geoff poked his head into the reception area. 'Is Frankie here? Send him in, will you?'

Frankie Brave appeared like a silent apparition, pale and big-eyed, a scruff of tousled hair falling over his eyes.

'How's Stevie going?' I ventured.

Furrows of thought moved across Frankie's forehead then recognition lit up his eyes. 'Oh, you mean our new guitarist.'

another song about love

I nodded.

Frankie smiled. 'He's going great. I'm glad you discovered him.'

'I miss him,' I replied.

'Stevie told me you're going solo. Is that what brings you here?'

'Yes, I've just been playing Geoff some demo tapes that I did with Scarlet Sisters.'

'Great little band you had there. I hope Geoff's going to do something good for you.'

On hearing his name, Geoff sprang into action. 'We sure are. I reckon *Number One* will be hot on the dance charts once we get a release.' Geoff grinned then steered Frankie towards his office and closed the door.

'We'll have to talk about image at this meeting,' Jules instructed me. 'We need something to project, something definite. We have to sell this thing, you know, so bring your ideas along. Next Monday arvo, two-thirty suit you?'

I nodded.

'I'll see you then,' Jules replied.

I hesitated, feeling there must be something else to say, but Jules was already busy with something else.

The following Monday, I sat by the window in Geoff's office as Jules pitched to Phil.

'We think Lillie's image should be womanly, but not too mature, somewhere in between,' Jules explained. 'We'll be working hard on the body too.

She'll need to lose weight. With exercise and beauty treatments and a new hairstyle, we'll have a more contemporary look that fits the style of the song. It's a wonderful dance number, don't you think? Of course we'll need some finance to carry this off professionally.'

Phil's reply came slow and easy. 'If you come up with an image for Lillie that suits, I'll come up with the dollars for the recording. You can't sell a song without an image. What about two grand down, as a guarantee of goodwill? I'll give you a month. Will that do?'

Jules was all smiles as we shook on the deal.

I'd been smiling so hard my face ached. There was no precedence in my life for this occasion. No protocol I could look up in a book titled, 'How To Handle Your First Record Deal'. I wanted to yell, 'Yippee!' but it felt more appropriate to stand at attention and salute. I mumbled something like, 'Glad you liked the song,' but Phil was already talking to Jules about the Frankie Brave deal.

I waved goodbye and descended once again to the street below. Jules was right. I needed to smarten up my image. With daily exercise and diet, I could lose weight easily. Determined to achieve my goal, I made a vow to myself and hummed it like a mantra over the rhythm of the tram on the tracks going home.

another song about love

Early next morning, I arrived at the city baths for my first swim. In the change room, I caught sight of my body in the mirror. The soft skin of my belly and breasts, the way my flesh moved as I walked, embarrassed me. I squeezed into my bathers and plunged into the pool. When the shock of the water cleared my head, I slowly swam the first lap to the other end.

Every morning for the rest of the week I arrived at the pool ready to do laps. The old red brick building made me feel like I was at school again and I took the front steps with increasing purpose, as the muscles in my legs grew stronger. At first one lap was all I could manage and I struggled to get to the other end. The next time I pushed myself harder and swam a little further, the next day a little further again. The rhythm of the strokes mesmerised me as I ploughed up and down, forgetting time and space, until I dragged myself up and over the side of the pool and sat on the edge. Soon I was swimming fifty laps a day. Attending the gymnasium at the pool as well, I lifted weights and took aerobics classes as often as I could. When I got home I cooked a nutritious meal for Jesse and me. Sometimes I didn't eat at all. Watching Jesse devour his food, I told myself it was good to miss a few meals and hasten the process of losing weight. Every morning I stood hesitantly on the scales and slowly lowered myself, sighing with relief at every kilo lost.

JANIE CONWAY HERRON

My house was quieter now. No band, no lovers. Even my friends had stopped calling round. René and Jemma rarely visited anymore. They'd set up such tight parameters around their life together, I felt as if Jesse and I were on the outside looking in. It made me envious. Watching René and Jemma's intimacy undermined my doubts about monogamy. Remembering how close I came to destroying my life trying to please Matt, I wondered why my need for approval made me do this. Wendy was insistent I give up on men and try being with a woman, but somewhere in the back of my mind I still had a rosy image of being with one man. That image made a lie of any pretence of being in a relationship with a woman or of having lots of lovers at one time.

René was full of good advice for me too. 'Be happy with the way you are, Lillie. In my country, we like big women. You are beautiful the way you are. Isn't she, Jemma?'

I was tempted to point out that Jemma was a skinny blond. Weeks went by without me visiting them.

Wendy was my main support. She regularly accompanied me to the pool and did laps with me. One day she brought out a camera. As I changed into my bathers the camera clicked in quick succession. I laughed as I posed, waist pulled in, breasts sticking out, waiting for the next click. Afterwards we paraded like comic fashion models, mincing our way to the

another song about love

edge of the pool where the other swimmers were doing laps. I looked down into the water as another swimmer stared back at me. Pausing for a second, he pushed himself off from the wall and swam out into the lane reserved for serious swimmers. I shrugged at Wendy then we dived in to start our own laps.

As we sat sipping juices after our swim, the serious swimmer appeared and asked if he could join us. 'My name is Pedro,' he said, winking at me as if I was part of some conspiracy.

Wendy was swift and acerbic in reply. 'Oh, so we have another Speedy Gonzales, do we? Did your parents call you Pedro because you're quick in the pool or fast on the uptake with women?'

Pedro was unfazed. 'Perhaps I'm a little of both,' he replied.

'I'm Lillie and this is my good friend Wendy, ' I gushed. 'Are you a regular at this pool?'

'I come here most days. I like the discipline. It helps with the unruliness of the rest of my life.'

'That's a good way to put it,' I answered enthusiastically. 'I imagine I'm coming here for the same reason.'

On the way home, Wendy berated me.

'I can't believe how you came on to that guy. What is it with you and men? You're like a siren beckoning the sailors in to shore.'

'Lay off, will you?' I protested. 'I was just having a bit of fun.'

'I know you Lillie. I saw how Pedro looked at you too. If he's a regular at the pool, you two will be thick as thieves in no time. When it's all over, it'll be me picking up the pieces, once again.'

'Christ Wendy, thanks for the vote of confidence,' I replied. 'I thought it was just a bit of flirtation.'

'You've got this great ideal that you spout all the time. All is fair in love and war. Everyone is civilised and just sleeps with each other, no strings attached. But that's not what I see. I think you're a serial monogamist.'

'A what?' I laughed.

'A serial monogamist is someone who goes from one lover to another, without looking back. That's what you are. You think you're some kind of free spirit just loving anyone you want, but you've been through a series of disastrous relationships since you split from Joe. Why don't you give yourself a rest for a while? When you do find someone you like a lot, man or woman – I don't care what – just take it slowly, okay?'

'Okay,' I replied. 'I'll try to take things slowly. You never know there might not be a next time.'

'And pigs can fly,' Wendy chuckled. 'I can't imagine you ever being alone for long.'

another song about love

It took me twenty minutes to struggle into the dress. Clinging tightly to my body, the material felt like a second skin. When I lifted my arms long hairs sprouted over the top of the material. I felt like a gorilla in a tutu.

Gingerly, I opened the door to Jules' office. Up the other end of the room, Jules and her dressmaker friend inspected me from top to toe.

'The hairy legs'll have to go,' Jules observed.

'And under the arms,' said the dressmaker.

I felt embarrassed. 'I can shave my legs if you like,' I offered. What would Wendy think of me now? She'd see me as a traitor to the women's movement for sure.

Jules had another solution, one that had never crossed my mind. 'We'll send you to a beautician for a wax. I'll make an appointment for next week just before we have our meeting with Phil. That suit you?'

At Veronica and Suzie's salon the following week, Veronica was in a chatty mood as she applied hot wax to my legs. 'We get all sorts in here, even men sometimes.'

'Really? Do you get to know them well?' I braced myself in wait for the next strip to be whipped quickly and deftly from my leg.

'Oh yes, it's such an intimate job. People tell you all their secrets.' Like ripping Elastoplast from a wound, Veronica removed the wax. I grimaced as she whipped off every piece of wax then picked off the small bits with tweezers. 'There you go, those legs look much better.'

I ran my hand down the silky-smooth expanse of coffee-coloured skin and felt pleased with myself.

'Last stages. Soon you'll be ready for the big presentation.' Susie angled the dryer over my head. 'Here, read this while your hair's drying.' She handed me a magazine. 'It might give you some inspiration.'

As I began leafing through, a page fell open at an article on Frankie with a close-up photo. He stared off into the distance, somewhere beyond the border of the photo, the angle of his head accentuating his jaw line. His shock of tangled hair was plastered down flat while the biceps of his tattooed arm were flexed. It gave him a deceptively muscular look that disguised his skinny frame. A well-placed headline read: 'FRANKIE BRAVES EUROPE'. Something about the picture lied. In spite of Frankie's name, he was fragile to meet, shy and indifferent, lacking the machismo this photo implied. I wondered whether he had gone through a change of image as profound as mine.

Susie pulled the dryer back and checked my hair. 'Nearly done. We'll do your face while we wait for your hair to dry a bit more.' Veronica pored over me with a pair of tweezers, plucking out the stray hairs between my eyebrows, while Susie got the makeup ready. They fussed over me for more than an hour, slowly transforming my face by blending colours to

another song about love

highlight the contours and accentuating the fullness of my lips, cheekbones and the lids of my eyes.

At the back of the salon, my clothes were all laid out; the fine black lace pantyhose, the suede dress and stiletto heels. This time I didn't have to struggle to fit into the dress. It fitted me like a glove, close but not too tight. I eased my feet into the high heels and did up the ankle strap. The shoes added inches to my height as I tottered back to the salon and sat down. Veronica and Susie set to work on my hair. Normally straight, my hair became a mass of black curls with a layer of bright red fanning out over the top. The sides and back had been shaved and sculpted. Susie cut a small hair here and there, plumped up one side and then flattened the other. Standing behind me, her hands on both sides of my chin, she checked the symmetry of her design in the mirror and nodded with satisfaction. As they gave me one final check Veronica and Susie whispered, 'Don't you look stunning? Aren't you our little star?'

Jules' assistant Tom came to pick me up. When he opened the door for me, his outstretched hand stopped me from falling. 'Come on,' he said, unaware of the fine line between chivalry and chauvinism. 'You'll have to get used to this when you're a rock star.'

I leant on Tom's arm and remembered Jules' words. 'Get the highest heels you can, your legs will look longer.' And I had.

'Just treat it like part of a performance,' Wendy advised as she helped me practise walking in heels with a book on my head. 'They practise walking like this in all the best deportment schools.'

I made it to the lift, with Tom there to steady me. We sailed up to the nineteenth floor, where Jules fussed around me, pulling my dress down, smoothing a crease here and there, before knocking on Geoff's door.

When he opened it, Geoff's jaw dropped.

Phil sat bolt upright. Forced by the dignity of the occasion, he stood up and extended his hand to me. 'How did you do it? You look so, uh...err...so different...so...o...'

I moved over to the window, turned deftly on my heels and faced them.

Geoff moved in closer. 'She looks that good and writes great songs too.'

For a long moment we all stood gaping at each other until Phil brought us back to the reason for being there. 'When can we sign the papers?' he asked.

Suddenly everyone was smiling and I felt something like joy rising from the pit of my stomach. With champagne corks popping, we made more plans. 'Overseas tours' … 'could be a hit in Europe.'.... 'Oh, yes for sure, I like it, great idea.' Pat, pat, grab, hold, kiss... Everyone in the office congratulated me. Someone had a camera. Click, click, I was frozen alongside Jules and Geoff in front of the gold records on the wall and pictures of other musicians beaming their success into the room. In almost all of them, Geoff or Jules was leaning on a shoulder, or shaking

another song about love

someone's hand. As the celebrations continued I sat down and pulled my shoes from my aching feet. When I massaged them, there was blood on my hands. It reminded me of another pair of shoes from long ago.

At fifteen I decided to return to ballet classes but not to the same ballet school. The academy had moved away from the city to a place too far for me to travel to after school. Michel Rosenthal recommended another school, run by a former dancing partner of his. Here in a class of other pubescent dancers, I prepared for my first point lesson. Flexing our toes and stretching our calf muscles, we pushed our feet into our new toe shoes. The wooden blocks inside my pink satin slippers encased my big toes so firmly they could take my full weight. I arched my foot, rose up on my toes, and pirouetted.

'Left, left, left, right, right ... plié, up, up, up on your toes,' the teacher shouted, clapping out the rhythm to the class with her small pink hands. 'Now glissé, left leg out, now bend, turn, up, up, up on your toes, now turn, clap, clap, clap.'

Over in the corner, a girl stopped dancing. She was crying, but the teacher kept yelling. 'No, no, no! You must not stop! Not until there's blood on your shoes!' When the class finished, I looked down at my aching feet. When I took my toe shoes off, the insides were stained red. But I was proud of the pain and the blood. This suffering for art was virtuous.

335

JANIE CONWAY HERRON

A few months later, Michel came to a class. I was excited to see my old mentor sitting up the front. He nodded and smiled at me as we gathered in one corner of the room and prepared to perform our individual dance pieces. When it was my turn, I took a deep breath and stepped out, leaping into my first jeté. Suddenly conscious of my budding breasts bouncing against my chest, I stumbled into a pirouette then stopped dancing. When I looked across at Michel, the expression on his face told me I was never going to be the dancer I wanted to be when I was a young girl. Feeling fat and ashamed, I ran from the class, from the look on Michel's face and from my dreams of becoming a ballerina.

Now I was dreaming a different dream. It was clearly within reach even if I was still suffering for my art. I put my high heels back on, pushed away the awful memories and turned to face the others celebrating my success. Smiling, I accepted another glass of champagne.

Every day after dropping Jesse off at school I arrived at the pool. When Pedro was there, our smiles shone across the water. Bodies glistening, we ventured closer to each other. Soon, we walked to Pedro's place, feet bouncing along the pavement. As we sat in his kitchen

another song about love

drinking coffee, I picked up an old guitar leaning against the wall, and played a few chords.

Pedro leant forward. 'Sing a song for me,' he asked. His look was intense, the intimacy between us exquisite.

As I sang, the words and melody danced over the chords I played. I looked up and Pedro's eyes were riveted on me.

'You are gorgeous you know that, Lillie? You sing and play beautifully and you're also extremely desirable.' He took my hand and led me down the hall to his bedroom. Slowly he removed all my clothes. As I stood there completely naked, Pedro's gaze travelled blatantly all over my body. Embarrassed, I stared at the floor.

'Look at me, Lillie,' Pedro commanded.

I looked up, barely able to maintain my gaze as Pedro took off his clothes. When he took out a condom from a bedside drawer my mortification was complete. 'I haven't used one of these in a long time,' I whispered.

'You should,' Pedro answered. 'We are living in dangerous times and a girl as free with herself as you are should make sure she is protected.' He pressed on my shoulders until I knelt in front of him then handed me the condom. Softly caressing him I rolled the condom over his erection. Pedro pulled me up and kissed me, first on the mouth then all over my body. I felt long and lean under his touch as desire slowly immersed me in intense passion. We lay together for a long time after making love, touching and talking, discovering each other's secrets.

When I told Pedro I was over thirty, he laughed.

'But I still feel like a teenager,' I added.

'You sure do,' Pedro answered and I was flattered.

That evening I lay in a bath at home, soaking in sweet-smelling water. I was pleased with the boniness of my hips and the way my belly fell away from them, flat and tight. When I put my feet up on the end of the bath and flexed my heels, the muscles in my calves pulled tight and smooth. There was no excess flesh at all.

Jesse leaned over the edge of the bath, playing on the surface of the water with his hands. 'You look weird, Mum,' he giggled.

'Why? Come on, out with it.' I flicked a thin spray of water at him.

'Your tits look thin and they float about in the water.' Jesse covered his face with his hands.

'So what should they look like?'

'Aw Mu-um!' Jesse's face turned scarlet.

'Come on, tell me.'

'They should be all, oh you know, like this.' Jesse mimed the shape of a voluptuous woman with his hands.

'You've been looking at too many girly magazines.'

'What magazines?' Jesse looked puzzled.

another song about love

'Magazines with lots of photos of naked women in them.'

Jesse grinned. 'You could be in one of those magazines, Mum.'

'No, I couldn't do that. It's too degrading.'

'Oh?'

'When something's degrading it makes you feel really bad.'

'Why do those women have their photos taken then?'

'I don't think they realise they feel bad until it's too late.'

Moving his hand across the surface of the water, Jesse watched the tiny ripples move towards the edge of the bath. 'I like it when you're not going out all the time like you used to.'

I flicked another small spray of water at him. 'I like it too, Jesse.'

A grin spread across Jesse's face and he slapped the water hard.

After some months of meeting at the pool, I brought Pedro home. I checked Jesse's reactions as the three of us spent the evening together. Always careful to include him in the conversation, Pedro paid great attention to what Jesse had to say. Jesse responded by opening up and sharing his world with Pedro. When the two of them stretched out on the floor, absorbed in Jesse's extensive *Marvel Comic* collection, Jesse rested his chin in his hands in the exact way Pedro did, laughed at every joke Pedro made, swaggered down the hall after Pedro as he took him for a drive to the all-nighter to buy milk.

When Pedro announced he was going home, Jesse's face fell. 'Can't you stay? Mum won't mind, will you, Mum?'

Pedro looked at me.

I swallowed hard. 'Pedro can stay if he wants to.'

Jesse grinned as Pedro answered, 'I'd really like to.'

Later that night Pedro offered me some speed. 'It will help you lose weight,' he said as he divided the white powder into lines on a mirror.

'I thought you liked me just as I am,' I protested. 'You're the one who insists that I don't need to lose weight.'

'Yes, but you're the one who thinks you still need to. You won't feel like eating if you have this, but you'll feel great.' He rolled a ten-dollar bill into a fine tube and tried to hand it to me.

I shook my head. 'If you want to use powders, use them away from my house. I don't want to know about them and I don't want them anywhere near Jesse The last time I used speed, I ended up spending an afternoon in a cop shop in Wangaratta where they charged me with possession. Luckily, they let me off with a fine and a bond for good behaviour. I swore off any white powders after that. They're too dangerous, too addictive. Ganja's different. It's far less harmful than alcohol in my opinion. Since being busted, I'm careful to never have any on me.'

Pedro kept offering me the rolled-up note. 'Trust me, you'll feel really good. I just like to have some every once in a while. There's no danger of getting addicted and I'd never do this in front of Jesse. I don't do needles or anything. I use it to get a bit high every now and then. Relax and enjoy. You won't regret it.'

In a moment of weakness, I decided to have some. Just this once, I told myself. It would be all right, especially if Jesse didn't know about it. Cautiously, I inhaled. Seconds later I couldn't stop smiling. Talking fast, I lay up close to Pedro as my dreams came flying out. Pedro listened intently. I could feel the tight smoothness of his body and the intensity of his desire as he held me close.

'I want to be an inspiration to you,' he whispered. Kissing my neck he murmured, 'I'll never let you go. I want to be with you forever.'

Secure in his declaration, I relaxed into the safety of Pedro's assurance. I didn't notice the fear behind it, or the tight wire of his affection closing in on me.

15

THE EAGLE SONG

THE STUDIO WAS COMPLETELY DARK when I arrived so I stood in the dim light near the mixing desk and waited for the others to arrive. Louis, my producer, had chosen this studio because it was one of the first in Australia to make the switch from analogue to digital recording. Inside the studio were separate booths for the drummer and vocalist, plus a grand piano and plenty of elbowroom for the rest of the musicians. Struck with admiration for anyone who could understand the array of buttons, slides, faders and digital delays on the mixing panel, I stretched my arms out along the edge of the mixing desk and tried to imagine spending my whole life in such a place. Some engineers did, never seeing daylight. That was the main difficulty, I decided. When a pasty face appeared in the doorway, I was certain it must belong to the sound engineer and I was right.

'Hi, I'm Theo. I'll be working with you today. Louis in yet?' He flicked a switch and the place flooded with light.

'No, just me,' I said, blinking in the sudden brightness. 'I thought I'd come early and check the studio out.'

'You're keen.' Theo continued turning on switches.

When Louis appeared accompanied by Josh, I snapped to attention. Josh's reputation as a drummer was legend.

'How're you going, man?' Josh's handshake was firm, his look direct. 'All ready for the big gig?'

'Yep,' I lied, as my nervousness increased.

'Yeah, me too,' Josh grinned. His cheerfulness was infectious, but it was hard to get used to Louis. This enigmatic, grumpy man was well respected in the music industry. I needed him to joke me along and give me confidence, but this was serious business for an up-and-coming producer. He was probably just as anxious as I was.

'Got a version of the song for me to listen to?' Josh asked.

344

another song about love

Theo slipped the demo on and my heart leapt into my mouth. Josh listened attentively at first, then halfway through the song he grinned. 'Wow, this is fantastic! Trevor and I can play something really funky on it. Yeah, I dig it.'

I laughed with relief.

Bass player Trevor jammed on the feel with Josh until they got it right. When Rossco joined in with some funky guitar licks, I could hardly believe what I was hearing. My simple song sounded amazing. Even Louis managed to smile. Toes were tapping as we listened back to the track. My dreams were becoming a reality at last. I had to pinch myself to remember that it was me, Lillie Bloom, in the studio with some of the best musicians in the country. That evening, I sprawled out on the back seat of a taxi as it cruised through suburban streets with my song playing incessantly in my head. Light rain fell and the car tires hissed through the puddles, the wipers echoing the beat of the song we'd been working on all day.

At home, the house was in darkness apart from a thin sliver of light filtering out from under Jesse's bedroom door. Jesse was asleep, curled up under the blankets, while Pedro lay fully clothed on top of the covers, his snores blowing at the pages of the *Star Wars* comic lying across his face.

Recently Pedro had been staying at my place most evenings. We hadn't discussed his moving in but more and more of his possessions had appeared at my house. Pedro's big soup pot appeared one night when he'd decided to cook for us. His doona arrived when the winter cold set in. His favourite music and most of his clothes also arrived in bits and pieces. Pedro enjoyed the feeling of family that Jesse and I provided, and I was relieved to have Pedro's companionship, particularly on nights like this when I had to work late. Knowing there was someone I could trust to look after Jesse made all the difference.

I tugged at Pedro's sleeve. When he opened one eye I put my fingers over my lips and lead him into the bedroom. We lay together, talking. Pedro wrapped his arms around me while I told him all about the recording session, savouring every detail of what had happened.

I practised my vocals daily, singing along to the backing tracks Louis had dubbed off. He wanted me to sing the song an octave lower. It wasn't easy. The lower notes in the original melody were hard for me to reach but Louis insisted I'd been singing out of my range for most of my life. All those years of reaching for the high notes – the measure of being a good female folk singer – had been a mistake. I decided to change the melody, leaving out the lowest notes altogether.

At the vocal session the following week I felt so unsure of myself Pedro came with me for support. But as soon as we were in the studio, I became overly conscious of him sitting next to me holding my hand.

another song about love

Louis was in an unusually jovial mood, falling into easy banter with Theo as they set up for the vocals. He turned towards me. 'You ready, Lillie?'

I peeled my hand out of Pedro's and made my way into the vocal booth.

'Now I want you to sing the song in as many different ways as you can,' Louis instructed. 'We'll record each version separately and then mix down the best bits from each take. I've worked this way before and it's a good method. We often pick up on some really spontaneous things. We'll play it through a couple of times, and then try for the first take. Alright Lillie, here comes the countdown.'

When the verse started, I began singing. Two bars into the song, Louis interrupted me. 'Hold on there Lillie, you've changed the melody.'

My pulse rate went up so high I could hear my own heart beat in the headphones. 'I can't get the low notes when I start down an octave,' I stammered.

Louis mumbled something inaudible and then said loudly. 'Yes you can, just go for it. We can drop in the low parts later.'

'Okay, I'll try.' I waited for the song to start up again, then sang the original melody as Louis had instructed. On some of the low notes, my voice almost disappeared but I struggled to the end.

Louis seemed pleased. 'Good one, Lillie. Now try singing along with yourself.'

As I sang along with my own voice, I couldn't decipher whether I was hearing what I was currently singing or what had already been recorded. I tried for the lower notes and one or two times I got them.

'And again,' Louis instructed.

By the third time, I was used to Louis' way of working. He asked me to sing a third above the melody, then the next time a fifth, until we reached an octave above the way I had originally sung it.

Louis invited me into the mixing booth and played all the tracks through one by one while explaining his method. 'We'll mark down all the best bits from each track and then mix them onto a separate track. I want you to listen through and tell me which ones you like the best.'

By the time I'd listened to the third and fourth tracks, I wasn't sure which one I liked or even which take I'd been listening to. Watching Theo taking elaborate notes for Louis, I understood why they made such a great team. But this team was used to having the final say. Although they tried to include me, the final decision usually came down to either Theo or Louis. As they argued over the finer points of different takes, I didn't have the confidence to argue about the quality of my voice or any other aspect of my singing. I sat silently next to Pedro while the dynamic duo completed a final mix-down for the day.

On the way home, I asked Pedro what he thought. When he didn't answer, my anxiety grew.

'Pedro, I asked you a question,' I said as calmly as I could.

'And I heard it.'

another song about love

'Well?'

'Well, what?'

'What the hell do you think?'

'What the hell does it matter what I think?'

'It matters a lot.'

'I didn't like it.'

'Didn't like what?'

'I didn't like the way you ended up sounding.'

'What didn't you like?'

'I don't know. I'm not a musician I'm a carpenter. I just think those guys were playing games and you let them walk all over you.'

'Playing games?' I laughed. 'Louis and Theo are professionals.'

'So why ask me? What the hell would I know?' By the time Pedro pulled into the curb outside my house we were both yelling.

'I wish you'd never come to the bloody session,' I shouted and slammed the car door.

'The feeling's mutual, darling,' Pedro snarled, before putting the car into gear and taking off up the street, screeching tires echoing his anger.

'Bastard,' I muttered and slammed the front door. Exhausted, I got into bed. Pulling the covers up around ears still ringing with the sound of my own voice, I fell asleep. I woke to Jessie's gentle tap on my shoulder.

'It's only me, Mum,' he said quietly. 'Pedro picked me up from Sam's place after school. We brought some dinner home for you.'

JANIE CONWAY HERRON

Pedro had laid the table. All traces of his anger had gone and his constant smile forced me to smile in return. 'I thought you might like a pizza from our favourite restaurant.' As Pedro pulled out a chair for me, I wondered if Jesse had sensed the tension between us. I looked from Pedro to Jesse, feeling trapped by the apprehension in their eager smiles as they waited for me to start eating. I smiled back and picked at my food. Both of them ate heartily, not noticing my anxiety.

I watched as Jules, Geoff and Phil listened to the mix of the song. Phil and Jules were frowning but Geoff was smiling.

'It's lost some of the original quality of the song, the bouncy light feel it used to have,' Phil said. 'What's happened to the vocals? They don't seem to stand out like before.'

I held back a sigh. I agreed but I didn't know what to do about it.

Phil did. 'I think we should remix the vocals. Bring them up front more. They just don't stand out enough. Don't you agree?'

Now it was Geoff's turn to frown. 'We don't want to blow out the budget on a remix, do we?

Phil was adamant. 'It definitely needs one. If we sell it to a record company, we'll make our money back.'

another song about love

Geoff eased back into his seat. 'So long as you realise that Jules and I don't have any money to put into it.'

A bemused smile spread across Phil's face. 'Don't worry, Geoff, I'm familiar with the way you work.'

'So what's the plan, boys?' Jules interjected. 'We have to get this girl working. It's no use waiting until we get record company interest. We need to move on it now.'

Geoff was unperturbed. 'Get the agency to work on it. Start local, then tour nationally.'

'But she needs a band for that,' Jules replied.

Geoff turned to me. 'What about the guys who played on the record? Could they play with you?'

Surprised by the thought of playing with such professionals I whispered, 'They'd need to be paid, though.'

'Of course they'll get paid!' Geoff roared. 'We won't be sending you out for peanuts. We're not that cheap.'

When the second mix was complete, Louis dubbed it off for me.

'I hope you're happy. Play it to Geoff and Phil. Make sure they give the nod, then you can start flogging the song to the record companies. Be careful of Geoff, though. He's got a habit of leaving people high and dry,' Louis advised.

'But he and Jules are getting me gigs,' I replied.

'So they should. That's their job. They'll be making sure they get their cut of any action. It's up to you to make sure you get yours.'

I steered the conversation towards something more positive. 'I enjoy playing. I can't wait to start doing gigs again.'

'Since Frankie got his new line-up, Josh and Trevor are looking for some live gigs,' Louis answered. 'I'll give you Josh's number.' He scrawled out a phone number and handed it to me.

I folded the note up carefully and put it in my purse. 'Thanks, I really appreciate that.'

'Give us a ring when you're ready to record your first album.'

'That'd be a dream come true,' I laughed.

'You're a good songwriter,' Louis replied. 'You should really be making albums not singles. Keep hold of the dream and it'll come true one day.'

I spent most of that evening hovering near the telephone. Finally I rang Josh's number but hung up before anyone answered.

Pedro looked up from the television. 'Who was that you were ringing?'

Without knowing why, I lied. 'I was ringing Wendy, but she's engaged.'

'Looking for someone to gossip with, are you?' Pedro mimed a mouth opening and closing with his hand.

another song about love

I chose not to answer him. I wasn't going to let an argument with Pedro spoil my day.

The next morning, Pedro worked early shift and Jesse had left for school by eight-thirty. I waited until ten before ringing Josh.

A sleepy male voice answered the phone.

I swallowed hard. 'Sorry, did I wake you up?'

'Yeah, but that's okay. Who's speaking?'

'Lillie, Lillie Bloom.'

'Oh hi, Lillie. Good to hear from you.'

I had rehearsed small talk, but nervousness made me get down to business. 'I was talking to Louis about getting a band together and he said you might be interested. He gave me your phone number, I hope that's okay.' In the silence that followed I could hear my breathing resonate in the earpiece.

'Might be, might be really interested,' Josh answered.

'Really?' I forgot to hide my amazement.

'Yeah. Why not? I haven't got much on. Since Frankie went to Europe I haven't been playing many live gigs. One thing, though.'

'What?'

'Trevor and I are a package. I don't like playing with any old bass player.'

'I was going to ask you about that.'

'We make a pretty cool rhythm section.'

'You all made short work of the session the other day.'

'I'm very partial to that sort of feel. Rossco might be interested too. He doubles on sax and he told me he really enjoyed what we did the other day. Give me a couple of days and I'll get back to you. We could have a pretty hot band here.'

By the time Pedro came home, my excitement was stoked even further by a phone call from Josh to say that Trevor and Rossco were interested.

I skipped around Pedro as he unpacked his tools. 'I can hardly believe it, Pedro. All my dreams are coming true at last.'

'That's great, Lillie,' Pedro replied, but the tone of his voice implied something else.

'What's wrong?' I asked.

'Nothing.'

'Don't you want me to get a band together?'

'Why does everything have to revolve around you?' Pedro snapped the television on and turned the sound up loud.

'It doesn't,' I yelled.

'Well, shut up then.'

I didn't speak to Pedro for the rest of the evening. Throwing him the occasional hurt look, I concentrated on hiding the conflict from Jesse as I served them both dinner. After saying good night to Jesse, I soaked in a long, hot bath and went to bed. When Pedro slid under the covers I pretended to be asleep, stiffening as he tried to pull me close.

another song about love

In the morning, I got Jesse off to school and headed for the pool. The strong regular stroke of the laps dissolved the tension churning inside me.

'We've got a bite from Desert Records,' Jules rang to inform me.

'From Derrick?'

'Yeah. He said you went to see him in Sydney. He's really impressed with the new song. He's going to be in Melbourne on Friday. Can you make it into the office?'

'Sure,' I answered, feeling slightly disappointed. With all the talk of overseas promotion, I'd imagined signing with a bigger company.

'How's the band going?' Jules asked.

'Really good, we're rehearsing at my place on the weekend.'

'Good girl, I'll book some gigs for next month. A few good supports should generate some interest.'

At the mere mention of supports, my heart sank again. 'These guys are used to getting paid real money, not peanuts.'

'You can't go out for top dollar straight away, Lillie. We'll get as much for you as we can, but you have to remember you're a virtual unknown.'

JANIE CONWAY HERRON

I scribbled dollar signs on the note pad next to the phone. 'I do have fans, Jules. Scarlet Sisters was a really popular band. We always went over well.'

'We're aware of your popularity, that's what we're building on. There's no use putting you out for too much. They just won't book you.'

The following morning I sat drinking a short black coffee while furtively checking my make-up in a pocket mirror. I'd abandoned the tightly fitting dress and the high heels, opting for a red and white T-shirt, black jeans, boots and leather jacket. I fluffed out the bottom of my hair and put more lipstick on before walking down Collins Street.

Derrick stood up as soon as I walked into the room.

'She's looking good, isn't she?' Jules commented.

'Err, yes.' Derrick sat back down.

'So you liked the new version of my song?' I gave him a warm smile.

'Yes, I do, and I'm glad to see you took my advice and went solo. Those session musos are top players.'

'The bass player and drummer are in my band now.'

Derrick was impressed. 'So when are we looking at releasing?' As he said this, I realised Jules and Derrick had been involved in a lot of prior dealing without consulting me. They were well into the bargaining stage.

'What kind of deal are you offering?' I asked.

'A one-off distribution deal with an option; we're a small company but we do well for our clients.' Derrick beamed at me then stood up and dusted himself off. The action signified the meeting was over. 'I'll leave you two lovely ladies to talk then you can get back to me.' When Jules hustled him towards the door he turned towards me. 'I'm here for a few days. Perhaps we can meet again after you've had some time to think it over.'

'What do you think?' Jules asked me after Derrick left.

'I was hoping for something better, I think.'

'You can't hope for much better on a first deal. A smaller company is going to do more for you. You need the personal approach when you're just starting out.'

I wanted to point out that more than ten years' experience wasn't exactly starting out, but it seemed like an admission of failure.

Jules rang Phil to explain the deal, then handed me the phone.

'What are your feelings on this, Lillie?' Phil's warm voice on the other end of the phone was reassuring.

'I'm not sure. I guess I was hoping for something bigger.'

'Ditto, but Jules is right. This is only the beginning. Desert Records are as reputable an independent as you'll get.'

'So what do you think?'

After a long pause, Phil said. 'I think it's as good as we're going to get.'

'So you think I should sign.'

'That's my advice. It's up to you, though. You're the artist.'

'Okay,' I replied, but I wasn't at all sure it was the right thing to do.

For the first rehearsal, I borrowed a PA from Anna and set it up in the lounge room. Conscious of my poverty, I spent the whole morning cleaning. I scrubbed the old linoleum in the hall on my hands and knees until it shone, dusted the shelves, even cleaned the windows. I moved all the furniture against the walls, clearing as large a space as possible for the band. Pedro arrived just as I was putting the finishing touches to a flower arrangement on the kitchen table.

'What's the occasion?' he asked.

I sensed suspicion in his voice. 'Josh, Trevor and the guitarist are arriving for rehearsal any minute. It's our first rehearsal and I really want it to go well.'

'Oh, I see. So, we're impressing the boys with flowers are we?'

another song about love

I let his comment fall into silence.

But when Josh, Trevor and Rossco arrived, Pedro offered beers all round, shared the joint that Trevor rolled, even helped set up. By the time they were ready to rehearse, Pedro had endeared himself to all three men.

'What shall we start with?' Trevor slapped the bass and started playing a riff. Josh came in with a rhythm and they fell easily into jamming together. Rossco joined in adding a funky melody, his spidery body swaying over the guitar in time to the rhythm the three of them set up. I hesitated, trying to find the right key.

'A minor, the same as *Number One*,' Trevor yelled. Right on cue, they shifted into the opening bars of the song we had just recorded and carried me off with them.

By the end of rehearsal we had the basics of most of the songs worked out. Trevor rolled another joint, while Pedro brought out more beer.

'A few more rehearsals and we'll be ready to rock and roll.' Trevor took a long toke on the joint and passed it to Pedro.

'The agency says they're going to start booking gigs for us,' I replied.

'Really?' Rossco looked surprised. 'Who's doing your bookings?'

'Jules and Geoff.'

'Louis told me they were managing you.' Josh frowned.

359

'Don't you like them?'

'Put it this way, I've known a few people who got burnt.'

'They've got me a record deal.'

'Yeah? Who're you signing with?'

'Desert Records.'

Josh and Trevor broke into laughter. 'So Derrick's signed you, has he?'

'You know him?'

'Derrick, Trevor and I had our first band together. Derrick was the singer, but I think he makes a better record company director.'

'So you think he's all right?'

'You could do worse.'

When Jesse arrived home, he walked over to Josh's drums, tapped the snare and looked around.

'Play a bit, do you?' Josh asked casually.

'A bit.' Jesse beamed.

'Want to have a jam?' Josh picked up Trevor's bass.

Trevor lifted Jesse onto the seat then handed him some sticks. He held the sticks up in the air waiting for the band to start, while his feet dangled from the stool. Josh and Rossco broke into a simple riff and Trevor picked up my guitar. When Jesse began tapping on the symbol nearest to him it was perfectly in time.

'Hey, this boy's got good rhythm,' Josh declared as Jesse changed to the snare and kicked the

another song about love

bass drum with his foot. With Trevor and Josh's encouragement, he even attempted a few faltering rolls on the toms. He kept the rhythm going, concentrating hard until he came to a stumbling stop.

Trevor shook his hand. 'Hey man, that was good. Nice playing with you.'

Bursting with excitement, Jesse wriggled off the stool and looked across at me, his chest puffed up with pride.

'Yeah, we'll have to do it again,' Josh joined in. 'Keep that up and you'll be playing with your mum in no time.'

'Really?' Jesse looked ready to believe anything.

'In a few years you'll be putting me out of a job if I'm not careful.'

I stood back and looked at my signature on the page, the curl of the 'L', the neat circle over the 'i'. Jules took a photo of Derrick and I holding it.

As the flash bulb went off, Derrick took out his wallet and asked where the nearest pub was.

At a wine bar on Collins Street, Derrick ordered two bottles of sparkling and put them on the table. 'Time to celebrate,' he yelled, as the cork flew into the air. 'To a great future for us all.' He raised his glass.

JANIE CONWAY HERRON

After hours of drinking, only Jules was sober. As we stood swaying together on the corner, a voice inside my head told me I should ring home but I was too drunk to make the call. I sat in front as Jules drove through the city streets. Derrick leaned over from the back, falling all over us both. When Jules dropped me off, Derrick stumbled out of the back seat and fell against me. His hands were all over me.

'I really like you, Lillie,' he drawled. 'I think we'll make a great team.'

I pushed him away and Jules opened the front passenger door just in time to catch Derrick before his legs gave way. I closed the door and stumbled back onto the nature strip as Jules revved the engine and roared away.

When I burst into the lounge room waving the contract above my head, Pedro turned off the television.

'Where the hell have you been?'

'I've been signing the record contract. You knew that.'

'Like hell.' Pedro's voice was quietly menacing.

'Where's Jesse?' I tried to sound sober and responsible.

'He's staying over at some new friend's place. He rang earlier to see if it was alright. I said you'd ring when you got back, but he's probably in bed now.'

I tried to peel back the layers of alcohol, to make sense of the dark look on Pedro's face as he

another song about love

loomed towards me. When his open hand made sharp contact with my cheek, the contract slid out of my hand and fluttered to the floor.

'Bastard!' I yelled, my anger rising in a swift sudden surge. Then Pedro hit me again. Shocked into silence, I watched him move round me like a boxer in a ring, his face contorted with rage, his fists raised, as if he expected me to hit back. I stood still for a long moment then, eyes fixed on his face, bent down and picked up the contract. Transfixed, Pedro stood there, knees bent, fists still raised. I turned away from him, walked down the hall and shut the bedroom door.

I woke the next morning to the sound of the telephone. Pedro opened the bedroom door and held out the phone.

'It's for you.'

When I sat up, a sharp pain stabbed at the side of my face. I stood naked and shivering, trying to listen to Jules.

'I'm a bit worried about getting the money for a film clip. The contract with Desert Records is only for distribution, there's no money in it for publicity.'

'What about Phil?' I pressed the painful spot on my cheek.

'He's already put up the money for the recording. I don't think he'll be too pleased about fronting for the clip after paying for that second mix.'

'Can't you ask him?' I felt for broken teeth.

'Alright, if that's what you want. See if you can dig up some friends who can help you out, then call me back.' Jules hung up and I put the phone down.

Pedro was leaning against the wall. 'You know what?' he sneered.

'What?'

'You're getting too skinny.'

'Never.' I brushed past him, got back into bed and waited for the sound of his footsteps to disappear down the hall. Instead, I felt the pressure of his weight on the bedclothes.

'Lillie,' Pedro whispered.

I didn't answer.

'I promise not to hit you again.' Pedro pulled back the bedclothes and I cringed. 'I love you, Lillie,' he pleaded.

I closed my eyes.

'Do you love me?' Pedro persisted.

'Sometimes,' I replied, opening my eyes and trying to smile.

With Wendy and Anna's help, we were able to get the clip together for next to nothing. Driven by necessity I borrowed money, goods and time from friends. My parents chipped in too, sending me a generous cheque and best wishes for my success. Amy, a graduate from film school, offered to direct the clip, Wendy offered to do lights, while a student friend of Amy's offered to be on camera. Even Susie said she'd do makeup and wardrobe 'just for the fun of it.'

Pedro took a week off work to design and build the set. The more he helped, the less he felt threatened by my music career. The backyard of the house filled with the bits and pieces he'd collected. He worked late into the night happy to feel needed.

On the night before the shoot I found it impossible to sleep and sat up, watching Pedro work. By six o'clock in the morning I still hadn't slept.

Pedro prepared me a line of speed. 'There's plenty more of this to keep you going,' he said cheerfully as he beckoned me over to a tiny mirror.

As I leant over, I caught sight of my reflection. The angle accentuated the shadows under my eyes and for a moment I felt alarmed at the sight of the dark hollows staring back at me. 'I hope I look better on video,' I laughed, as the speed hit my nostrils.

The warehouse where the shoot was taking place was a hive of activity. Wendy waved at me from high up in the roof where she was hanging the last of the lights and I waved back enthusiastically.

'Ready for the big day?' Amy's young face beamed. Her vitality would inspire the cast of extras who had rung since word circulated that I needed volunteers to be dancers in a nightclub.

Amy took my arm. 'We've set up a dressing room for you over here. If you need anything, just give us a yell.' Then she disappeared, leaving me alone in a neon-lit corner. At one end a table was spread with cosmetics. A mirror, surrounded by light bulbs, threw out such harsh light the room disappeared into black behind me, leaving an image of my gaunt face staring back at me. When Susie's smiling face appeared beside me, she looked like an angel, her wild blond hair making a halo round her head.

'I've come to put the finishing touches on your transformation.' Her voice sounded hollow as if it was coming from a long way off. She got out the leather bodice I'd had made especially for the clip. The tight fit was designed to push my breasts up and accentuate my cleavage. As Susie pulled the laces at the back in as tight as she could, I lifted my breasts into the shallow cups. In the short space of time since my last fitting I had lost so much weight that the bodice was too big. The stiff bones made it stand out and my breasts fell onto my chest like deflated balloons.

'You're getting too thin,' Susie hissed as she stuffed tissues underneath my breasts so there was a hint of cleavage.

I stood sideways and looked at myself in the mirror, running my hands over my stomach, watching my legs as I pulled back my skirt. I had an image. For the first time since I was a young girl, it was one I liked.

Out in the warehouse, the final touches to the set were completed. A surreal dance club had been created. Not in my wildest dreams had I imagined it could look so good. Dozens of smiling faces greeted me as the extras milled around the set, waiting for the action to begin.

'Hey!' A voice called from above me. High up in the scaffolding, Wendy and Pedro were adjusting the last of the lights. A shaft of pink light fell around me and their faces disappeared into the darkness of the roof. I blew a kiss and walked out into the middle of the floor. I was ready. The music began and I walked towards the camera, smiling into the huge lens as it followed me. As I mimed the song I knew so well, I remembered the dancer inside me. My grace had returned. I was multi-coloured, bright as a shooting star.

In an interview for a magazine, a journalist asked me how I felt being moulded to an image. I hesitated, remembering an old self who'd have rebelled against the idea. But I felt differently now. I enjoyed fitting an image. It was only a surface impression. The real Lillie existed in my songs.

On the way home from the interview, I was startled by a dark shadow over my head. When I looked up, a giant eagle was hovering above me. Its piercing stare stopped me in my tracks as it landed on the chimney of the house next door. I smiled as I thought of days on the beach with my mother, her whispering shells and her great love for those majestic birds. I pictured Mum standing on the balcony of her seaside home, searching the ocean with her binoculars for the beautiful soaring birds. If only I could get on the next plane and be by her side. But I had another life now, a thousand miles away from my parents. There was no time to go visit them. When I waved at the bird its wings fluttered and it hopped from one foot to another.

Neither Jesse nor Pedro had come home so I went into the lounge room and took my guitar out of its case. I could feel a new song taking shape. As my hands flew over the fret board the notes fell into place. By the time Jesse came home from school I had a melody and chords plus a rough draft of the words.

'Did you see the eagle outside?' I asked as he dumped his school bag on the table and came over for a hug.

'No. What eagle? Eagles don't live in the city, do they?'

'I couldn't believe it myself. It was sitting on the roof, staring at me.'

'That's scary.' Jesse pulled in closer.

'The eagle doesn't want to hurt you, silly. It's got better things to do.' I wrapped my arms around him. 'Shall we go look for it?'

Jesse rushed out the front door and looked up into the sky but the eagle had gone. We headed towards the shops in search of the beautiful creature. As dusk descended we turned back towards home,

another song about love

disappointed. When we turned into our street, Jesse stopped and pointed at the roof of our house. The eagle was sitting on top of the chimney. Stealthily we crept up to the fence.

'How come he's here?' Jesse asked.

'I don't know, perhaps he got lost and he's trying to find his way home.'

'He must be lonely all by himself. Perhaps we could get him to come inside.' Jesse put on his best wide-eyed pleading look as he tugged my sleeve.

'We can't do that, Jesse. He's a wild animal. He needs to be out in nature. Besides you have a cat. Cats and birds don't mix, remember?'

'Oh, yes, I forgot about that,' Jesse replied.

'It might pay us a visit every now and then,' I comforted him. 'Give him a wave and see what he does.'

Jesse waved as hard as he could. The eagle turned, fixing us both with a piercing one-eyed stare and began dancing, its gigantic wings held at half mast.

Later that evening I told Pedro about seeing the eagle. Riding the wave of my own enthusiasm, I tried to raise his interest. 'I even started to write a song about it. It's called, *The Eagle Song*. Do want to hear it?'

'Another time maybe,' Pedro sighed. 'It's late and I've been doing hard labour all day. I just need some time out.'

As Pedro turned on the television, I swallowed my disappointment and curled up on the couch next to him. When I woke some hours later, Pedro had gone to bed. Quietly I slipped into Jesse's room and crawled in beside him.

After the film clip was completed, Pedro started sulking again. Our moods see-sawed up and down like ill winds blowing in and out of each other's lives. As Pedro drove me to rehearsal one evening we travelled in silence but the air sparked with the tension of unsaid things. When I reached over and rested my hand on Pedro's leg, he muttered something under his breath that sounded like a threat.

'What's wrong?' I asked, my voice thick with a cold adding to the tightness in my chest.

'Nothing. Fucking nothing!' Pedro snarled. 'Just leave me alone.'

'Okay, I will then,' I withdrew my hand and leant my hot head against the car door.

Pedro screeched to such a sudden stop that my head hit the dashboard. 'Get out, will you! I'm sick of being your fucking lackey. You treat me like one of your handbags, just taking me out when you need me,' he yelled. 'Get yourself to rehearsal for a change!' When I got out of the car, Pedro drove off through a puddle and water sprayed all over me. Walking straight ahead, I watched his taillights disappear into the distance. When he returned he pulled up alongside me and beckoned me into the car with his head. I felt like a streetwalker being picked up. As I got into the car

another song about love

Pedro apologised, adding that he didn't want to be angry with me.

'But what can you expect when you act like that?'

'Like what?'

'You know.'

'No, I don't know.'

'Yes, you do.'

'Look, I don't!'

'Oh, forget it, will you. Here, put this jumper on. We'd better get you to rehearsal. You'll be late now.'

At rehearsal I feigned cheerfulness. 'Sorry I'm late, but I've come down with this awful flu. I guess you're all ready to go now, huh?' I quipped. As I plugged into my amp I whispered to Pedro. 'You wouldn't have any of that speed, would you?'

'Nah,' Pedro answered, as he reached into his bag, 'but take some of these, they'll make you feel better.'

I swallowed the tablets with a gulp of whisky. The warmth hit my aching chest and spread out into my body as I launched into the first song.

Pedro crouched in the corner watching me, waiting for me to smile or glance towards one of the other band members. I closed my eyes and soared away from his prying gaze, playing louder, sinking into the music and making it swirl around me. When the song finished, Pedro had gone.

371

At the end of rehearsal, Josh asked me if I needed a lift home.

'It looks like I might need one,' I shrugged. 'Thanks.'

As we drove through the rainy night, Josh tapped a rhythm on the wheel of his car in syncopation with the steady beat of the windscreen wipers.

'You okay?' I asked.

'Yeah, sure.' Josh kept tapping.

I leant forward so that I could see his face. 'No, you're not. You never play badly but your heart wasn't in the music this evening.'

Josh avoided my gaze but his words were frank. 'You're right. I just don't think the band is firing at the moment. It's because you're not on top of things.' Josh turned towards me, eyebrows lifted in inquiry.

'You're right,' I answered quietly, 'but I haven't got a solution right now.'

Josh slowed down and pulled up outside my house. 'Take it easy, Lillie. You're too strung out. You'll burn out if you're not careful. You're getting to be skin and bone too.' He paused, looking directly at me. 'The band's counting on you, not me. You can get a drummer any old time. Take more care of yourself. Don't let Pedro get under your skin. Too much speed's making him paranoid, that's all.'

I pulled my guitar over the back seat and got out of the car. Blowing Josh a kiss through the car

another song about love

window I caught a glimpse of Pedro's face in my bedroom window. Then the curtain dropped.

Within a few days Pedro was yelling at me again, standing right up close, his face twisted with anger. This time it was about the way I looked at men, leading them on, flirting with them. I yelled back, pointing furiously at my chest where my wildly beating heart was hurting far too much. With the other hand, I swept everything off the mantelpiece and sent it crashing to the floor. I threw things round the room. Objects crashed and bounced off the walls. When Pedro threw himself on top of me I broke free of him and ran out into the street. People stared as they drove past, but nobody stopped. Running blindly, I arrived back home to find the house was silent. Pedro had disappeared.

All the fight had left me. I stared at the mess then started cleaning up. When I'd finished, I sat by the kitchen window and let the sun warm my aching bones.

When Jesse came home from school, I could see fear in his face. I knew I looked awful, my eyes dark, my face pale, my top lip swollen and a big purple patch on my cheek. When I tried to stand up, I had to hold my back like an old woman.

'Pedro and I had a little fight,' I explained as I picked up the telephone. 'How about you go and stay with Sam and Antonia tonight?'

JANIE CONWAY HERRON

'No!' Jesse screamed. 'I want to stay with you! I need to look after you.'

I held him tight to comfort him. When he'd gone to sleep, I rang Wendy.

'What's wrong, Lil'?' Wendy's voice strained through my sobs.

'Can you come over?'

'Now?'

'Please?'

I left the front door open and curled up at one end of the couch. When Wendy arrived, she coaxed the story out of me.

'How long will it take you to realise you need to stop everything? Stop right now,' she advised. 'Not in two months' time, after you've done this or that gig. Take a look in the mirror. You look like a ghost.'

'But I can't stop.' I've come too far to give up now. I've got the record launch and all that publicity to do. They're even talking about a national tour! Oh, it's all hopeless.' I dropped my head onto my arms.

'Look, Lillie.' Wendy lifted my head. 'You talk about being an independent woman and not relying on one person for all your emotional stability, but every time you get into a relationship, you lose yourself trying to please whatever guy you've attached yourself to.'

'No, I don't. Not with everyone. Eddie and I were never like that.'

'That's because Eddie was always going to go back to Queensland. You didn't know whether you'd see him again. You had no expectations, that's why it worked.'

'That was only a year ago. It seems like another lifetime. I feel like such a failure. I just want a chance to feel brilliant for once instead of feeling second rate. But I may as well give up. I'm useless.'

Wendy folded me in her arms. 'Where's your sense of adventure? Remember how we used to ride round on the milkman's cart early in the morning? You were the leader of the pack back then. Remember the things we got up to?'

'Yes, like pissing in the gutter.' I smiled through my tears.

'You need to find that kind of courage again. Forget about all of those guys, Matt, Pedro, whoever. They're not worth it. Forget whatever drugs you're using to get yourself through. Forget being famous too. It's eating you up, Lillie. For your own sake and for Jesse's sake too, you need to pull yourself together whether you make it in the music business or not.'

The next morning, Jesse refused to go to school unless I walked with him. I dabbed some make up on my bruised face, tied my hair up in a scarf and took out my trusty sunglasses. Their heart-shaped lenses seemed outrageous when compared to the state of my real heart, fleshy and beating like crazy against my ribs.

As I took Jesse by the hand I looked up and spied the eagle. 'Quick there he is, give him a wave,' I urged.

JANIE CONWAY HERRON

Jesse waved and the eagle gave a little dance. 'Mr Johns told us the eagle has been captured by someone and its wings have been clipped.'

I looked up. The eagle's eye was fixed on us. Rather than pride, I could see sadness. It had never occurred to me that our eagle was imprisoned.

I arrived at the record launch totally wired. Jules had paid a road crew to set up so the band had maximum time to mix with the crowd before we went on. When somebody handed me a joint, I took it.

'You want me to tune your guitar for you?' one of the roadies asked.

'Thanks,' I answered through a haze of speed and ganja.

I walked on stage to a full house. Across a sea of bobbing heads, I could see Geoff, Jules, Phil, Derrick and Louis standing together. Beyond them I could just make out the silhouetted figures of Wendy and Anna. I picked up my guitar and struck an angry-sounding chord that rang out across the room. Josh, Trevor and Rossco set up a tight rhythm. After each song the audience went wild. Someone placed another glass of port next to me and I drank it steadily. As a blur of faces stared at me from the dance floor, I closed my eyes to steady myself. Nobody noticed my inebriated state. Even Josh was fired up, riding the wave of success the evening had brought. He started up the rhythm of each song grinning like a Cheshire cat. Tight and crisp, the band kept me together. After three encores, the applause died out.

As the champagne corks popped I shook people's hands, thanked them for coming and responded positively to the flood of compliments. Though I smiled constantly I wasn't really there. Faces loomed up close, but I didn't recognise them. Bodies pressed against mine, but I didn't feel them. People's voices sounded as if they were coming down a drainpipe. Nodding, I thanked them over and over again.

As the party continued, the hum of voices sounded like ocean waves. I sank to the floor and cupped my hand round my ear listening to the roar. When Wendy came over, I held it out. 'See, I've got the ocean in my hand, want to hear it?'

'Sure, Lil', after I get you home.' Wendy helped me out through the back room and put me in the car. When she put me to bed and sat by my side, I smiled up at her through a haze of inebriation.

Wendy didn't smile back. 'You really need to get help you know. Not in a month or two, or next year, but now. You shouldn't put it off any longer.'

'You're not going to leave me alone here tonight are you?' My hand tightened around Wendy's.

'No,' Wendy assured me, 'I'll ring Anna and let her know I'll be staying here tonight. She suggested I take you back to your place while she went home to relieve the babysitter. Jesse will be happy hanging out with Sam and Ant for another day.'

Jules rang me a couple of mornings later. 'Hey, that was great the other night, wasn't it?' I croaked. 'There were lots of people there.'

'Yes, it was, Lillie,' Jules replied, 'and the band sounded great too. You should get some good reviews. There were plenty of press there. Where did you get to, by the way? We were wondering what happened.'

'I needed to get back for my son, Jesse,' I lied.

'That's a shame,' Jules replied. 'I was hoping to get a moment for a chat while the energy was positive and high. Sorry to call you so early, but we need you to come for a special meeting. Can you come tomorrow?'

'Okay, I'll see you then.' I put the phone down.

The next day I sat in Jules' office, hiding behind a floppy black hat and my trusty heart-shaped sunglasses. Jules' words felt like sharp raindrops falling on my shoulders, pricking my skin with pins and needles.

'We're going to close the management side of things. It's not making enough money to warrant keeping it on. Geoff will be keeping a few of the more established acts like Frankie, but that's all. This means you will have to look after things yourself, or find new management, Lillie. We've still got that national tour lined up for next month. You can either do the publicity yourself, or hire a publicist. Publicists cost money but they're worth it. Think about it and give us a ring in a couple of days.'

When Jules put her arm around my shoulders, a part of me wanted to reach out and ask her for help but I was numb with the effort of keeping myself together. The last thing I wanted was to break down in front of Jules.

I rang the band to tell them I'd decided not to work for a while. The shell of my body could walk and talk but inside there was nothing left.

'Well, that's life, I guess,' Josh replied before hanging up. He was the last person I told. After that, it was all over. The music had stopped.

That night I dreamt about a candle throwing an orange light against the dark blue of the night sky. It flickered in the breeze coming in through a broken window and almost went out. I protected the flame from the wind with my hand. As I stood back to watch it burn, a long brass snuffer hovered over the top of the flame, waiting to put it out. As it was about to descend, I realised the flame was my soul. If it went out it would make me a walking shell of a body without the ability to create. The flame shrank away from the candle snuffer and I woke just before it slowly lowered itself over the candle.

I had one last phone call to make. In their retirement, my parents had found a companionship with each other that had seemed impossible when I was growing up. If my father knew what was really going on he'd be on the next plane to get me. That was the last thing I wanted to happen. But I missed them both and longed for those nights when I'd lie in bed with Mum, talking until dawn crept over the skyline. The dial tone went on for ages before I heard my mother's voice.

'Lillie darling, how wonderful to hear from you!' The warm sound of my mother's voice almost brought me undone.

'I'm a bit sick, Mum,' I blurted out.

'What's wrong? You sound terrible.'

'I'm just exhausted,' I said, holding back the need to tell her everything.

'Why don't you come and stay with us for a while?' Mum offered.

'I can't right now. I've got things I need to sort out first.' I disguised the reality of going into hospital through a veil of half-truths. Mum was the one person I knew who'd been through something similar to me. I wasn't sure if I was protecting her or myself with my subterfuge. I took a deep breath. 'I was wondering if you'd look after Jesse for a week or two. The holidays are starting soon so he won't need to miss too much school if he comes up now.'

'Of course,' Mum replied. 'I'll get your father to book a plane. You should come too. The sun's shining, the ocean's blue and the eagles come circling every day.'

'We've got our very own eagle down here in Melbourne too.'

'Really? I didn't think they could survive in the city.'

'This one's had its wings clipped. It can't fly away.'

'Fancy clipping a wild bird's wings. Humans are strange, aren't they? You come up and see us as soon as you can. We'd be overjoyed to have Jesse up here and you know we'd love to see you too. Try and get here as soon as you can.'

'I will,' I answered. I knew Jesse would tell them everything once he got there. But by that time, I'd be in hospital.

I packed a bag and waited. When Wendy arrived with Jesse, the sight of his big, frightened eyes made my own fill with tears.

'Come on, Lillie, pull yourself together,' Wendy hissed in my ear. 'Jesse wants to make sure that you're going to a nice place.'

'Mummy's just tired, isn't she?' I heard Jesse ask.

'She just needs to rest, then she'll be alright,' Wendy reassured him.

I lay down on the back seat while Wendy drove. Telephone wires, treetops and blue sky flew past the car window at a rapid rate. Then a familiar song came on the car radio.

'Hey Lil', they're playing your song,' Wendy boomed.

'Yeah, Mum, it's going to be a hit.' I could hear the squeak of Jesse's excitement as he squirmed on the vinyl seat. When I reached up and ruffled his hair he grabbed my hand and held it. At the hospital he clung to my legs.

I knelt down to face him. 'I know this is a hard thing to do, but you'll have to be brave for a little while. When you get to Nanna's place, everything's going to get better. Nanna and Pop live right by the ocean. You'll be able to go swimming every day. You'll love it.'

'Will you be coming too?' Jesse sniffed.

'I'll come very soon, I promise.'

Gently, Wendy prised Jesse away from me. 'We have to let your mum rest so she can get better as soon as possible and join you at your grandparents' place.'

As they drove away, Jesse scrambled over into the back seat and waved furiously. I waved back, watching his grinning face get smaller as the car disappeared from view.

another song about love

After what seemed like an eternity, a nurse ushered me into a room filled with other patients. They looked up as I entered then went on with whatever they were doing. I stood in the middle of the room. A couch in the corner by the long windows offered a safe haven. The warmth of the sun sank comfortingly into my skin as I stretched my legs out. When I closed my eyes, I could see my life strung out before me in an endless array of moments, like picture postcards from an old lover in some far off place. As I felt my way back through the tunnel that had brought me here, I remembered. Thoughts crept across the floor, snaking their way into corners, or hiding behind the curtains that hung heavy in the afternoon sun.

The windows in the hospital framed a view of green hills and purple haze, park benches and forest walks. But I needed to rest. My wrists fluttered in a vague, pale way as I lifted my hands. My heart beat way too hard, my soul felt like it was floating upwards into my throat. Caught inside the reflections of my mind, I let them carry me out over the hills towards the horizon.

Somewhere close to me, a young man played the guitar and sang old sixties songs in a high-pitched voice. They sounded more like Christian hymns than the rebellious, hopeful songs I remembered.

When he saw me look at him, he smiled. 'Play guitar, do you?'

'A little.' My voice was so small I could hardly hear myself speak.

JANIE CONWAY HERRON

The young man leant forward and offered me his guitar. 'Would you like to play some now?'

'Not now, maybe later,' I whispered as my eyes settled on the horizon.

EPILOGUE

MANY YEARS HAVE PASSED SINCE then, but sometimes I can still see myself through those young-woman eyes. As a teenager, music was my solace. The sound of the guitar, the way the strings resonated inside the body of the instrument, touched a place deep inside me. Then the words came and turned the music into songs. They were love songs. Love – powerful and insidious – wove its way through every aspect of my life. Love killed the music in me, yet without it, I would never have sung a single song.

JANIE CONWAY HERRON

As soon as I left hospital I headed north, to be with family. Mum and Dad had enrolled Jesse at their local school so I decided we should stay on. Now we have our own place close to the beach. I'm grateful to be here with the sun shining and the surf rolling in.

Jesse often goes busking in town on the weekends. He doesn't want to play professionally he told me, but he makes a good living from the tourists who flock to this small coastal town. When he was younger, people often asked him whether he wanted to be a musician. He always answered, 'No, no way,' as if music was the last thing he wanted to be involved in. When he turned fifteen, he asked me to teach him guitar. Surprised and pleased, I started with a simple three-chord song. Jesse became bored with that very quickly.

'Will you to teach me *The Eagle Song*?' he asked, after only a few sessions.

I hesitated, concerned that the chords were difficult, but I only had to show him once. From that point on there was no stopping him. He was still adamant he wasn't going to become a professional musician though. 'No Mum, I just want to enjoy playing. I'm happy jamming with friends.'

Recently, I went to a gig at our local hall to see Jesse play with a few of those friends. To my surprise, the band invited me to join them. As I made my way through the audience and onto stage, Jesse started up the opening riff to *The Eagle Song*. He grinned at me as the rest of the band joined in. I closed my eyes, gave

another song about love

myself over to the sound of Jesse's soaring guitar and began to sing. Within seconds, the hall was rocking. Outside, the night sky was full of shining stars and the fresh smell of salt sea air as our music mingled with the whispering waves licking into shore.

ACKNOWLEDGEMENTS

I would like to acknowledge that *Another Song About Love* was completed on Widjabul/Wayabul country and pay my respects to elders, past, present and emerging, from the land that has provided me with a sense of home and spiritual sustenance for the last twenty years.

The following people helped me along the way with the many iterations of *Another Song About Love*. Thanks to Amanda Lohrey for supervising early drafts of an experimental piece called 'Spotlighting' that I completed for my masters at The University of Technology. This manuscript provided the foundational material for what evolved into *Another Song About Love*. Thanks and appreciation also to, Professor Anna Gibbs, Jude McGee, Associate Professor Maarten Renés, John Ryan, Dr Moya Costello, Dr Maria Simms, Christine Strelan and my granddaughter Vashti Illanya for reading drafts of the manuscript and providing much needed feedback at crucial times in the evolution of the novel. Also heartfelt thanks to Vashti for the beautiful cover image. It captures an essential essence of being a woman that I've been trying to portray in words.

Thanks also to Ben Ellis of Tall Story for all his care, creativity and wisdom in designing such a beautiful looking book.

Thanks also to my colleagues in the writing program at Southern Cross University for providing the kind of writerly friendship that helped sustain my enthusiasm for this project.

Extra special thanks, to my husband, Peter for his constant companionship, love and support. His attentive listening, as I read each chapter to him, helped me find the rhythm of my words, while his camera work and vision for the clip of the song, *The Ocean in Me*, expressed our love of the ocean perfectly.

I am particularly indebted to my son, Tamlin Tregonning, for helping me realise the musical part of this project. I couldn't have done it without his enthusiasm for my songs plus his musical genius on guitars, bass, drums, keyboard and vocals as well as production and song writing. Thanks also to, Billie McArthy, Jess Ciampa, Stuart Vandergraff, Jim Pennell and my brother Jim Conway. Your unique musical contributions helped make my songs sound so good. Thanks also to Geoff Lee, engineer at Zen studios for 'being there' the whole time and helping keep us all on track. Special thanks to Scott Keanie for assistance with mixing sound and editing of the film clip, *The Ocean in Me*.

The recording of the collection of fifteen songs that accompanies the novel was partially supported by research funds I acquired as an academic in the School of Arts and Social Sciences at Southern Cross

University. This project was also assisted by a Pozible crowdfunding campaign. Thanks so much to all those wonderful supporters whose pledges to the campaign helped me complete my project of novel and songs and make my creative dreams come true.

Note: While this novel is based on real times, places and events, it is a work of fiction and the characters portrayed come from the author's imagination. Any resemblance to known people is entirely coincidental.